MONSTER OF FATE

Little Secret
Little Truth

Immortals of Lionswood Academy
Pawn takes Knight
Knight take Bishop
Bishop takes Rook

Princes of Rosewood Hall
Prince of Thorns

AS ELIZABETH STEVENS

unvamped
the Trouble with Hate is…
Keeping Up Appearances
Being Not Good
Popped
the Art of Breaking Up

Accidentally Perfect Books
Accidentally Perfect
Perfectly Accidental

AVAILABLE ON WATTPAD
the Danu Cycle
Gryffynhall
Elfhaven
Innisfail

THE VAMPIRES OF KNIGHTSBRIDGE #1

MONSTER OF FATE

ELIZABETH STEVENS WRITING AS

SCARLETT KNOX

KINKY
SIREN

Kinky Siren
An imprint of Sleeping Dragon Books

Monster of Fate
by Scarlett Knox

Print ISBN: 978-1925928631
Digital ISBN: 978-1925928624

Cover art by: Izzie Duffield

Worldwide Electronic & Digital Rights
Worldwide English Language Print Rights

Scarlett,
Welcome to the ranks. Officially.

CONTENTS

Author's Note

This is a dark, angsty, contemporary paranormal, enemies-to-lovers, stepsibling romance with some bully elements and enough steam to melt your screen. Do not engage in public consumption unless your poker face is impenetrable.

Do not read if you don't like vampires, fated mates, alpha stepbrothers claiming what's theirs, a feisty heroine discovering the hidden secrets of her new stepfamily, complicated love triangles full of passion, dirty words, and a little bit of death.

This story features the heroine in romantic/sexual situations with two love interests. While not considered cheating by the characters, you may have different feelings. Proceed with caution.

This book has an Australia narrator and is therefore written using Australian English. This will affect the spelling, grammar and syntax you may be used to. It might come across as typos, awkward sentences, poor grammar, or missed/wrong words. In the majority of cases (I won't claim it's infallible, despite all best efforts), this is intentional and just an Aussie way of speaking (it took my US beta readers a bit to get used to). I can't say 'the' Aussie way, since we seem to differ even within the same state. Just think of us as a weird mix of British and US vernacular and colloquialisms, but with our own randomness thrown in. I still hope you enjoy it, though!

Contains possible triggers.

CHAPTER ONE

"I'm seeing someone new."

I looked up at my mum's outburst and wasn't sure if there was a follow up coming, or if I was supposed to give her my paltry excuse for congratulations now. When she said nothing, I assumed the latter.

"And it's a Tuesday. Both things that happen on a weekly basis," I said to her as I looked back down at my book.

She sighed like I wasn't being fair and maybe I wasn't. I tried to feel bad about my words, but I couldn't find it in myself.

"I thought we agreed we wouldn't talk about them?" I reminded her.

She joined me at the table. "I know."

"We pretend they don't exist, and we can go about our lives in blissful ignorance."

It was legitimately the only way we'd been able to have any normal mother-daughter relationship; pretend her string of lovers didn't exist. She kept that part of her life separate, and we got on with ours.

"Except…" she nudged.

"Except if it means something," I finished with a nod.

I looked at her as something hit me. She was looking at me like she was waiting for the other shoe to drop. It did. A ten-tonne cement shoe right on my head.

"Don't tell me this one actually means something," I begged.

She smiled at me hopefully and I felt the wind knocked right out of me. The last time this happened, she uprooted my whole life and then dumped him the next week only to uproot me again, and not back to my previous life. After that, we'd made our deal and I hadn't met another of her short-term beaus.

The problem with my mother, as much as I loved her, was that she needed to love. She was driven to love. It was one reason she'd kept me despite getting pregnant at such a young age. And she had so much love to give – and I mean that in only the best way – that one person – me – wasn't enough. But she always picked the wrong guys. At least she also got out once she realised that, instead of staying with them. She'd learnt that lesson the hard way, but she'd never let it catch her, or me, out again.

Mum fiddled with the cross at her neck. "He's asked me to move in with him."

I blinked. "Then he's even more delusional than you."

"We've been…together nearly a year." Her voice was small, like she knew I'd disapprove or not even believe her.

Like anything I thought had ever stopped her before.

"When do I need to be packed?" I sighed, resigned.

She smiled in relief. She'd honestly thought I'd fight her. I'd learnt there was no point. She'd get her way eventually. I was still a minor and she was my legal guardian. If she wanted to move us again, then me fighting would only upset us both and for absolutely no other outcome.

She patted the table excitedly. "Pack a bag and we'll leave tomorrow."

Tomorrow? I'd literally just bought all my stuff for the new school year, and I'd started reading the materials. Why had she let me waste the money if she knew we were moving tomorrow? But I knew better than to ask more questions. They'd be answered in time. Me voicing them now wasn't going to change a thing. May as well go for the ride and see where life took me. After all, where would the fun be if I had all the spoilers beforehand?

"What about all the rest of our stuff?" I asked. We didn't have much in our two-bedroom unit, but it was ours.

She grinned. "Etienne is having his people come by to pack it all up and bring it to us."

Etienne.

He sounded like a man who was used to control and did not like to lose a single shred of it. I was already looking forward to meeting him.

"Do I need my passport? How far are we going?" I asked her.

I'd meant it sarcastically, so was not at all prepared for her giddy response to be, "Yes. Definitely. They won't let you out of the country without it. Even on a private plane."

She clasped my hand where it rested on the table, then headed out. I was left sitting there with my now unnecessary Year Twelve SACE books and a feeling of impending doom. Logically, I knew the impending doom was just displeasure; my lazy arse didn't want to have to pack a bag for God knew where or for God knew how long. If Mum had planned for our belongings to follow us, then I suspected we were going forever.

But we'd played that game before.

Had I had anyone to say goodbye to, I'd have called them or driven to their house or something.

I didn't.

Have anyone.

Except Mum.

So, instead, I spent a solitary night trying to work out what to pack. My only clue had been 'for Winter' as Mum had hauled my suitcase into my room. Winter suggested Northern Hemisphere, but how cold? We lived in the south of Australia. It was starting to get mighty cold in Winter here, but we didn't have snow to contend with. Yet.

Starting with the basics, I set about filling my suitcase to bursting.

"Don't worry about luggage weight limit," Mum said as she flitted by my room at one point. "Etienne said he doubted even *I* could pack enough to begin to worry the pilots." As she continued on her way, she laughed the laugh of the truly happy…and infatuated.

It was difficult to remain cynical. It was difficult to begrudge her happiness.

It was difficult, but not impossible.

As I walked out of my room the next morning, I wasn't sure how I felt about strangers going through my things. Mum assured me they were professionals and wouldn't linger about my lingerie. She thought the idea whimsical and amusing, I was mortified to think I might have left even a scrap of underwear behind for them to find.

But my mortification was nothing in the face of my mother's optimism and it carried us through the car trip to the airport in the black SUV with the blacked-out windows. It carried us through the backdoor customs desk reserved for private flights. It carried us through my tiny mind completely blowing over the fanciness of the plane and the way the staff served us like we were royalty. It carried us through the flight, the fuel stop, and then I blissfully fell asleep only to be awoken when the plane was on the ground again.

I checked my phone, but even roaming wasn't getting any bars wherever we were.

I'd have been more annoyed if there'd been anyone back home to talk to.

"Mademoiselle Basset," a man said to us as we walked down the steps of the plane onto the tarmac. His accent was hard to place, but my ignorance thought it might be eastern European. "Monsieur le Rege waits for you at the manor."

By this point, I was expecting luxury – the guy had sent his private plane for us after all – so I didn't bat my sleep-filled eyes at the notion that Mum's beau lived in a manor. It just kinda seemed expected.

Go with the flow, I reminded myself as I took a look around and the wind blew a sudden chill through me.

The place was beautiful. If you liked to be surrounded by dark greens and browns and greys and a thick layer of fog over everything. There was a slight drizzle in the air, and I felt damp seeping into my clothes, not that anyone else seemed bothered.

The guy who'd greeted us put us into another black SUV with blacked-out windows, and we set off on another long journey, this time winding up and up and up into the mountains. The colour palette didn't change, and the fog seemed to only get thicker, but the driver navigated up the road like he'd done it a million times.

My eyes felt heavy, and I drifted off to sleep again, glad I'd saved my playlists onto my phone, and it hadn't yet run out of batteries.

The next thing I knew, Mum was shaking me gently.

"Evie," she whispered. Her nickname for me. "We're here."

I blinked and rubbed my eyes, looking out the window to find the sun had long set. We drove through what looked like big gates and up a long drive. Finally, looming up out of the dark was more than just a manor and it was lit up brighter than a Christmas tree. It was the kind of building you saw on British period shows. Lady Catherine wished she had a place this big.

As we pulled up, the driver said something quietly, and I realised he was wearing an earpiece. Presumably it was attached to someone at the house, or some fancy guardhouse.

He rolled the car to a stop at the front doors just as they opened, and even more light spilled outside.

"Monsieur le Rege and the rest of the family are waiting for you in the parlour," the driver said as someone came to open Mum's door.

"Mademoiselle Basset," the man said, with that same vague eastern European accent. "Welcome home."

"Thank you, Mortas," Mum said as though she knew him. She looked back to me as she got out. "Come on, Evie. They're waiting."

I slid over and followed her out. If this was my Princess Mia moment, then it was not everything I'd hoped for and more.

I kept following Mum, who somehow seemed to know exactly where she was going and nodding to the staff as though she'd seen them before.

She walked into the parlour like she belonged in the place, and I saw her beeline for the man by the fireplace. There was also a girl and an older woman, standing like they were waiting to greet us, and a couple of well-dressed people around the very fringes of the room as though they were waiting to serve us.

"Darling," Mum cried happily as she hurried over to the man, and he had nothing but a warm embrace for her.

So, this was her new beau?

Etienne looked to be a man in his mid-forties, maybe his fifties. He had light brown hair and, when he looked at me over Mum's shoulder, I saw deep hazel eyes containing a shrewd intelligence. He was fit; tall and slim, but not gangly. He wore a three-piece suit in what movies had reliably told me was tweed, complete with pocket watch. He and his manor – and his manner, actually – looked like they'd definitely stepped out of another time. There were just so many different periods going on that I couldn't pinpoint what was the most prominent.

The history nerd in me was going nuts. Internally.

"Evangeline, it really is a pleasure to meet you," he said as he let go of Mum and came over to me. It seemed everyone in this country had the same vague accent. That was going to be fun.

I tried not to scrunch my face in displeasure, the way my real name in the mouths of others always made me. I hated the name Evangeline. My name. I always had. It sounded wanky and pretentious. Mum still called me it or Evie but, at school, I went by my middle name Selena, or Lena for short. No one but my mum had called me Evangeline for years.

I had a feeling that Etienne would call me whatever my mum

7

wanted me called, my thoughts and feelings be damned.

"It's nice to meet you," I told him.

His smile for me was warm as well. He looked open, sincere, and honest. No warning bells clanged in my head immediately. So far, so good. I guessed.

"Please, let me introduce you to my daughter, Artemia." He indicated the girl to the side of the room, and she stepped forward.

She was already as tall as me, but she looked younger. Her skin was pristine, almost like porcelain. Her hair was a shining dark blonde, long and luscious and dead straight down to her elbows, with a simple pink ribbon as a headband. Her eyes, like her father's, were a deep hazel. Artemia, despite the strangeness of her name, at least looked more like a normal modern teenager in pastel pink heels, light washed jeans, and a matching sweater set in bright blue.

"Welcome to *Manoir le Rege*," she said with a smile as wide as the one on her father's face. Her's though was slightly more cunning, like we were in on a joke together. "It'll be nice to have a sister finally."

Well, if anything was going to win me over, that would be it. I'd always wanted a sister as well. I didn't have a chance to return the sentiment though as Mum intervened.

"Etienne also has a son," she said, like I needed an explanation.

"Erasmus," Etienne said, his voice losing some of its warmth.

"Yes," said the older woman as she stepped up. "Though he seems to believe good manners are not for the likes of him."

I'd have guessed her age to be in her sixties or seventies and she was clearly in no danger of losing her prime. She had ash blonde hair that I couldn't tell if it hadn't started greying yet or if she dyed it. Her eyes were as blue as the summer sky as she looked me over with a discernment to put Etienne to shame. I could already tell she was a no-nonsense sort of woman, but I sensed a kindness in her that would be freely given once earned.

Etienne chuckled. "Teenagers."

The woman didn't seem to think it as funny as him.

"Come, Mother. Give him a break." Etienne turned back to me. "This is my mother, Violet. She lives with us and–"

"Mainly sticks her nose into everyone's business," Artemia said, but fondly.

"Call me Grandma Vi, dear," she said as she clasped my hands and looked deep into my eyes. She seemed to be searching for something, but I didn't know what. Finally, when I was starting to sweat from nerves under her scrutiny, she said, "It's lovely having you here."

I nodded. "Thanks. It's…nice to be here."

"You don't need to be polite," Etienne said tenderly. "I'm sure it's a big change."

I gave him a slightly less stunned nod. "Thanks. It might take some adjusting."

Artemia grinned at me, like she knew how all this looked and was reassuring me it wasn't impossible for teenagers to be teenagers here. I had to admit, despite the suddenness and the major upheaval this all was, these people seemed…fine. Nice and genuine and actually happy to have me there.

"Shall we go through to dinner?" Grandma Vi said. "The two of you must be famished."

Okay, I was rethinking my previous statement. Something

about the way she said famished sounded…ominous, but the expression on her face was harmless enough, so I choked it up to a million years of travel making my brain funny.

"Yes. They took great care of us, but travelling always leaves me so hungry," Mum said as she took Etienne's arm, and they walked out.

Grandma Vi followed, and Artemia didn't move until she'd kicked her head and I'd fallen into step with her.

"We've only just gone on winter break," she said. "So, you've got four weeks until school starts."

I nodded, as though I had any idea the plan was for me to attend school here in four weeks' time. "You go there, too?"

"Knightsbridge Academy?" she said, like she was helping me out but we didn't have to admit that, and I nodded. She smiled. "Yes. Year Nine, though. I'm only fifteen. My brother's nineteen."

So, if their school system was anything like ours, then he wouldn't be going to school with us. Okay.

Well, that had given me quite a nice amount of information I wouldn't have to ask for or awkwardly pretend I already knew. Artemia looked at me like that was exactly why she'd given it to me.

I had a feeling I was going to like Artemia.

More well-dressed staff, in their black ties and three-piece suits and white shirts, directed us to seats in the dining room. Etienne sat at the head, with Mum on his left and Grandma Vi at his right. I sat next to Grandma Vi, with an empty chair across from me next to Mum, and Artemia sat in the next one over. I assumed the empty chair belonged to Erasmus. The way Grandma

Vi glared at it as she sat down told me pretty much all I needed to know about the absentee, and I wasn't going to bother giving him a second thought.

As the staff set about filling our glasses with a dark red wine, even Artemia's, Mum took Etienne's hand.

"Didn't we…have some news, darling?" she said slowly.

Etienne looked at the door as though his missing son was going to appear through it. When no one did walk through it, he sighed, picked up his glass and stood up. "I was hoping Erasmus would be here for this, but that's what he gets for sulking." Etienne held out a hand for Mum and she stood to join him. "We're going to be married."

Mum exclaimed in happiness as they hugged, and I couldn't help looking around the room. Artemia and Grandma Vi were both smiling, but I didn't think it reached their eyes. What did they think of this? Clearly Mum had – somehow – been here before; us moving in and the news was obviously less of a shock to the people who lived here than it all had been to me. But I didn't think that meant they liked it any more than I did.

"When's…?" I started as I fiddled with the base of my glass. "Uh, when's the big day? Do you have a date?"

"The twenty-ninth," Mum said, looking like her smile was going to split her face in half. Her happiness made it a little easier to stomach, but she and I had been here before.

I blinked. "Of January?"

"Everything is already in motion," Etienne said as Mum brandished her left hand at me, and I saw the giant bauble on her third finger I was sure hadn't been there half an hour ago.

Holy hand grenade.

Her engagement ring looked old. Like way more than just vintage glamour. And expensive. Though, judging by the size and contents of *Manoir le Rege*, money wasn't something Etienne was lacking.

I forced a smile for Mum. "It's beautiful. That's great."

Forget my resigned acceptance of going to Knightsbridge Academy in four weeks, that whole being here forever thing was starting to seem most likely.

Artemia, Grandma Vi and I all raised our glasses with a chorused, "Congratulations."

"Of course, you and Artemia will be my bridesmaids," Mum gushed.

As I took a sip, and felt the wine go straight to my head, I looked to Artemia and was glad when we shared a wry look. *Look at us, being all sisterly and shit.*

"Of course," she told my mum. "We'd be honoured."

I nodded. "Sure. As long as the dresses aren't hideous."

Mum clasped her hands. "I promise, they won't be hideous."

After that, the first course – the *first* freaking course – was served and talk came mainly from Mum and Etienne talking about their plans for the wedding. Grandma Vi interjected to disagree with some choice or other, multiple times. Artemia came to our parents' defence every time. And I just sat there, nodding and smiling at appropriate intervals, and thought about how lucky it was that we didn't have anyone back home.

No one to miss us.

No one who'd complain about a missed wedding invite.

It all seemed quite convenient.

Etienne and his family could kill us and live off the meat of our corpses through the rest of Winter and there'd be no one left to care. I wasn't getting murder house vibes or anything from them, but – just saying – it could happen.

After dinner, I was left to my own devices. Artemia showed me to my room and made apologies she couldn't hang out, but she had other things to do. With friends, because she was normal.

"I'd invite you along, but…" she said.

I shook my head, both of us pausing as Mum and Etienne giggled up another flight of stairs. Ten points if you guessed what they were off to do. "No. I get it. It's fine. You and your friends don't want some old woman hanging out with you," I teased and she smiled widely.

"Hardly an old woman," she said. "But when you're a bit more settled, maybe you'll come out and meet some people? I imagine it would be nice to know more than just me before school starts."

The chance of that was zero, but I didn't want to shit all over her optimism. "Maybe. Yeah."

I had the feeling she knew the chances were zero, and kudos to her that it didn't break her optimism. "Great. Well, I'll see you tomorrow?"

I nodded. "Sure."

"Night, Evangeline," she called as she hurried back down the stairs.

"Night," I muttered to the manor at large before I took a breath and pushed into my room.

I hadn't expected my own room. Even in a manor, I'd assumed I'd be stuffed away in some corner, not just down the hall from the owner's real daughter. When I opened the door?

"Holy freaking shit," I breathed.

The manor was ridiculous enough, but my room? I had my own ensuite that was larger than my entire bedroom back home. I had a brand-new computer and the latest phone sitting on my desk just waiting for me to boot them up. I had the world's biggest four poster bed with curtains pulled back to reveal way more pillows than any one person needed. There was a fireplace, complete with warming flickering flames.

And the colours? The colours were all one hundred percent me; dusky purples and ashen roses, silvers and grey-blues. The wood was all white-washed, making it look vintage and avoiding the starkness of seamless white. The icing on the cake? There wasn't a single flower or floral pattern in sight.

It was perfect. Ridiculously perfect.

The kind of perfect that had been planned all just for me by people who knew me and cared about me.

And all I could think was what kind of crazy world had we fallen into.

I went over to the giant dark rose velvet curtains along one wall and peeked through them. They were heavier than I expected. Inside was a window seat and the chill of the mountain Winter that was apparently now my home. I hoped it would be a nice place to sit in Summer and read. But the frosty air would suit my purposes at present most nicely.

I grabbed a blanket off the bed and curled up in the window seat, staring at the full moon high above the trees. I could almost hear the mournful call of wolves from deep in the woods. It sent my heart racing at what else might hide in those trees, and I smiled at my imagination. In an effort to dispel the nervous anxiety, I drew little wolves in the condensation on the window.

They danced in the moonlight as I fell asleep.

CHAPTER TWO

I woke the next morning in my own bed, having no idea how I'd got there. I assumed I'd woken, no doubt as cold as a popsicle on the verge of hibernation and burrowed under the blankets. Because I woke toasty warm. Almost too warm actually, with the fire still roaring merrily away.

As I sat up, I looked around and again wondered what kind of crazy hell we'd fallen into. Stuff like this didn't happen to us. To any normal person. They didn't get whisked away, unquestioning, to far off countries on the other side of the world and dropped in the lap of luxury.

Certainly not without some major consequences.

Time would reveal the consequences, I supposed. Until then, I may as well enjoy the decadence.

I saw my suitcase sitting against the double doors that led to the wardrobe. Everything would be crinkly, but crinkly would beat clothes I'd been wearing for…however many hours it had been since we'd left home. Usually, if we travelled, I lived out of my suitcase. But we weren't travelling, we were moving, so unpacking it was.

First on the to-do list was set up my music so I could have it playing while I unpacked. It took me very little time to set up the computer and new phone, and soon my favourite playlist was blaring out over the speakers on the desk.

"Evie?" I heard Mum ask a little while later and I popped my head out of the robe, into the bedroom to see her looking for me.

"Hey, Mum."

"How are you doing?" she asked, concern marring her features.

"Fine. Unpacking. Why?"

"You missed breakfast."

"Breakfast is a…thing?" I guessed.

"All meals are things, Evie," she chastised fondly. "More importantly, all meals are things we have as a…family."

I wasn't going to debate her word choice.

"So…I'm meant to have breakfast, lunch and dinner with…the family," I said carefully.

"It's not mandatory. Per se. But what is mandatory is prior notice of an absence."

I smirked. "I'm guessing Erasmus didn't give notice."

She tried not to smile; I could see it on her face. "No. He didn't. He told his father he would be here for our arrival, left the day before, and hasn't been seen since. Artemia assures Etienne that Erasmus fine, but I know he's worried."

I could see she was as well. So, despite my firm belief that Erasmus was undoubtedly some unattractive, uninteresting, wet towel of a boy, I tried to comfort her.

"I'm sure he *is* fine," I said gently.

She smiled. "Even still, you'll be coming to lunch."

I wasn't sure if it was a question or an order. I was impressed with her. One night in her new home and she was already so much more…confident and assertive and…whole somehow.

I nodded anyway. "Uh, yeah. What time?"

"Time enough for you to shower and change," she said pointedly.

I smiled. "Yep. Good point. I'll see you down there soon."

"Half an hour, Evie," she said as she started slipping out the door and she didn't take her eyes off me until I nodded.

"Okay, shower…" I muttered, feeling an incomprehensible flutter of nerves in my chest.

I needed to get out of these unfamiliar walls. Even unfamiliar outdoors was better than the sudden stifling heat that clawed at me.

"Maybe it'll brighten up and I'll go for a walk," I told myself as I got into the shower.

I knew it was a futile hope but, by the time I was jogging down to lunch, I was set on a walk. As a rule, I didn't go in for exercise. It seemed a waste, a cruel mockery to the litre of ice cream you'd eaten the night before. But a stroll wasn't exactly exercise, and it would be nice to get some idea of where Mum expected me to live for the foreseeable future.

At the bottom of the stairs, I realised I didn't know where I was or where I was meant to go.

Taking a gamble, I turned right and realised pretty quickly I was in the wrong part of the manor. The walls were plain cream, the floors suddenly a simple dark brown wood with no carpet runners. There were no portraits in ornate frames on the walls and most of the bulbs were bare or in a simple sconce.

As I rounded a corner, I saw someone in a room at the end of the corridor. There was a carcass they were draining of blood. The shape of the carcass looked familiar… Then they looked up, saw me, and someone else in the room closed the door.

"Can I help, mademoiselle?" another of the staff asked at my elbow and I jumped.

"Help?" I laughed self-consciously. "Sorry. Just… I could have sworn they had a person hanging up there." Another ridiculous self-conscious laugh.

I must have been going mad. Jet-lagged to the extreme. To think they had a person strung up and were draining them of blood!

"Must have been a pig or something," I said, realising this person must have thought I was bonkers, going on about people strung up in their fancy manor.

The servant nodded. "Must have, mademoiselle. Can I help you find your way?"

"Lunch," I said. "I'm looking for lunch."

They inclined their head. "I will take you to the luncheon room, mademoiselle."

"Thanks. Is that like a whole room just for lunch?" I asked as I followed them.

"Indeed, mademoiselle."

"Right. And does every meal have their own room?"

"Indeed, mademoiselle. The breakfast room. The luncheon room. The dining room. Then, for Sundays, the terrace, conservatory, and solar."

Holy hand grenades. "And I suppose there's the banquet hall and ballroom for special occasions," I teased.

Like so many of my jokes of late, it backfired.

"Indeed, mademoiselle." They pointed to a door. "The luncheon room, mademoiselle."

"Uh, thanks." By the time I looked back, they were gone.

Etienne, Mum, Grandma Vi and Artemia were waiting for me when I barrelled into the luncheon room.

"Evangeline," Etienne said. "Lovely for you to join us."

I nodded as I slid into my seat. "Sorry. Not a big breakfast person and didn't realise it was a whole thing."

Etienne smiled. "Your mother suggested as such. No matter. You know now. Breakfast will be served until ten while you're on break, so come down when you like."

I nodded again. "Thanks." I leant forward as I thought of something. "Listen, I don't suppose this place has a map?"

Instead of answering me, they all just chuckled and commented on how amusing I was. Not exactly the answer I'd been looking for. Not even a joke, and it had backfired.

"Still no Erasmus?" Mum asked as we ate.

I caught the look Artemia threw to her before turning it on her father. Etienne seemed to return it, but Mum missed it. I hadn't, though, and there was obviously something about Erasmus' absence. I wasn't sure what kind of something, but I was sure it was the kind of something the newbies weren't familiar enough to be privy to.

"No. Sadly, he has been…held up. And what do you have planned for this afternoon, Evangeline?" Etienne asked, turning his attention to me like I was enough to swing the conversation in a totally different direction.

I swallowed my mouthful and looked around the table to a sea of expectant faces. Even the servants seemed expectant.

"Uh, I thought I'd go for a walk…I guess… Get the lay of the land."

Etienne nodded perfunctorily. "Just do not wander too far. There is all manner of beasts in these woods with a desire to kill you."

I huffed a short laugh. "Trust me, I'm used to it. Everything in Australia either *can* kill you or wants to." Another (semi)joke that backfired.

"Trust *me*," he said carefully. "Even your Australian upbringing will not have prepared you for the things that lurk in those woods."

Artemia cleared her throat almost pointedly.

"So," Etienne seemed to add cheerfully as an afterthought. "Please be careful and stay close to the house."

Okay. Weird. But sure, why not? These people knew their home better than me.

I nodded. "I will. Thanks."

Mum smiled at me warmly, a thank you for trying. It wasn't that difficult. So far, Etienne seemed perfect for her; same penchant for naming his kids weird shit, throwing himself into the relationship with the speed of a fighter jet doing a flyby over Clipsal, and he didn't set off any warning signals. He was already doing three times better than her previous choices.

As we ate, I had to wonder why meals were a forced family affair. Other than making it easier on the staff – which, now I thought about it was a perfectly valid reason – it seemed pointless from a family point of view.

The conversation was all, "Bit of sun this morning."

"How nice."

"Have you looked in on the greenhouse?"

"Not today."

"I thought our guests might enjoy dinner out on the weekend."

"We'll see."

"What if Erasmus is back?"

"Then he can pay out of his ungrateful pockets."

I liked Grandma Vi. I couldn't say I disliked any of them, but I *liked* her. She seemed like a proper grandma: spoke her mind, didn't put up with anyone's shit, and complained about whatever she damned well wanted. Most of my knowledge of family came from pop culture, but every story needed a sassy granny.

"If you'll excuse me," Etienne said. "I have some business in town this afternoon. Mortas will see to your every whim."

"And what am I?" Grandma Vi asked, her voice full of authority. "I was mistress of this house when you were still wet behind the ears, boy. I think I can handle an afternoon."

Etienne inclined his head with a small smirk. "Of course, Mother. Forgive me."

"Use this time to corral your son home and I may," she said meaningfully.

"Until tonight, ladies." Etienne bowed and swept out of the room.

Mum watched him go like she was enthralled by him. I just rolled my eyes, finished my lunch, and beat a hasty retreat back to my room for a jacket to try to provide some protection against the relentless misery that could be seen out every window.

"Take heed of my father's warning," Artemia said as I crossed back over the entry hall on my way out.

I looked up to see her on the stairs. "Okay."

"The woods aren't all that safe. Are you sure you don't want to stay in? We could watch a movie or something."

Here was someone else who was trying, and I appreciated it more than I'd say. But I needed to get out for a minute to myself.

"Thanks, Artemia—"

"Mia, please," she said with a smile.

I grinned. "Mia. Call me Lena."

She inclined her head. "Lena."

"I'll take you up on that movie another day, but I need some fresh air."

"Well, you'll find precious little out there with all the fog. But it is fresher than inside."

I smiled. "Thanks. I'll see you later."

"Later, then."

As I ducked out the front doors, nodding to the morose Mortas on the way out, I pulled my collar up against the drizzle and dicked about, being indecisive as to which way to go.

"Might I suggest left, mademoiselle?" Mortas called from the safety of the door when I'd changed direction for the seventh time.

I gave him a salute, "Thanks," and tried left.

My feet crunched pleasantly on the snow, and I'll admit it was a novel experience. But that was about where the novelty ended. I slipped over numerous times. If I hit a bank of soft snow, my leg disappeared, or it was just really difficult to walk through. But it felt like it would be giving up if I turned and headed back to the manor so soon.

If I turned around, I could still see it behind me, despite how long and far it felt like I'd been walking.

A shrill cry sounded above me, and I looked up to see a raven perched in a tree. Even it seemed to be goading me on, like it agreed that turning back now would make me pathetic or weak.

"Oh, yeah?" I muttered to it. "That a dare?"

So, on I went. Not so much the stroll through the woods I'd intended, and far more like exercise. And still I continued, getting grumpier as I went, and the fog seeming to get thicker with every step, and the raven seeming to follow.

I'd been forced to leave the glorious heat of an Australian summer for this? This constant cloud cover. Practically drizzling rain twenty-four-seven. I didn't know where we were exactly, but if I'd had any reception on my supposedly wonderful new phone, or still been in range of the manor wifi, then I'd have googled 'place with the most cloud and rain. Not England'.

The fog by now was thick, as much as the Australian knew about fog. I could see maybe all of four trees ahead of me, but that probably equated to like five metres. Which was actually not that many after I'd thought about it and the word 'lost' was starting to play around my head.

"This probably counts as not close to the house," I muttered to myself as I stopped and looked around.

"And who might be missing you?" came a tantalising voice, and I wanted to say I didn't melt at the sound of it. I'd given up trying to place the accent, but the way it danced from his lips to my ears made it my favourite accent in the whole world.

I kept looking around, losing all that remained of my bearings, until I saw a male shape standing where I was sure there'd been empty fog seconds before.

He was walking towards me, the fog making him look like he was solidifying out of it, as the raven settled on a branch above him. When he was close enough to see his face, my heart stuttered in my chest, my stomach bottomed out, and I was pretty sure I did melt.

The guy was gorgeous. Hands down freaking gorgeous. The stuff your dirtiest daydreams and hottest fantasies were made out of. Well, mine, anyway.

Chiselled cheekbones. Sweeping dark brown hair and the palest blue eyes I'd ever seen in real life. I didn't know they made blue eyes that pale outside of the TV. He was tall, and the way he filled out those dark jeans and that dark red long-sleeved tee that clung to his muscles under a black coat? Utter perfection.

As he walked towards me, he held himself with the kind of dominant confidence and arrogance that had the power to send me to my knees at his feet. He moved with a grace I could never even dream of having, like he spent hours a day just perfecting his walk to make everyone swoon when he passed. And I'd bet he looked even better going than he did coming.

"You're new to Knightsbridge," he said. Somehow his voice seemed to curl around me in the fog, like a comforting presence.

I nodded, pretending there wasn't the beginnings of a raging crush smouldering deep inside me and that one more word out of him would be enough to fan the flames into an irrepressible obsession.

No one ever said I wasn't highly dramatic or a bit tragic.

"I am," I told him.

He gave a single nod as he took another step towards me. My chest fluttered wildly and I vaguely registered that I was no longer totally annoyed with this place I was being forced to call home.

"Are you attending the Academy next term?" he asked,

looking at me through thick, dark eyelashes.

"I am."

"Are you capable of saying anything else?" he teased.

I bit my lip, playing coy, before answering, "I am."

A half smile blossomed across his face, making him even more beautiful. "Well played," he said, and I heard the amusement in his voice.

"I'm Lena," I said quickly. Too quickly. Did he even care?

"Call me Rune," he replied. Just as quickly.

A stark cry came from the trees, and he gave another smirk. I looked up and saw the raven was still on its branch, seemingly watching us.

"I should let you get back," Rune said. "No doubt someone is missing you by now."

I shook my head as I looked down to watch my foot kick a stick. "I doubt it. I'm sure they don't even know I'm lost. I guess that's what I get for wandering too far from home."

"Well, I'm glad you did."

"Really? Why?"

"Because I found you."

Well, damn.

The boy had game, I had to give him that.

Why did I have to be such a sucker for game?

"I'll see you at school," he said.

I took a step forward. "Maybe I'll get lost again sometime before then."

He inclined his head again and the ghost of that previous half smile played at his lips. "Maybe you will."

I watched him walk away, being swallowed by the fog like he

was dissolving into it. The raven seemed to keep a beady eye on me for a moment longer before swooping away.

Feeling like any further walking couldn't be nearly as interesting as that, I looked around to try to see where I was and if I could work out what direction I needed to go in. The fog seemed thinner, and I saw a very road-shaped indent in the snow. I wandered to it and found a very conveniently placed sign with a direction pointing towards the le Rege manor.

I stuck my hands in my pockets and hurried along back to the manor. I felt a ridiculous smile threatening on my face the whole way back and had to keep shaking my head to clear it. But there was a bubble of something in my chest that accompanied the thought that maybe Knightsbridge wouldn't be so bad after all.

CHAPTER THREE

It had been the first time I'd bumped into Rune while utterly lost in fog, but it wasn't the last. What wasn't lost was the knowledge that maybe I did get lost on purpose in the hope I'd see him again.

For the next couple of days, as I made an afternoon constitutional a habit, I only saw the raven. If it was even the same one. That seemed pretty unlikely to me, but then what did I know about ravens? It might have been a crow for all I knew about birds. But it – being many or one – watched me carefully.

The next time I finally saw Rune on my walk, he seemed to appear out of nowhere again, with the same sinfully delicious half smile on his face.

I wanted to say that I didn't warm and perk up instantly at the sight of him, but that would have been a bold-faced lie. And I'd learned young that lying to yourself was a dangerous game; you could lie to the world, but never should to yourself.

"Lena," he said with a nod and the raven cried mournfully. Rune seemed to look at it like they were conversing silently, but then he turned back to me. "Lost again?"

"I am," I joked.

Humour lit his features and breathing was suddenly a little more difficult. "On purpose?"

I nodded noncommittally. "Perhaps."

"Good." He took another step towards me, and my feet matched his like I was on autopilot, or something far more celestial was pulling us together. "You never said where you were staying."

As enamoured with him as I was, telling a strange guy where I lived was maybe not the best idea. Yet. "I didn't."

"I sense you're not going to."

"You sense right. The force is strong with this one."

Even amusedly quizzical, he was sexy. "The force?"

I frowned. Who didn't at least know of *Star Wars*? "You know." I put my hand over my mouth to mimic Vader. "Luke, I am your father."

He nodded. "Right. Of course." He looked around. As one, we both took another step towards each other. "Will you tell me anything about you?"

Another mutual step closer. I shrugged. "Will you tell me anything about *you*?" I countered.

We were close enough that our clothes almost brushed against each other and my whole body hummed at his nearness. I tingled. Goosebumps flared in nervous anticipation that he might actually touch me.

He looked down at me, all suave and sexy cockiness. It might have just been wishful thinking, but the look deep in his eyes had me believing he wanted to touch me as much as I wanted him to touch me. I was captivated by those eyes. So pale. Framed by such dark lashes. I couldn't look away if I'd wanted to. Something pinned me to him in a way I'd never felt before.

"What would you want to know?" he asked. His voice was

echoey, like I was hearing it from a distance or while I was underwater.

Everything in my head was him. How would his kiss taste? What would his hands feel like on my body? My nose tingled with something almost smoky citrus along with the freshness of new snow.

My senses felt heightened, and my head had this weird combination of clarity and fuzziness. He was all clarity. Everything else was a distant memory, irrelevant and unnecessary.

I could feel every single beat of my heart, heavy and steady and sure against my ribs.

The sting of the cold against my face was bracing and acute.

"Everything," I breathed.

His eyes searched mine and my body took another step towards him. His hands went to my arms to steady me where I stumbled into his body. Something crackled between us. Something that was already fanning this rabid crush into an eternal passion that I was both terrified of and ready for it to utterly destroy me.

Then, the raven cried again, and Rune stepped away from me.

"I'm sure I will see you again, Lena." Was it my imagination? Or was his voice as choked as my throat felt?

I nodded. "At school, at least."

He also nodded. "At least."

He seemed hesitant to go, but he finally walked away and left me once more in the enveloping fog. It seemed to wrap around me, and I almost convinced myself that I felt hands caress me. His hands.

As my cheeks heated horribly at my ridiculousness, I forced my feet to take me back to the manor. I ran straight up to my room and locked the door to give me the privacy I needed to soothe some of the deep ache of longing that Rune had caused in me.

A few days later, I walked out the front doors of the manor and saw a – the? – raven perched atop one of the giant statues in the drive. It regarded me with its little head cocked sideways. I felt like it was judging me, but I had no idea if I passed or not.

"Don't suppose you know if I'll see Rune today, do you?" I asked it, like I was actually going to get an answer out of it, and like it had actually been the same raven I'd been seeing all week. "Or if you'll cock block me again if I do?"

The raven gave its shrill caw, and I felt my cheeks heat.

"No, of course it can't understand you, idiot," I muttered to myself. "Let alone have any idea you're crushing obsessively over mystery boy."

It felt like I walked twice as far as usual before I saw Rune leaning against a stone wall, staring down into a river. The raven, who had seemed to be following me from the manor, finally came to rest on a lamppost above his head.

"It seems you found me today," Rune said, without looking away from the river.

"Did I?" I asked, coming to stop next to him. I leant back against the wall, half-sitting on it, and he finally looked at me.

"Or perhaps you were led," he teased.

The raven shrieked, but I didn't know if it was agreeing or arguing. Whatever it was, it seemed to make Rune smile.

"Is there always this much fog?" I asked him.

"In Knightsbridge, yes. Something about the…" He seemed to

be searching for the right words. "Environment."

I nodded, like I understood anything about the environment. "Oh."

"Have you been this far from home before?" he asked, casually, like he totally wasn't fishing for information.

"Considering I don't know how far away I am from where I started, or how many circles I went in to get here, I can't answer that. *If*," I continued, not wanting to put him off entirely but not sure how much I should give away, "you're referring to my accent. No. This is my first time out of Australia."

He looked at me with a frown like he was trying to work something out, then he smiled. "Well, welcome to Knightsbridge, Lena…"

The way he finished that sentence sounded very much like he wanted my last name. I looked down to hide a smile at his efforts. "Just Lena will be fine. Rune…?"

He chuckled but looked confused about something. "Just Rune will do."

I pulled myself up on to the wall proper. But of course, I bungled it totally and started falling backwards. Rune was between my legs in a second. His arm was wrapped tightly around my waist, and my body was hard against his. My centre was against him, and my legs had wrapped around his body in an effort of self-preservation.

My breath was embarrassingly shallow, but everything in me sizzled and tingled and I had never wanted anyone to close the gap between us more than I did right then. I didn't know why I hadn't already. I wasn't usually the kind of girl to hold back from something I wanted. Not when everything in me was telling me he wanted it, too.

We seemed to sway towards each other. Then he took a deep breath, helped me get my feet under me and took a visceral step back.

"You want to be careful," he said.

I nodded. "I will. Thanks."

This time, he didn't seem to feel the need to hurry off. But when we stood in a silence – that wasn't uncomfortable but extended – for long enough, I cleared my throat.

"I guess I should find my way back."

"I guess you should. If you told me where you lived, I could walk you back."

I smirked. "Maybe on our…fifth meeting," I suggested, pulling a random number out of my head.

"I look forward to it."

I gave him an awkward nod as I started walking away in the direction that I thought I'd come from. The raven once again seemed to follow me or…maybe as Rune had suggested, it was leading me back.

"So, you don't hate me after all?" I asked it before I went inside.

It gave a caw, then flew away. I got the feeling it didn't hate me, but that didn't mean it actually liked me either.

About two weeks after I'd arrived in Knightsbridge, I was pretty sure that raven had something – everything – to do with him. I had seen it without him plenty, but it always left after I saw him, and I wouldn't see it for the rest of my walk, except the one time it seemed to fly me home.

As I walked along that day, the raven keeping me company, I

found myself talking to it.

"So does anything dictate on what days or under what circumstances I see Rune?"

It answered, but I didn't understand it.

"You just think sometimes it'd be nice to let me find him? Or is it fate?" I teased.

I laughed at the idea of fate, but the raven seemed to have very strong feelings about it. I still didn't understand what they were though.

"Okay, keep your feathers on," I told it, thinking I was being quite clever. The raven didn't seem to think I was very clever.

Rune appeared in front of me, and the raven seemed to shout at him. Rune frowned and paused. My heart crashed at the look on his face, the stance of his body. Was he avoiding me?

Whether he was or not, he turned to go. My feet carried me quickly forwards against all better judgement. My hand lighted on his arm and he looked at it like it confused him before he turned to me. His eyebrow rose quizzically as he waited for me to say something.

But I was too busy getting lost in those mesmerising eyes. Too busy wondering what his kiss tasted like. Too busy wondering if it was too cold for more than just a kiss or whether our combined body heat would be enough to justify getting all our clothes off.

My heart raced. My stomach fluttered. Heat pooled deep in me. And I felt flushed.

He blinked slowly and the spell was broken.

"Before you go, Rune–"

I didn't need to come up with a good excuse as to why I was moments away from fondling a veritable stranger because that stranger wrapped me in his arms and kissed me.

My heart stopped entirely. My stomach dropped right down to the depths of Hell. In my head was just him. I smelled fresh snow and something smoky with a touch of citrus about him. And he tasted…like all my wildest dreams come true.

As his tongue claimed mine, I wrapped my arms around his shoulders and reached up on tip toe so my body moulded with his. His hand blazed a searing path up my side, and I definitely melted for him. My hands fisted his jacket like I couldn't get him close enough. One of my hands slid up into his hair. One of his ran up my leg like he was about to coax it around his hip.

"Lena," he groaned against my lips, and I'd never heard such need before.

The raven cried its mournful caw, almost like a warning, once more and, by the time I opened my eyes, both it and Rune were gone.

The chill of the wind was in stark contrast to the warmth of his kiss.

And holy hells, what a kiss it had been.

It had been hands down the best kiss of my life, leaving me wanting so very much more. So, of course he disappeared into thin air with only the vaguest notion that I might see him at school in two bloody weeks, or around the woods the next day.

I sighed, looking around. I wasn't sure if I was hoping to see Rune again so soon, or if I was resigned that the only thing I might see was the way back to the manor.

So, when I realised the fog had thinned again somewhat and realised the manor was actually not that far away, I was surprised.

But at least it was a fairly short walk back to the privacy of my locked bedroom where I could lose myself to the memory of Rune's kiss until I shattered with a silent breath of his name on my lips.

CHAPTER FOUR

The bridesmaid dresses were, in fact, not hideous. They were the opposite of hideous. They were glamour and sophistication and, provided my body didn't change too much over time, it was a dress I could pull out for any and all future soirees, and feel like I'd be the most overdressed person in whatever room I entered.

Okay, that was a slight exaggeration. It did require heels, but it did look good. Better on Mia than me, but I still pulled it off well.

I wouldn't mind Rune pulling it off...

A deep red, floor length, A-line chiffon gown. The bodice was tight and covered in lace. The neckline hugged my throat, and lace sleeves ended in stiff points over my hands. There was a great giant split up one side, but the way the whole dress was put together meant the skirt could fall with the split unnoticeable.

The last two weeks of January had been filled with fittings – both for my bridesmaid dress and my new school uniform – and menu tastings and flower choices, and no sign of Rune.

I didn't see him, but I saw the raven who seemed his constant companion. I couldn't tell if it didn't like me or whether it watched me with the typical apathy of animals in regards to humanity. I was sure it was apathy, but something niggled at me and told me it really didn't like me.

By the time the twenty-ninth rolled around, I hadn't had much chance to think about the enigmatic mystery boy who might very well have the power to capture my heart with nothing more than a single kiss. It didn't mean I didn't think about him every chance I got, I just got little chance.

"How many people are coming?" I asked Mia as we stood on the top landing and watched the elegant servants putting all the last-minute touches together on the morning of the big wedding.

The back of the manor had a large stone terrace that had to be kept cleared of snow. There were fires and flower arrangements and ice sculptures to place appropriately so nothing melted or caught on fire. There were tables and a bar to be moved. There was the arch and the chairs for the ceremony. It was little wonder they'd left it all until the morning of.

I didn't know much about party set-up or about the work of servants, but it seemed like they worked quickly. Really quickly. Like I was watching a time-lapse video, everything just started coming together before my very eyes.

"Most of the town." Mia nodded and amended, "Probably nearly all of it? Everyone over fifty definitely."

It was a weird line to draw given Mum and Etienne's ages, but then what did I know about the inhabitants of Knightsbridge?

"The youth of Knightsbridge too cool for a winter wedding?" I joked.

Mia looked at me for a moment like that wasn't the reason at all. But it was kind of hard to take her seriously with the rollers in her hair, especially when she grinned. "Something like that," she said.

"Is it normal for weddings to happen in winter here?" I asked her, thinking that it seemed an awful lot more work than it needed to be if it had been at any other time of year. "And why outside?"

Mia smirked like she had a secret. "Quite normal."

"Don't get me wrong. The snow is pretty and all. But all the work that's going into it?" I shook my head. "It just seems a lot."

"I guess our parents just couldn't wait."

I snorted. "Yeah. Like they've been waiting for their wedding night?"

Mia nudged me companionably. "We shouldn't begrudge them their happiness."

I nodded in agreement. "And I don't. I just don't know why a piece of paper is so important that she had to put us in lace in the middle of winter."

Mia laughed. "That's your main concern?"

"One. It's *one* of my concerns. I'm also worried that my hair will freeze into some horrible mass of curls, and I'll never get them out."

She nodded but, as she opened her mouth to reply, we both heard my mum's disappointed, "Oh, no!"

"Mum?" I ran to my room, where she was getting ready, and we found her reading a note in her hands.

She looked up as she dropped her hands in her lap emphatically and pouted.

"What's wrong?" I asked her, all ready to be indignant and go on the war path for her. "Has he cancelled the wedding?"

Mum frowned. "What? No." She waved the note. "Etienne tells me that there's still no news of Erasmus' return. You don't know anything, do you, Artemia?" she asked Mia, while I felt a little twinge of something sweet that Mum and Etienne were exchanging notes on the morning of their wedding.

Mia shook her head. "I haven't heard, sorry. Every time I bring up the wedding, he ignores it."

Which proved that Mia was still in contact with her brother even if no one else was.

I had to wonder what game Erasmus was playing. If indeed it was a game. I wasn't exactly all that thrilled at being dragged across half the world only to find that we were here for a wedding, but Mum legitimately seemed happy and carefree for the first time in my life. And Etienne seemed the same. Mia had been right when she said we shouldn't begrudge them their happiness. It was a minor inconvenience in my life, but I could make it work. I wasn't going to chuck such a wobbly that I disappeared for a month. Unlike some people. And there was no way I would have missed their wedding to make a point that honestly didn't matter in the grand scheme of life.

Mum sighed. "Etienne will be so disappointed if he misses it. He was so hoping Erasmus would be back in time. Could you try him again, dear?"

Mia nodded and pulled her phone out of her bra strap. Her fingers moved dexterously over the keyboard before she put it away again. "If he doesn't reply in an hour, I'll call him."

"Will he be able to make it back in time if he hasn't left already?" I asked.

Mia and Mum shared a look like I was the only person in the room who didn't know something, and they were going to keep me that way. I chose not to worry about it. I was sure there were a lot of things I didn't know, and there wasn't much I could do about it.

Go with the flow. No spoilers.

"If Erasmus so chooses, he could be here in moments," Mum said, looking impressively autocratically unimpressed. I shivered at the austerity and poise she had commanded since we'd arrived, but in a good way. But her words were what hit me more than her manner.

I filed her words away under weird and decided that Mum got to be hyperbolic and mysterious on her special day if she wanted to. After all, this was her first – and hopefully last – actual wedding.

A knock came at the door, and we turned to see Grandma Vi sticking her head in.

She didn't look all that much different than usual, and I wasn't sure if she was dressed for the wedding already or not. She wore a thick, dark grape coloured, floor-length dress made of satin with three-quarter sleeves and a thick collar, and a sash around the middle.

"Is everything okay?" I asked, totally still prepared for everything to go to shit.

Grandma Vi nodded. "Fine. Etienne would just like to see you girls before you get dressed."

Mia and I were still in pale pink bridesmaid satin robes, and Mum had a matching one in ivory with 'bride' on it. The night before hadn't exactly been the hen's night I'd have wished for Mum, but I didn't think I'd want to actually *be* at a typical hen's night for my own mother.

I felt a bit weird going to see my soon-to-be stepfather in just a robe, but Mia just shrugged and started following her grandmother out. So, I bucked it up, decided that Etienne wouldn't think twice about it unless he was a creeper – and then I'd be able to get Mum out of there if necessary – and followed Mia and Grandma Vi upstairs where Etienne was getting ready in their bedroom suite.

It was the first time I'd been in it and my jaw dropped. The suite was freaking huge. Enough space for comfortable couches around the fireplace. A small round table and chairs that I assumed were for lazy morning breakfasts. A ginormous bed on a raised dais that, like mine, had big curtains to draw around it.

Grandma Vi helped herself to a chair in front of the fire and crossed her legs elegantly while she waited for whatever we were there for.

"Where is he?" Etienne thundered when he saw Mia.

Mia didn't shrink back, she didn't tremble, and she didn't look scared of him.

"I don't know," Mia said, but it felt like she was implying she did but wouldn't say.

Etienne frowned. "What has he told you?"

I just stood at the edge of the conversation, wondering why on earth I'd been called in for this family matter. I wouldn't know who Erasmus was if I ran into him in the woods, how would I have any idea where he was? The vague thought floated through my head that Etienne knew that his daughter knew where Erasmus was, and now I was lumped in under the category of 'daughter'. It felt stupid to think it, but I couldn't help the flair of hope that these people were including me in their family, even if I felt like a total fish out of water in the room.

At least Etienne gave zero shits about my state of dress. Or rather, as few shits as he gave about Mia, so I could cross creeper off my list of red flags. It didn't mean he wasn't just very good at the game, but I was going into this whole bizarre scenario giving everything and everyone the benefit of the doubt, so he'd get a tick on this one.

"Well?" Etienne pressed when Mia didn't say anything.

Mia wrung her hands while Grandma Vi's face got more and more pinched in displeasure. Mia looked concerned, but I didn't know what about exactly. Grandma Vi just looked like she was ready to slap Erasmus upside the head as soon as she saw him.

"He won't tell me anything," Mia said earnestly. "Every time I bring up the wedding, he tells me he's done indulging your fantasies and there's no reason to be part of yet another mistake."

Ouch.

I was about ready to slap this Erasmus upside the head myself. What a douche! But I appreciated Mia not being quite so honest with Mum. She'd have been horrified to think that one of Etienne's kids didn't want him marrying her. Although, it sounded like it wasn't Mum and me that Erasmus opposed to, and just his dad marrying altogether.

Then that made me think of something.

Another mistake...?

Has Etienne been married before? Quite likely to Erasmus and Mia's mum. But just *how* many times had he been married before?

"You tell him," Etienne told her sternly. "You tell him that if he misses his father's wedding then there will be hell to pay."

"The boy will *wish* for hell once I'm through with him," Grandma Vi muttered, more to herself than the rest of the room.

"Just get him here," Etienne snapped, and I saw there was

definitely a temper in him. It looked like it could be held at bay and not take him over completely, so I'd be wary, but not worried. Yet.

"I'll do what I can," Mia promised.

"Well, do it better!"

"Leave the girl alone, Etienne!" Grandma Vi chided. Her voice was soft, but it held a forceful authority that seemed effortless. "Do not blame her for her brother's disobedience."

Etienne growled then swept from the room.

"I'm sorry you had to witness that, Evangeline," she said to me as she stood up. "My grandson oft acts like a prize idiot, but you can see where he gets it from." She went over and took Mia's hands. "Do what you can, my dear, but we all know Erasmus is as tameable as his father."

Mia nodded to her, and Grandma Vi glided out of the room. Mum and Etienne's suite. Which felt weird that they'd been the ones to leave. Once the adults were gone, Mia dropped into a chair and breathed out heavily. Clearly, we weren't going anywhere just yet.

"Nothing like a wedding to bring out the family crazy," she said with a sour chuckle.

"Erasmus certainly seems to piss off your dad."

A small smile crossed Mia's face and there was a sign of deep fondness for her brother. "He does. They annoy each other. I'm not sure they realise just how similar they are. My brother spends his life doing anything and everything to…annoy my father. My father does the same to my brother, but I'm not sure, for him, it's a conscious decision."

"After everything I've heard about him, I don't know if I want to meet this Erasmus or not," I told her.

"Pfft," she scoffed, looking at me with a wry smirk like she knew the answer to that. "All the girls want to meet him. Most of the guys, too. No. Just everyone. I don't see the appeal personally, but apparently he does. Appeal, that is. To the masses." She seemed exasperated about that. "He's suave, brooding, dark, gorgeous. Or so I hear damn near every day of my life. At school, they worship him. The adults are even worse. The whole of Knightsbridge would probably happily die for him."

Well, that was certainly not what I expected. Here, I'd pictured him being this crotchety, pernickety old man trapped in a young man's body, more Mr Collins than Heathcliff. Mia made him sound…intriguing. Which was probably not a good thing, because Erasmus wasn't exactly available. Not to me anyway. In a few hours, he was going to be my stepbrother, to say nothing of the fact that he was unlikely to be interested in a little old me.

I smiled at her. "I'd like to think I'm not quite so tragic that what appeals to the masses automatically appeals to me."

"You like more substance to your men?" she teased.

"Who doesn't?"

Mia grinned and we shared a look like she knew we both knew that was bullshit. And, I mean, it was. What about mystery forest guy? He was clearly the 'appeal to the masses' type and I was smitten. Obsessively so.

"Come on," she said, and she hauled herself out of the chair. "Let's forget my brother and get back to your mum."

I inclined my head in agreement. "We don't want her sitting down there by herself on her wedding day."

"No," Mia laughed. "Who else would make sure my father

44

doesn't try to sneak a glimpse of her before the ceremony."

She held her elbow out and I took it before walking out of the room.

Mum didn't seem bothered that we'd been gone, she was happily sitting at the dressing table in my room having her hair and makeup done while some lovely classical music washed through the room.

"There you both are," she said warmly when she saw us.

Time passed quickly and we did forget all about Erasmus as we drank mimosas and got dressed for the wedding. It was hard to have reservations about the speed of everything when Mum seemed so legitimately happy, when Mia was so sincerely welcoming and lovely. Hanging out with them and singing to music and being all girly and ridiculous was one of the most – no, *the* most – relaxing time of my whole life.

If this, this happiness and untroubled-ness, was what her marriage to Etienne and our life in Knightsbridge was going to be, then I couldn't be against it. For the first time in my life, I felt like I might have finally found my home.

When Mortas gave us the okay, we picked up our bouquets and got Mum down the stairs in her satin and lace fish-tail gown. Mia carried her train while Mum held my arm and laughed about how she should have picked a different silhouette.

"Nonsense," I told her. "You look amazing."

And she did. She looked stunning. Perfect. I wasn't going to bring up any of the useless random white wedding trivia that was swirling in my head, because I knew that it would sound like I was berating her or doubting her. Still, she looked at me like she knew what I was thinking, and I gave her my biggest smile in comfort and encouragement.

The bridal march started up and Mia preceded us all outside. My heart fluttered madly, and I didn't really know why. I focussed on Mia's back and started my ever-so-less graceful glide down the aisle. Etienne's eyes were exactly where they should be; on my mum as she followed behind. And his face said everything I needed to know about this marriage. He was all-in. No one could fake the kind of absolute happiness and joy that shone deep in his eyes. I hoped.

Mia and I took our place to the side, and I watched as Mum took Etienne's hands and the officiant began the service. It was my chance to look around at the gathered guests. Both sides of the aisle were full up, despite my certainty that Mum didn't know any of these people, at least not well enough for them to sit on her side.

But it wasn't the fact that both sides were full that confused me the most.

Because it looked like the occupants of le Rege manor weren't the only ones in the middle of a multi-time period revival faire. All the guests looked like they'd stepped out of different time periods in the last five or six hundred years. Finally, my love of period drama and all things history seemed vaguely useful.

There were women with bustles – actual freaking bustles – on their very heavy-looking satin dresses. There were men in – no joke – tights and knee-length pants like they'd just stepped off an Austen set. Women in white lace gowns like they were off to Hanging Rock. Bridgerton-style ball gowns in ever so less bright colours made quite the appearance. There were some Rockabilly outfits. A couple of flappers. And a few in something they probably got since the turn of the last century. Gothic fashion seemed a favourite. Sideburns prevailed. One man even had those poofy pants you associate with Shakespeare.

It was simultaneously bananas and awesome, but did make me wonder – again – what kind of weird-arse place I'd found myself in. If they were this into dressing up and obvious individualism, then maybe it wasn't so bad after all. I could live in a place where you got to unabashedly be yourself, no matter what that self was.

I did notice though the way they looked at me and Mum intently. They whispered behind hands and programmes and fans. It wasn't particularly odd, I imagined, to be focussed on the bridal party at a wedding, but it felt like they weren't quite so interested in Mia. It made some sort of sense, given we were the newbies to town. I guessed.

After the ceremony, as I followed Mum and Etienne through the well-wishers, I realised the guests were still watching us carefully. It wasn't just the look of normal wedding guests, all awe-struck over how beautiful the wedding party looked or commenting on what they would have done better. I realised it was different. Calculating. With a hint of something almost, but not quite, sinister in it. I couldn't figure out their intentions, for good or ill, and that made me uneasy.

For the first time since we'd arrived in Knightsbridge, I wasn't sure how welcome we really were. I didn't feel like we were about to be run out of town, but there was the potential for one wrong step to have them whipping out their torches and pitchforks. There was a tension through the whole party, as though they were just waiting for someone to mess up royally. If my past luck was any indication, that someone would be me.

But those that Etienne or Mia introduced me to smiled politely and didn't act like I was left wanting. I didn't get the third degree. By the time the cake had been cut and the party had become much less formal, I'd decided that I was over-reacting. Of course, they were wary of and interested in us. Mum and I were unknowns. We were new to town, and I'd only left the manor to go for walks since we arrived. The only other person I'd met had been Rune, who I couldn't help but look for among the guests.

Though, true to Mia's prediction, most of them seemed to be middle-aged or over. Those who were young enough to be school-aged were most definitely not Rune.

"Evangeline," Etienne said, and I pulled my eyes off the crowd.

"Yes?"

He passed me a glass of Champagne. "I just wanted to thank you for helping us make today so perfect."

I felt like he was thanking me for much more than that, but I shrugged. "Mum's happy and that's all that matters."

He nodded. "It does, but that doesn't mean you had to purport yourself with the grace and decorum you have."

I felt my cheeks flush and smiled. "Oh… Well. Thank you, Etienne."

From the corner of my eye, I thought I saw the flap of black wings against the lights, but Etienne distracted me.

His eyes narrowed and I thought he was angry with me for some reason, but then I realised he was looking behind me and he said to someone else, "You finally grace us with your presence."

Was this finally the mysterious Erasmus?

"I wouldn't have missed your wedding," came their reply.

Wait.

I knew that voice.

How did I know that voice?

Something in me was warning me not to turn around. Great big honking red lights. *Don't do it*. Something was telling me I didn't want to know who belonged to that voice. But I had to know where I knew that voice from.

"You very nearly did," Etienne said coolly.

I started to turn.

"And yet, here I am…"

And finally saw his face.

"…Father."

Shit.

My dirtiest daydream, the kiss I would never forget, the guy who had starred in my hottest fantasies for the past two weeks? I guess he had found out where I lived on our fifth meeting after all…

Because he was my new stepbrother.

And being wrapped in a pristine, perfectly fitting navy suit wasn't doing anything to help me move on from thinking about him in the most unholy of ways. Even with that heavy scowl so firmly indented on his gorgeous face.

"Erasmus," Etienne said, "meet Evangeline."

Rune looked at me. There was the briefest flash of recognition on his face and then…nothing. I may as well have been a rug on the floor for all the bothers he could clearly give about me.

"Where is Artemia?" he asked Etienne, as though bored already.

"Erasmus," Etienne snapped. "Don't you want to say hello to

your new sister?”

Rune's gaze raked over my body, but there was only ice in it. “Stepsister.”

“Regardless,” Etienne pressed.

Rune sighed like he was surrounded by idiots. “Hello, Evangeline.”

It was a far cry from the huskily groaned way my name had last come from his lips. It was all ice and venom. Clearly Rune and Erasmus were two very different people.

I inclined my head. “Hello…Erasmus.”

Etienne smiled like everything was better now. “There, now. Was that so hard?”

“I've played your little game, Father. Since you won't let me play mine, you might be so good as to tell me where Artemia is.”

Etienne seemed to realise he'd lost whatever battle they were fighting. “She's helping your mother–”

“Stepmother,” Rune said harshly. “I will find her. Good night.” He spared me the briefest nod possible, then disappeared.

“Forgive Erasmus,” Etienne said to me. “He's…adjusting.”

I took a deep breath. “Aren't we all?” I replied, forcing a smile I certainly didn't feel.

Etienne inclined his head. “Indeed. Some,” he seemed to be meaning me here, “more graciously than others.” When I said nothing, he finished, “If you'll excuse me, dear. I think it's time I danced with my wife again.”

“Of course. It's your party. Have at it. Her.” I frowned and stopped talking, not keen to know where that train of thought would take me.

Etienne gave me a weird short bow and swept away, leaving

me free to slink up to my room.

I changed and sat in the window seat to watch the party continue on below me as I unwound my hair from the complicated chignon it had been wound into. I told myself I wasn't thinking about Rune, and his kiss or how his hands would feel on my body. I told myself I wasn't attracted to a guy who was clearly cold and distant and rude. I told myself I wasn't wondering if he'd be able to get from his room to mine without being seen. I told myself that I wasn't imagining the things he could do to me in the safety of the cold, dark night.

I told myself all these things, but it didn't make any of them true.

CHAPTER FIVE

The next Monday, while I was fixing my tie, there was a knock on my door.

"Come in," I said, absently.

In the reflection, I saw Mum poke her head around the doorway. No honeymoon for them just yet. "You decent?"

I smiled to her. "As decent as I'll ever be."

She walked into the room, closing the door behind her, and looked at me like all her dreams come true. Her eyes shone with unshed tears. "You look awesome," she said softly.

I took a deep breath as I looked myself over.

There wasn't much to be done with my auburn hair or my green eyes, but the grey and maroon uniform was tailored to within an inch of its life. The seamstress who'd spent an afternoon pinning me up had made sure of it.

Maroon plaid skirt falling just short of my knees, knee-high white socks and black mary-jane shoes with a tiny heel, white shirt, maroon and silver tie, grey sweater, and grey blazer with maroon piping and the Academy's insignia on the breast pocket. I looked like a proper little private school kid. And I'd never been a private school kid.

As Mum helped me do my tie up – she *had* been a private

school kid before me – I knew that this was what she'd wanted for me from the start. The apology in her eyes wasn't for uprooting my life again or surrounding me with strangers. It was for not being able to give me this life sooner. No matter how complicated our relationship was or how much I might disagree with some of her decisions, I couldn't stay mad at the purity of her heart. I loved her and I knew she loved me with everything she was.

"Think I'll pass Etienne's approval?" I teased.

Mum hugged me. "If he can find anything wrong with you, then we're packing up and leaving."

I knew she didn't mean it. Even if Etienne was the wrong guy – again – she'd stay because he could give me a future she never could on her own. I hated that and appreciated it. But, as long as he wasn't raising a hand to her, then who she married was her choice. She did look happy, and I'd have to be happy with that.

"Let's get some breakfast in you and then you three had better be on your way. Don't want to be late for your first day."

I frowned as Mum led me out of the room, snatching up my bag as I passed it. "Three?" I asked.

She nodded as she glided gracefully down the stairs. Whatever she and Etienne were, it really did look good on her.

"Yes. Three. You, Artemia and Erasmus."

I paused on the stairs. "Erasmus goes to the Academy?"

Of course, he did. He'd told me as much the first day we'd met in the woods. When he'd just been Rune. But the only way I was getting through this whole thing was to pretend Rune and Erasmus were two different people.

She nodded again, coming back to tug my arm gently when I didn't follow by myself. "He's in his final year, so you'll have a few months for him to show you the ropes before going it on your own."

"I don't need him to show me the ropes. I've got Mia for that, haven't I?"

"Artemia's still intermediate, Evie." Still the nickname I despised. "You'll be at opposite ends of the campus most of the time."

Well, shit.

Starting a new school was daunting enough. Starting it halfway through the school year when my compatriots at home were just starting from the beginning was enough to have me worried that I wouldn't just be six months behind but miles behind. Now I wouldn't even have Mia to lean on?

Double, triple, a million times shit.

Mia, Grandma Vi, and Etienne were in the breakfast room when Mum and I got down there.

"Morning, my love," Etienne said to Mum, helping her into her chair and kissing her lightly. "Good morning, Evangeline." I nodded to him and bit my tongue on my thoughts about him using my full name. "Well, how's this? All my girls with me for breakfast. A very pleasant start to the day."

Mia and I shared a smile.

Having never had a sibling, it really did feel like I had one now. I seemed to know she was bemoaning the wistful nonsense of a doting parent and sharing that feeling with me. While I wasn't sure yet if Etienne doted on me, I agreed with the sentiment.

"Are you ready for your first day?" Mia asked me as the butler brought me eggs and bacon and coffee.

I shrugged. "I think so. I don't really know what to expect so

I don't really know what to be prepared for."

Mia grinned. "Any questions, just come and find me."

"Why bother when I'll already be there?" Rune's voice broke over me like an ice-cold wave, but at the same time like intense heat.

I didn't care for it.

He walked to the seat at the table across from me, his eyes roving over the parts of my body he could see. I repaid the favour and, annoyingly, cared a whole lot more for the view than I did my reaction to him.

He filled out his uniform perfectly. Of course, he did. Like mine, it had been tailored to fit him like a glove. Nay, a second skin. Never before had anyone looked so good in a school uniform of all things. The grey trousers wrapped around his legs in a way that made my fingers jealous. His shirt and tie were the same as mine and Mia's, but his sweater was maroon with a grey stripe and his blazer was maroon with grey piping. I guessed I'd find out soon if that was the boys' uniform or reserved for final years.

"Erasmus. Evangeline. My office before you leave," Etienne said as he got up from the table.

I snuck a look over to Rune. He behaved as though he hadn't heard his father, but he was in Etienne's office when I finally got there.

"Come, Evangeline," Etienne said to me.

I walked over to him, and he leant down so we were at equal head height.

He looked deep into my eyes and spoke carefully. "Whatever you may see or hear at school, all is well and normal, and you are safe."

I blinked. "Um… Okay, thanks for the tip."

Now Etienne blinked. He gripped my chin with vice-like fingers and forced my eyes to stare even deeper into his own, like that was possible. I could smell the guy's breath. I was breathing it. It wasn't unpleasant as far as smells went, but I didn't exactly enjoy doing something so intimate with my stepfather.

"Whatever you may see or hear at school, all is well and normal, and you are safe," he repeated.

I blinked again. "Thanks, but I heard you the first time."

"Erasmus!" Etienne barked and Rune stepped forward with a boredom that must have taken years to perfect.

"Father?"

"You said you compelled her."

Rune grinned and there was nothing pleasant about it, despite what the heat pooling in my stomach might be trying to tell me.

"I never said I used compulsion."

Etienne roared and turned angrily. His arm swiped a vase off the table beside him, launching it a full ten metres across the room. When it shattered against the wall, I flinched out of sheer habit. Ten years later and I still flinched.

"What are we going to do now?" Etienne asked Rune.

Rune shrugged. "This was your idea, not mine. I said we could keep the mother alive long enough if we had to."

Pardon?

Etienne tutted. "It is better this way. For everyone."

"So, why haven't you tried compelling her before now?" Rune's voice was snide.

"I have been…preoccupied," Etienne answered.

"You've been playing honeymoon with your new toy," Rune

accused.

Etienne was like a thundercloud. "You will not speak to me like that."

I mean, it seemed he did, though.

"You wouldn't be in this mess," Rune spat at him, "if you'd pulled it out of her long enough to try compelling her daughter."

"Whoa…" I chuckled humourlessly. "I don't need to know about their…" Both Etienne and Rune were glaring at me for interrupting them. "What our parents get up to is their business…" I said slowly.

I certainly didn't need to know about my mother's sex life. I didn't currently have one of my own to speak of, unless you counted dirty dreams about my stepbrother. I didn't really care about other people's, least of all the woman who gave me life.

"Then you are tasked with keeping her safe," Etienne told Rune like it was a threat.

"Once again, making your problems my problems," Rune growled back at him, and I had to wonder who actually held the authority in this dynamic.

"Erasmus…" Etienne warned.

"She'll need to be told the truth," Rune said like I wasn't in the room. I didn't doubt he wished that was true.

"She is right here," I pointed out, thinking now seemed like a really good time to be telling me whatever truth there was to be told.

Etienne pinched the bridge of his nose and spoke to Rune. "There is not enough time today. Keep her safe and we will talk about this soon."

"As you command, *Father*," Rune replied, dropping into a

mocking bow. "Come, Evangeline." He swept out of the room, and I hurried after him.

Having added layers appropriate for the outside weather, Rune drove us to school. Mia insisted on sitting in the backseat so I could get the full view of Knightsbridge Academy as we rolled up the drive. And, I had to say, I was glad she did. The burning form of my million questions after Etienne's study, and of Rune at my side, was something I could do without, but they were all-but forgotten as the car crested a rise and the gates of Knightsbridge loomed out of the never-ending fog.

They were great wrought iron monstrosities, emblazoned with the school crest. The drive wasn't as long as the one to *Manoir le Rege*, but I'd still have hated being dropped at the gates in the morning.

We drove around one of the huge gothic-inspired buildings to what looked like a student carpark. There weren't very many cars, though. Either we were very early or…

"There are a lot of boarders," Mia said as though she could read my mind.

As we got out of the car, I nodded, still astounded by my surroundings. My little history nerd heart was going nuts at the architecture. Growing up in Australia, I didn't realise that places like this really existed. Little pockets of history like they'd been frozen in time and protected from destruction and decay.

The buildings weren't the only thing that was amazing.

Every student on campus was unreasonably attractive. They were graceful and perfect. There wasn't a hair out of place. There wasn't a pimple or scar or blemish on any of them. Their uniforms were all, unsurprisingly, tailored to their individual body shapes, which all seemed perfect no matter what they were.

"I'm in some kind of multi-verse," I muttered to myself as Mia smiled at me.

"I'll see you after school," she said. "Rune will show you to administration."

"Will I?" Rune asked, like he was bored. His boredom was, quite frankly, getting boring.

"Ten minutes," Mia told him. "Ten minutes and you can go back to pretending your little sisters don't exist."

"Thank fuck," Rune said. "This way, then."

I followed him, noting the way every single student got out of his way. They stopped and stared at him as he passed like he was the air they all needed to continue living. They were all so busy focussing on him that barely anyone saw little old me. He strode through them all, basking in it but not acknowledging it.

Finally, we got to what looked like offices and found a man waiting for us. There was a woman behind the desk and a girl with thick curly black hair sitting on a chair against the wall like she was waiting her turn.

"Dean Soyer," Rune said, seeming to wield far more authority than anyone else in that room. "This is my...stepsister, Evangeline le Rege."

I'm sorry? What, now? When had *my* name changed?

"Evangeline," Dean Soyer looked at me with the bored disinterest that dealing with a bunch of teenagers on a daily basis would give any sane man. "Welcome to Knightsbridge Academy."

"Lena," I said, glaring at Rune's back. "I go by Lena."

Dean Soyer inclined his head. "I'm sure you do." He snapped

his finger and the girl jumped up and hurried to his side. "Evangeline, this is Amaris. She will show you around." His eyes slid to Rune carefully. "Your…brother–"

"Stepbrother."

The dean looked between us like that had been an interesting interruption on Rune's part. "Rune," he said slowly, "has other responsibilities."

"Responsibilities. Don't care. Take your pick," Rune said before striding out of the room. He paused at the door, gave me a look as though he didn't even care about me enough to dislike me. "Oh, she's not compellable and no one's told her anything. Have fun," he added totally insincerely before he disappeared.

Something in me started to crumble at the hate he'd had for me since the weekend, then I bucked the fuck up and just felt angry. Like, I was *well* aware I'd thought there was something potent between us and then we'd found out who we actually were to each other. But seriously? He didn't have to be a complete dick about it. We did have to live together and go to school together, the least we could do was be civil about it.

"Not compel…" the dean muttered, then looked at me. "I see." He and Amaris shared a look that I'm sure they understood. "Be careful, then."

Amaris nodded then nudged me, "Come on. I'll show you to your locker, then the basics."

We headed outside again.

"Lena, was it?" she asked.

I nodded. "Uh, preferably, yeah."

She grinned at me. "I get it. Ama."

I nodded. "Ama, okay."

She helped me find my locker to drop my bag, then did the general things of dining hall, toilets, and first lesson – which we shared. She also found me a map or, rather, convinced another, much smaller student to give me theirs.

"Okay, you'll be all right from here? Get your first books and stuff?" Ama asked. "There's just something I need to do before class."

I nodded, map in hand. "I think I can find my way there."

She touched a hand to my arm. "Thanks. I'll see you there."

I nodded. "Sure."

I headed back inside as she headed in the opposite direction, towards a building she hadn't taken me anywhere near. I didn't have much chance to think about that though as a body rushed across the corridor, forcing me to pause mid-step.

The body pinned Rune to the lockers at his back. He caught my eye with a cocky smirk before letting her kiss him hungrily. His hands were all up her skirt, fisting it as he dragged it up her legs, as hers were in his hair and grabbing his jumper. Their bodies pressed together tightly, and I was sure she was grinding against his leg.

To say a little green monster of jealousy didn't rise up in me at the sight would have been a lie, but he was my stepbrother and surely there were like laws in place or something – at least some moral code – that said stepsiblings getting together was a bit weird to say the least.

"Where have you been?" I heard her moan at him.

"Travelling," he answered, his eyes flickering to me again for a second.

I kept on the path to my own locker and realised it was just across the corridor from them – from his. Because of course it was. I couldn't say for sure that these were those consequences I'd been waiting for, but I wasn't surprised that fate was finding a way to kick all the hope out of my life just as I was starting to find it.

"I missed you," she continued in that breathy, moaning voice that I assumed was supposed to be sexy.

"I needed to go to the city," was Rune's reply.

Whatever the real reason was, his father had certainly not come up with something as simple as 'he's gone to the city'. So, I felt like that was a lie. Not in the least because I knew he'd been around somewhere during the holidays. Four times at minimum. I had to wonder what and where he'd been the rest of the time, though.

"To get away from the…humans?" she asked cryptically, throwing a look to me.

Wait. What?

Rune looked at me again. There was something mean in him. It played at his lips. It danced in his eyes. He wanted to hurt me. I had no idea why, but he did.

It seemed Rune and Erasmus weren't two different people after all. Clearly the guy I'd kissed in the woods had been toying with me, though I had no idea what he got out of it. Then again, guys like him got off on games without there needing to be an alternative motive.

"She's not compelled," he told the girl.

She frowned in surprise, then smirked. "Where does she think she is?" she whispered, making sure I heard.

"At school," was Rune's answer and she laughed, as though it was the most delusional thing possible.

I felt my cheeks heat and my heart pound in my chest.

Stupid Lena for thinking that Knightsbridge would be any different. I'd been inferior all my life. Poor. Damaged. Broken. Lacking. Here I'd been, stupidly thinking that for once I might find a real home. At least I'd been set to rights early enough to have not become entirely reliant on the delusion.

Grabbing my books, I ducked my head and made my way to my first lesson.

Ama met me at the door with a smile that had a piece of me desperately trying to retain that hope I'd so recently found.

"Find everything okay?" she asked, and I nodded as she led me to a seat.

She sat down at a table with four chairs, across from a guy with caramel skin and dark brown eyes and hair.

"Radu, they/them," they said happily, and I corrected my internal monologue.

"Lena, she/her," I answered, sitting next to Ama.

"Lena *le Rege*," Ama said pointedly like that was important.

Radu's eyes widened. They shared a knowing look with Ama, but I didn't know what it meant. "Really? Well, welcome to Knightsbridge, Lena. I'm sorry you're stuck living with Rune the Ruler."

I frowned in confusion as the classroom got on with finding their seats around us. "The what?"

Radu smirked. "le Rege means 'the ruler', but it's an apt description for Rune. Or what's between his legs, if the rumours are to be believed."

"He's a monster among monsters," Ama breathed softly,

leaning her chin on my shoulder.

A shiver ran through me and, seeing Rune walk past the classroom door, I knew it wasn't just Ama's voice in my ear. I swallowed hard.

Ama chuckled. "Oh, I see," she said as she pulled away from me again.

I blinked. "What?" I said quickly. "No." A self-conscious laugh.

Radu nodded. "No. Of course not."

"Oh, who's this?" asked a blonde girl as she sat at the table with us.

She was smiling as she sat beside Radu, and I noticed – shock horror – she had a very small, red mark like the threatening of a pimple on her chin. So, they weren't all as perfect as I'd thought. That was a comfort.

"This is Lena," Ama said.

"le Rege," Radu finished.

Even her eyes widened, then she was smiling at me again. "I'm Loren. Welcome to Knightsbridge."

"She's…" Ama started like she hoped I wouldn't hear her, "not compellable."

Radu and Loren both looked at her with wide mouths and eyes. "What?" they both breathed.

"What *exactly* does that mean?" I asked. "People keep saying that about me."

Loren's smile widened. "Just that you must be very strong minded."

"Is that a good thing?" I asked and they all tittered.

It was the sort of titter people did to placate you, but I felt like

64

it was intended good-naturedly at least.

"It is," Ama said forcibly. "You obviously know your own mind and who you are."

I sighed. "I wished it felt that way."

Loren put her hand on my arm comfortingly. "Our subconscious minds know what they're doing."

"Do they?" I asked, feeling like mine hadn't got the memo.

After all, why would I keep thinking about Rune the way I did if my subconscious knew what it was doing?

CHAPTER SIX

When we got home that afternoon, Mortas informed us that, "Your father has been called away on business, and your mother has gone with him."

"Stepmother," Rune snapped at him.

"Indeed, sir," Mortas said evenly, the picture-perfect objective servant. "Shall I be arranging dinner to be brought to your room tonight, sir?"

"Yes," Rune answered. "Did my father leave instructions about dealing with Evangeline?"

"Rune!" Mia hissed.

"Monsieur le Rege said Mademoiselle le Rege would be dealt with when he returns."

When Mum and Etienne got back, I was going to have some serious words about this whole 'Mademoiselle le Rege' thing. I knew bringing it up now would just give Rune something else to be a dick about.

Rune frowned at Mortas, then shrugged. "Fine. As long as I don't have to."

"When will he be back?" Mia asked Mortas.

"By the weekend."

"Rune, we can't leave Lena in the dark for a whole week!"

Rune looked at his sister like he honestly couldn't give a shit about how long I was left in the dark. Whatever was in the light, the fuss everyone was making over it, I wasn't sure I wanted to know what it was anyway. I could spend the rest of my time here – my life – blissfully in the dark. Couldn't I?

"As if it would be any different to her current state," Rune drawled.

"And what about the rest of Knightsbridge?"

Rune shrugged. "Much like Evangeline, they are not my problem." Then he strode up the stairs, leaving me with a very apologetic Mia and an apathetic Mortas.

Mia's shrug was more awkward. "I wish I could do more."

I nodded. "No. Sure. I'll… I'm sure whatever it is, I can deal with waiting."

She gave me a grimace that looked like it was trying to be a smile. "It's… It's better coming from my father."

I nodded again. "I'm sure it is."

She gave me another of those grimace-smiles and followed her brother up the stairs. "Let me know if you want to hang out." I nodded once more, but we both knew I wouldn't. "I'll see you for dinner?"

"I'll see you for dinner," I agreed.

By the time Mia was up the stairs, even Mortas was gone, and I was left feeling very much like a problem no one wanted to deal with. The kind of problem you just shoved into a corner, or a drawer, or a boarding school, or a mental facility and decided you didn't have to deal with it until you were ready, regardless of how ready the problem was.

It messed with that feeling of home and settled that had been sneaking in since we arrived. On one hand, I still felt it. I still felt the most at home I ever had. So, what did it say about me that the place I felt the most at home was also a place that wasn't shy about the fact it was hiding something from me?

Going about my own life for the rest of the week was very much like reading a book or watching a movie after you've been warned there's a huge twist. Like someone had yelled 'SPOILER ALERT' and I was busy sticking my head under the sand so I didn't ruin the story, but I was still curious as to what it was. And everyone treated me like they were very much aware of it.

Lunch at my old school was a madhouse. Lunch at Knightsbridge Academy was only a mess because I was the only one who didn't fit into the organised pattern of the dining hall.

"Come on," Radu chuckled as they grabbed my elbow and pulled me out of someone's way at lunch the next day.

"How do you navigate this?" I asked.

"Supernatural reflexes and a superior sense of fashion," Ama teased, winking at me.

Someone ran into me none too gently and I recognised her as the girl who'd been all over Rune at his locker the day before.

"Watch it, mortal," she sneered as she walked away.

"What in the ever-loving fuck did you do to get on Venette's radar this soon?" Ama asked me.

"Who?"

"Venette Blanc. She's hands down the nastiest ho in this place," Ama said.

"And Ama would know," Radu joked.

I forced a smile I only partially felt. "I have no idea."

Radu smacked Ama like they'd worked it out. "She lives with Rune. The little harpy queen's just jealous our Lena gets to share a roof with the Ruler."

Ama nodded. "That would do it. Bitch would spit on Violet le Rege if she thought it would get her anywhere with Rune."

"You know Grandma Vi?" I asked.

They both nodded.

"Everyone knows Grandma Vi," Ama said dismissively. "She may be matriarch of the le Rege household, but she holds significant sway with the whole town."

As they led me to the table Loren was already occupying, my eyes turned back, and I watched Venette sit down at a table beside Rune. She locked her eyes with me as she put her hand on his shoulder and whispered something in his ear. His hand paused on the way to his mouth as his eyes darted up to find mine and his mouth twisted in a devilish, crooked half-smirk. Then he put whatever it was in his mouth, sucking on his finger sensually before grabbing Venette's face and kissing her hard.

I told myself I felt nothing about it or him or this Venette. Ama had been right. Harpy queen was a good description of her. She had that angular, almost birdlike appearance and everything. She was just a million times more beautiful than any depiction of a harpy I'd ever come across.

I sat beside Radu, putting my back to Rune's table and tried to get engrossed in their conversation. But I felt the hairs at the back of my neck prickling, and I knew Rune's eyes were still on me, watching for my reaction, waiting to see if his performance destroyed me. I knew his type. My mum had dated a string of them and every one of my old schools had been full of them. Which probably went some way to describing the kind of schools I'd been to, but also proved that it didn't matter how exorbitant the school fees; arseholes lived and thrived in every economic echelon.

Annoyingly, Venette was in our year, and she was in more of my classes than would have been preferable. Luckily, Ama's timetable was the same as mine and she had no qualms about making sure Venette did nothing more to me than intimidation and basically fucking Rune at every possible moment in front of me. I wondered what the hell Venette got out of it, this shoving it in my face? It wasn't like I was falling to pieces over it, I didn't exude jealousy, and I gave them no hint I cared other than Rune's apparent surety I did. So, what did Venette get out of it? Was she so damned insecure that she had to make sure the stepsister knew who got to fuck him?

On Wednesday, I was finding my way to class without Ama when I bumped into someone. I looked up and "Sorry," was immediately on my lips. Some kind of stereotypical jock was standing in front of me, but he was smiling. Which, despite the inane arrogance of most jocks I'd ever met, instantly relaxed me. He had slate grey eyes and dark brown hair.

"No. I'm sorry," he said smoothly, taking a step back. "Salem Westmeyer. But my friends call me Strix."

Embarrassingly, I bit my lip nervously and tucked a piece of hair behind my ear. "Good for your friends, Salem," I told him.

"You're new, but I'm sure we could be friends." I wasn't sure if he was smooth or corny.

I smiled. "Maybe we could. I'm Lena."

He nodded. "I heard." I frowned quizzically. "It's a small place. Newbies tend to stand out and create a fair bit of talk. You've got History now?"

My eyes scanned the hallway, but I wasn't sure why. "Yeah."

"I'm next door in Math. Can I walk you?"

I caught his eyes, and I didn't hate what I saw in them. "I don't know. Can you?" I sassed.

He grinned. "May I?"

I shrugged as I adjusted my bag and started walking. "It's a free world."

He smirked. "I'm glad."

I snuck a look at him from the corner of my eyes. "I'll bet you are."

He laughed, clear and open. "Would it be forward of me to ask if you left anyone special behind when you moved?"

"What makes you think I moved?"

"The fact I've gone to school in Knightsbridge my whole life and never seen you before. Plus, your accent's a dead giveaway."

I smiled. "It *is* incredibly forward, but no. I can't say I've really ever had anyone special."

"Shame. A wonderful person like you should have someone special." Okay, I was leaning towards corny.

"I suppose you're offering, Strix?" Ama asked as she fell into step with us.

His shrug was all coy and cheeky. "I didn't say I was. I won't say I'm not."

Ama nodded, a twinkle in her eye. "Yeah, I'm sure you won't. Go away and leave Lena be. You know what Rune will do to you if he sees you talking to her?"

Strix gave her a warm grin. "He can certainly try, but I feel like who Lena talks to is up to her."

I liked him already. "Thank you, Strix. I think you're about the first person here to think that."

Ama frowned and I smirked at her to show I was taking the piss. Of her, at least. It was incredibly true for Venette.

"Just you watch yourself, Westmeyer," Ama said carefully. "I'd vouch for Lena any day, but you really think she's worth the shit Rune will not hesitate to rain down on you?"

Strix looked right into my eyes as he said, "I think she's worth finding out."

Okay, so my heart did a little flutter. Here was a ridiculously hot guy obviously flirting with me unashamedly and he gave zero shits about what my supposedly territorial stepbrother was going to think about that. It was kinda sexy. Not going to lie.

And Strix clearly wasn't put off by whatever apparent retribution Rune would rain down on him. Because he kept talking to me. Not like hour-long discussions, but he fell into step with me in the hall when we were going in the same direction, he said hello to me at every opportunity, he even winked at me when he saw me across a room or through a door. To say it didn't bring a bit of a goofy grin to my face would have been a lie. I didn't think I was going to fall for whatever he was trying on, but it was nice nonetheless.

Rune came up to me on Thursday at my locker, dropping to lean casually against the one beside mine.

"What?" I asked him, not bothering to look at him anymore than out the corner of my eye.

"Is that any way to greet your darling stepbrother?" he asked, his voice clearly not familial in *any* way.

I zipped up my bag and closed my locker calmly. Then, as I swung my bag onto my shoulder, I turned at just the right moment that my bag smacked him in the stomach. Fury burned in his eyes.

"So sorry," I said, saccharine sweet. "What can I help you with, dear brother?"

His jaw twitched in anger, and I just piled on the sarcastically innocent expression. "You left your textbook on the dining table this morning," was his answer. He lifted his hand – that I was sure had just been empty – and a book – that I was sure I'd just seen in my locker before I closed it – was between his fingers.

I frowned at him, knowing this had to be some kind of trick. I just didn't know what the hell kind of trick it could be. "Uh, thanks."

I reached out to take it and our fingers brushed. My eyes flew up to his face and I saw nothing on his that suggested he'd felt that jolt of something pass between us. Great. So, it was just me, then. Just me who was still clinging to this idea that there had been something between us in the forest. Just me who couldn't let go of it, despite reality staring me in the face and telling me in no uncertain terms that Rune was both off-limits and not at all interested.

I hated myself all over again.

Thankfully, I hated him more as well.

"Keep your shit in your room next time," he snarled.

"Why not just burn it then, *Erasmus*?" I sassed him. "More satisfying for you and less interaction with me. Clearly a missed opportunity."

He stepped up close to me. His nearness made my whole body zing, but I stamped it down and faced him off with all the angry defiance and hatred I could muster. "I so look forward to my father's return and watching him put you in your fucking place."

I smirked. "Oh, I'm sure he'll be so happy to know that. I'll tell Mum how much you've missed them."

His lips rippled in a snarl as he took one more step into me. Our bodies actually touched. He was almost a head taller than me, but he leant his face as close to mine as possible. "When you know the truth, *sister*," the moniker was the most scathingly sarcastic as I had ever heard, "you will be begging for me to end you," he promised, and a shiver ran through me.

"And just when I thought your family *weren't* a bunch of serial killing arseholes," I said flippantly. "Then again, I guess every family has that one disappointment."

He pressed forward and I met his strength as well as I could. "Remember this conversation," he growled. "It will not be long until I get to show you exactly what I'm capable of."

I rolled my eyes, even as my stomach quivered. "You think you're the first alpha douche hole bully who's tried that on?" I asked him and something flashed in his eyes too fast for me to catch it. "Think you're the first to threaten to rape me or beat me or whatever else your twisted little lack of imagination can come up with?" I scoffed. "You're all the fucking same, Erasmus, and you don't scare me."

"I will."

I had the audacity to pat him on the chest as I stepped away from him with a nod. "Sure. Okay. You let me know when that's supposed to be in effect, and I'll get right on it. Better yet, text me. You've got my number? Would be good to have that in writing. I wouldn't want to miss it."

He was actually gobsmacked, and I felt a wave of proud victory engulf me. Giving him a winning smile and a dicky little shit-stirring wave, I turned and headed off to find Ama, Radu and Loren.

I found Ama first, who had obviously seen me talking to Rune up the hallway. "What did he want?"

"Intimidation tactics. Clearly, Little Master Privilege has no idea what my old schools were like and the arseholes I've had to deal with."

Ama smirked, then her eyes slid behind me and she frowned. I turned to see Venette stalking towards us.

"Territorial much?" Ama muttered.

Venette shoved me hard, and Ama caught me against her chest.

"Keep your hands off Rune," Venette snarled.

Perhaps unwisely, because Venette was clearly used to being the Queen Bee to Rune's Prom King here, I was feeling bold. Bold and pissed off that I was being punished for being here when I would happily be anywhere else. "Not going to be a problem," I told her.

"He is mine."

I nodded, thinking that guys like Rune didn't belong to anyone, no matter how pretty or obsessed or delusional they were. "Good for you. Don't care."

"Stay away from him."

"I live with him," I reminded her. "Going to be difficult, but I promise to do my best."

She growled and it was decidedly not very attractive. Just as it looked like she was going to lunge at me, Ama slid me out of the way and took my place in front of Venette's fury.

"Back off," Ama told her firmly. "No one touches a le Rege." The reminder was tinged with humour, like there was more to the words than I could understand.

Venette's eyes slid to mine. "Soon," she promised before sashaying away to throw herself on Rune, and I huffed.

"What's with this 'soon', business?" I mumbled to myself. "Seriously, these arseholes need to get themselves a better life."

Ama snorted. "You're not as insignificant as you think, Lena." She took my arm as we went outside to find Radu and Loren.

"I would be more than happy being as insignificant as I think I am," I told her, and we shared a smile.

"You're a le Rege now," was her answer. "You will never be insignificant again."

I nodded. "That is not the comfort you seem to think it is."

Radu shaded their eyes as they looked up at us from their place on the lawn. "What's not a comfort?"

"Lena's bemoaning her significance," Ama explained as she sat down.

I dropped my bag next to her and sat as well with a shrug. "I revel in insignificance. Is that bad?"

Radu scoffed as they leant back on their hands, tipping their sunglasses to their eyes. "In Knightsbridge, that's a Class A felony, Lena," they said with a seriousness that was completely belied by the smirk playing at their lips.

I laughed and Ama nudged me companionably. "No," I said. "I guess the standout way to be significant in Knightsbridge is to be insignificant. That's literally the only way to be different to the rest of you and your almost literal perfection."

"Aw," Radu teased, bumping my knee with their foot companionably. "You think we're perfect?"

I rolled my eyes. "You know you're perfect."

"I may look utter perfection," Radu said. "But that is not going to help me pass this next English essay."

We got talking about the essay and tried to find ways to help Radu pass when Ama snorted. "Tame."

We all followed her gaze to see a couple of kids doing what looked like the Macarena across the lawn while Rune and a bunch of his friends laughed at them. Only, it wasn't the Macarena I'd learned in junior school.

Radu smirked. "Ama," they chastised.

She shrugged. "What? Rune made two kids have sex right there on the lawn in the middle of lunch last term. And this term, all he does is make them strip tease to some old dance? Forget tame. Lame."

They both looked at me. I couldn't pinpoint exactly what those looks said, but I was sure it wasn't something I wanted to know about.

"What?" I asked, biting back the question about *how* Rune made those kids do those things.

"Nothing," Ama said, a grin playing at her lips. "Just thinking about what's changed in Rune's life since last term."

Unbidden, the memory of his kiss ploughed into me. My heart pounded and heat pooled. Then my gut wrenched horribly, and I hated myself for being attracted to such an arse.

Ama's green eyes shone as she looked into mine. "I would

caution against your reaction to your stepbrother, Lena." Her voice was gentle, almost like a song. Her perfectly manicured finger nudged my chin, forcing me to look deeper into her eyes. "Venette is a vengeful bitch. She won't care how mortal you are. She will destroy you for even thinking about the man she claims is hers."

"Claims?" came out of me a whispered croak. Everything was too much for me to even bother with the fact everyone kept calling me mortal.

Her finger left my chin and she stepped away. My head felt suddenly clearer.

"Rune plays with her, strings her along like he actually entertains any feeling for her."

"He just likes she'll let him do whatever he wants to her," Radu said.

I felt the stirrings of heated cheeks as I imagined the implication of that statement.

"Whatever he wants?" I said, my eyes sliding to him across the quad.

Ama put her hands on my arms and her chin on my shoulder as she watched Rune with me. "Whatever he wants," she purred seductively in my ear.

Radu mimicked her stance over my other shoulder. "And Rune likes it dirty."

"Rough," Ama added.

"He likes them screaming."

"And not just in pleasure."

"If they bleed…?" Radu continued.

"All the better," Ama finished.

I swallowed. Hard.

My heart pounded in my chest again.

Looking at the boy – no, man – across the quad, I could believe every word. Not only did I believe every word, but I knew two things with a fiercely stark clarity that, now known, could never be unknown.

Firstly, I would let Rune le Rege do anything he wanted to me. I would scream for him. I would bleed for him. He didn't even need to ask. He could command it and I wouldn't hesitate.

Which made the second thing I knew achingly disappointing; Rune would never ask, he'd never command, because there was no way in this frozen Hell on earth that he'd ever want me.

After the day I'd had, I decided to go for a walk after we got home from school.

As I wandered through the fog-deep forest, I was sure I heard Rune's voice echoing around me. The fog thickened and I thought I could see a ghostly human shape appearing around me, then disappearing back into the gloom. The voice whispered insults. Much more of the same as he'd said at my locker, and that was the moment I knew I was going insane.

I was literally driving myself insane over the arsehole. Sure, he was sexy as hell, but goddamn he aggravated me. He thought he could just treat people like shit because he was what? Some rich kid?

"Yeah?" I called to the fog, not caring if he was actually out there or not. "Why don't you say that to my face?"

A disembodied chuckle on the wind I easily could have been imagining.

"You think you're the first rich kid to be a dick? Newsflash, Erasmus, you're not original. You're not special. You're just yet another jerk!"

Another chuckle, sounding somehow further away in my imagination.

I turned and headed back to the manor, deciding that a walk had been the stupidest idea. Rune's voice pestered me the whole way back, so quiet and distant I couldn't quite make out all the words. Just snippets. And it was not the sort of thing to repeat in polite society.

I fully intended to give him a piece of my mind when I got back, even fully knowing that it was all in said mind.

But when I did get back to the manor, Rune ignored me. He seemed so good at avoiding me, even what looked like a near-brush approaching turned into nothing. Every time my brain had registered that I was about to run into him around a corner or in the dining room, every time the thrill of just the idea of touching him ignited in me, he'd moved and was suddenly as far away as I could get, and I was left firmly believing that my mind was playing more very unfair tricks on me.

At school was no different.

He spent the rest of the week ignoring me, unless he and Venette were basically having sex anywhere near me, then he locked his eyes with mine like he was asking me if I wished it was me.

I mean, I did. But that was beside the point.

But I had Ama, Radu and Loren. Mia was as nice as could be

expected from a new 'sibling'. Even Strix was a pleasant distraction from Rune's shittery. Like everything else in life, there were pros and cons to my situation and the pros were outweighing the cons.

At least in number.

CHAPTER SEVEN

Our parents hadn't returned by the weekend after all, and I was still stuck in the weirdness that my mum had seen fit to leave me alone in. I was left feeling like Etienne was avoiding whatever talk it was I was supposed to have with him.

Mia was lovely and always checked in with me, but I could hardly tell her I was going insane. Especially when the focal point of my insanity was my lust/annoyance for her brother, my stepbrother.

Ama, Radu and Loren had welcomed me with open arms, and I did feel the most at home I had all my life. They included me in their conversations and invited me to go out with them, not that I'd taken them up on it yet.

There was this sense of settled-ness deep in me that, if I just ignored the weirdness, gave me the first feeling of peace I could really ever remember having. I sunk my claws deep into it and didn't want to let it go, despite everything in me telling me it would all be ruined soon. It made the encroaching feeling, that I was actually losing my mind, somewhat easier to bear.

Rune – *Erasmus* – was the only thing that rocked my peace. Just the thought of him threatened to crack the solidity of the ground beneath my feet and send me tumbling into an abyss.

I hated myself for it. Not because he was technically my stepbrother – although, I was sure plenty of people would have had an issue with it – but because he was clearly a sadistic arsehole. But I'd still bleed for him, and I'd very willingly scream for him.

On Sunday, I was exploring the house. I could easily play time period bingo with all the various things around me.

But it was the locked room at the end of a third-floor corridor that was bugging me. I didn't know why, but I'd walked past it like five times just that day and had the unshakable need to open it and see inside.

The sixth time I walked past it, I was sure there was a waft of cool air I hadn't noticed the other times. I debated my sanity for the umpteenth time that week as my hand reached out for the door handle; it had been locked every other time I'd tried it, so why would it be unlocked now?

Except, unlocked it was.

I didn't hesitate to enter.

The room was some kind of storeroom, almost attic, but set out like dozens of tiny… The only word I had for them was 'shrines'.

The one closest to the door looked like it was from the 70s or 80s. It was a wedding photo. A man who looked like Etienne, a full fifty- or forty-odd years ago, was dressed in a powder blue suit with a smiling woman beside him. This Etienne-copy was clearly the groom. Grandma Vi stood beside him, looking no different to the way she'd look at Etienne's wedding to my mother, just in a slightly different dress.

The next picture I saw looked like a war-era photo. The

Second World War. Another man who looked like Etienne, dressed in military garb with a woman in a fashionable white, wedding-looking dress. It was just the two of them.

I looked around the room some more and things just got weirder and weirder from there.

There was another man who looked like Etienne. Only this time it was a drawing, or painting. And everyone but the priest was wearing a ruff around their necks like it was the renaissance.

They were all wedding photos or paintings or drawings. Styled as though covering the last four or five hundred years. All accompanied by locks of hair and vials of dark red liquid, marriage certificates, and various trinkets like cups or jewellery or perfume bottles. And all of them with a man who bore a striking resemblance to Etienne. Not just of the familial kind, but the kind where he either had a really weird fetish and a penchant for commissioning really specific pieces of art or…

No.

The alternative wasn't even worth thinking about. Surely.

Except I couldn't *not* think it.

…or Etienne had not only lived for hundreds of years, but he'd married dozens of women. Like, every twenty years or so.

I stumbled backwards and ran into a very hard body.

"What are you doing in here?" Rune's voice curled around me the same way his hand curled around my arm.

I whirled to face him. I intended to say, 'nothing', but what came out was an almost reverent, "What is this place?"

Rune looked around the room. "Call it a shrine to my father's…" He paused as though trying to find the right word, "ambitions."

"There are dozens of women here."

"I have no doubt," he said, like he was bored.

"What happened to them? Where are they? There are… They all have wedding photos."

Rune sighed. "It's no concern of yours. You'd be better staying out of things that aren't your business."

"Not my business? It's totally my concern if my mum's just going to end up a discarded memory, thrown in here with the rest!"

"He loved them all. In his way."

"That is not a consolation, *Erasmus*," I said, and his head snapped to me.

"If you're looking for consolation, *little Angel*, you will not find it under this roof."

"Who are they?" I asked him.

He took a step towards me, as intimidating as it was a turn on. "Why don't you ask the question you *really* want to ask?" he purred.

My heart thudded in my chest. "What do you mean?"

He smirked and it was all predatory. "You haven't asked me if my father likes dressing up and playing at history, little Angel. You haven't asked why he hasn't aged in five hundred years. And you haven't asked what those little red vials are."

I swallowed hard, trying not to think about what was in those little vials, as much as I was trying not to think about lurching forward and just kissing him.

"Go on," he begged. "Ask me."

"Does your father like dressing up and playing at history?" I asked him, my voice wavering.

"No."

"Why hasn't he aged in five hundred years?"

"He's immortal." He said it like it was a joke, but it rang like truth.

I swallowed even harder as my brain was madly trying to put together connections that made absolutely no sense. The carcass on my first day at the manor. The red liquid they always drank. The way my mum just went along with everything. The fact that everyone was so perfect but seemed slightly out of sync with contemporary time. That Knightsbridge was closed off to the rest of the world to the point I couldn't even get a GPS signal.

"Go on, little Angel," Rune said, his voice a low rumble, daring me to continue. "Last question…"

I didn't need to ask what was in the vials. I seemed to know. Or guess. Or have gone totally mad.

"Why…?" I licked my lips and tried again. "Why does your father keep little vials of…blood?"

Rune licked the tip of his finger sensually. "One taste is all it takes to remember a whole lifetime."

I took a step back, my chest rising and falling rapidly as my heartbeat raced. "Vampires don't exist," I said, my voice barely a whisper.

Rune took a step towards me, his face dark and cocky. "Don't we?"

I shook my head. "No. You can't… *They* can't," I amended, thinking he had to be playing with me. It sounded exactly like him, to be honest.

Except, if I was being totally honest with myself, he could be playing with me, and it still be true. Telling me would mess with me more than not telling me.

"Tell me, little Angel," he said slowly. "Does the truth make you want me more than the lie?"

The insufferable prat! "I don't want you, Rune," I lied.

He smirked as he licked his lip. "Why? Are you worried I'll bite?" he teased. "Or are you more worried I won't?"

"Your sick games don't scare me."

"Maybe I'll do us both a favour and just taste you now." He lurched towards me with his teeth bared and I startled in shock, then sidled for the door. "All right," he called as I ran out of the room. "You tell yourself you don't want to feel me buried deep in you as I taste you."

Now he'd mentioned it, it was exactly what I wanted, and I had to wonder what in the hell was wrong with me. What was wrong with me that I wanted that? But more importantly, what was wrong with me that I was willing to believe not only did vampires exist, but that my mum had married our little duo into them?

I didn't stop running until I'd run quite literally into Mia.

"Lena!" she cried in surprise. "What's the matter? What's wrong."

I stumbled away from her. Rune had made me wary. I still couldn't believe I was entertaining the idea that my new stepfamily were vampires, but I'd be damned if my gut wasn't desperate for me to believe it. My gut was busy telling me that it made sense. That it was the only truth that made sense. But that didn't make sense in itself.

"Lena?" Mia asked again.

I shook my head and took another step away from her. "I…" I

pointed behind me upstairs and Mia followed my finger.

I saw her frown. "Rune," she snapped. "What did you do?"

"I just let the little mortal in on the truth, sister. Isn't that what you wanted?"

"Not like this!" Mia cried.

"What did you want me to do?" Rune asked her. "She found Father's shrine room and she had questions. I was just being a good *brother* and answering them for her."

Mia didn't seem to believe that he'd done it out of the goodness of his heart. "Just piss off and let me fix your mess, Rune," she sighed, sounding tired. "I think Lena's had enough of your *brotherly* help for one day."

"But I might not feel so very brotherly any other day." I could hear the sarcastic pout in his voice but refused to look at him.

"No," Mia said sternly. "But you have been warned."

I didn't know what Rune had been warned about or by who, but he made a sharp inhalation noise like a hiss, and then Mia visibly relaxed.

"You'll have questions…" she started.

"So many questions," I breathed.

The gut I was so heavily listening to about the existence of vampires was telling me to trust Mia. Which felt like the easiest of options. But I was currently not quite trusting its insistence on the existence of vampires, so whether I could trust Mia or not remained to be seen.

"So, this obviously isn't the ideal situation to be in," was how she chose to continue.

"It's not?"

She shook her head. "No. So, uh, our parents met and fell in love, as people do."

"As people do," I agreed.

"Father knew about you, and you weren't anticipated to be a problem–"

It was hard not to take offence. "I'm a problem?"

She gave me an apologetic grimace. "Not like that. Sorry, I haven't done this before and I'm not doing it very well. And Grandma Vi's gone 'til dinner… Let me start over." She bounced on her toes. "So, first things first…there's… Uh…"

"Uh huh?" I encouraged her.

"Vampires, right," she said quickly, like she wasn't sure how to put it.

I blinked again, feeling like all my worst fears were being confirmed and yet still hoping that she was going to turn around and claim February Fools or something. "Vampires?"

She nodded. "Yes."

"You're *worried* about vampires?" I tried, hoping that was actually the truth; that they were just some conspiracy weirdos and not actually monsters out of fiction.

"What? Oh, no. No, we *are* vampires."

Okay. I was either not the only one in this godforsaken place who'd lost their mind, or my gut was trustworthy. Good to know.

"I'd assumed Rune had told you that."

He pretty much had, but it didn't hurt to make certain that he wasn't just being a dick. "Did you have a bit much wine at lunch?" I asked.

She chuckled awkwardly. "No. That's… Uh, we don't… That's not wine."

"Okay, so you're vampires and you drink blood every meal at

the table and I've just not noticed." Point one was far-fetched enough. Point two seemed like something I would have noticed. *Should* have noticed.

She nodded. "Yes. I'm sensing that was sarcasm, though."

I didn't want to believe her, but I did. "Mia, I–"

"I'll…" She held up her hands. "Wait, I'll prove it. Okay, watch."

I did watch.

I watched as her face changed. Her irises changed from sparkling hazel to pitch black. I watched as her skin, already pale, paled further until it was a shade that could only be described as ashen. I watched as smoky, veiny tendrils snaked down her face under her eyes. She gave me a toothy grin to show me there were two very sharp fangs where her very normal-sized incisors had previously been.

I was out of explanations at that point, and full of apologies to my gut.

"Uh…" I said taking a step back.

Mia took a step forward, then paused and shook her head. Her face returned to normal, and she held up her hands again. "I know this is a lot."

I nodded, realising it was probably for the best that I was so readily accepting of the whole thing. "Actually, it kind of makes sense. I was sure I'd seen a body being drained of blood downstairs on my first day here."

"Uh…yeah, that's entirely possible."

"The weather is shite for anyone who won't burst into flames in the sun."

She frowned. "I mean, it's a severe irritant, but I don't think

90

anyone's actually burst into flames…"

"Everyone's freaking gorgeous and perfect and fabulous."

"Vampire genes do have some perks."

"The fog…" A thought struck me.

"The fog?" Mia asked, like she wanted to help me continue my roll.

"What other powers do you have?"

"We're super fast." She zipped about the room for good measure. "Strong." She looked around like she was checking if anyone was nearby, then slammed her fist into the wall next to her. Her tiny fist left an indent in the solid rock. "Uh, we can transform. I go in for a cat. Grandma Vi keeps it old school and goes bat. Rune's favourite is mist. Was that what you meant before?"

My mind was whirring, and I still wasn't sure if I believed her or not. "And the raven?"

"Atlas?" Mia said and I shrugged. "Yeah, no one's really sure what his deal is, but he's kind of like a familiar to Rune. Although, he's the only vampire anyone knows of with a familiar. But Atlas has been around since Rune was born, so they say."

"And that was…?"

She frowned. "That was what?"

"How long ago?"

"Nineteen and…a bit years ago," she answered uncertainly.

"Oh." I wasn't sure why that disappointed me. "So, you're not like pretending to be younger?"

She snorted. "Father and Grandma Vi, hard yes. Rune and me, no. All the students at Knightsbridge Academy are born vampires and the age we say we are. I'm actually fifteen and Rune's actually nineteen." She paused and a knowing smirk lit her face. "That wasn't the answer you were hoping for, was it?"

I found my smile for her sincere. "I'm not sure what answer I *was* hoping for."

"I know it's a lot but, since you're not compellable, we did have to tell you at some point. Though," she seemed to admit, "it could probably have been done with more tact."

But I was stuck on one word. "Compellable. People have been saying that a lot about me. What is that?"

"Uh, another power of ours. We can make humans do whatever we want. Make *most* humans do whatever we want," she amended, looking at me. "Do, think, feel. We control them and thus we control the knowledge of our world. You, on the other hand…"

"I can't be compelled to keep my mouth shut about the weird shit that goes on here," I said, understanding.

She nodded. "Bingo."

"Right. Bummer."

"Different word. Same sentiment," she said with a rueful grin. "What were you asking about fog before?"

I frowned. "I think your brother's been playing funny buggers."

"Ah. Sounds like him. Tormenting you as a disembodied voice? Appearing and disappearing so you think you've gone mad? That kind of thing?"

"That exact thing. How did you know?"

"Oh, he drove Margot White's older sister so insane she threw herself off the school tower."

I didn't know who Margot White was but… "He… What?"

She shrugged like it was nothing. "Made an awful mess. Imagine teasing fledging vampires with that much human blood. It was mayhem. They had to shut the school for a week, the blood lingered so."

There was way too much to unpack in that one sentence, so I just asked, "Fledgling vampires?"

She nodded. "Any vampire under fifty is a fledgling. We all learn control at different rates but, if we don't get it by then, we're just rogues."

Okay. I was getting way too deep in a lore I knew far too little about. A deep-sea dive when I should have been in the kiddies' pool kind of situation.

I shook my head. "You're right. This is a lot."

Though, I noticed, it did nothing for the impure thoughts I had about her brother. Even the story about Margot White's older sister.

As if I needed another reason to prove I'd gone mad.

"If you have any questions..." Mia said. She looked at my confused face and smiled. "*When* you know what your questions are, Grandma Vi and I will be here to answer them."

"My mum," I started, and she nodded. "She's compelled?"

"Yes and no. The love is real. It takes a truly skilled vampire to compel love, and even then... Lust is easy, but love is an untameable beast. But her acceptance of some of the...harder things is compelled."

I wasn't sure I wanted to know what the harder things were, so I moved on. "And no one can compel me?"

"I mean, Acheron might be able to." At my quizzical look, she explained. "Our oldest council member. But I would guess if

93

you're not compellable, then you're not compellable. I don't
know. It's never happened before."

"No human in your whole history has ever been
uncompellable?" I clarified, not much bothered about whether
that was actually a word or not given the current situation.

"Our history is way long, but not that I've heard. No. I'd think
it would have at least made its way into myth by now and even
then, I've not heard about it outside a fantasy book."

"I think you and I have a very different definition of a fantasy
book," I told her.

"I've always been interested in human fantasy, but never got
around to it. Can you give me some recommendations?"

I nodded, leaning into the weirdness. It had got me this far.
"Sure. I'll give you my human fantasy recs, and you give me
your…vampire fantasy recs."

Mia seemed inordinately excited by that idea. "Yes.
Definitely." She looked me over and her smile softened. "Are you
okay?"

I took a deep breath. "I don't know. I don't think it's really
kicked in yet. Like, I don't know. It seems to make sense but how
could it possibly be real?"

She nodded. "Some mortals have that reaction."

"Really?"

She nodded. "It's like you know there's more to the world,
you just need it shown to you. But you're told all your lives that
we're fiction, so your head needs some time to process what your
heart already knows."

"Yeah, I'm not sure my heart knows anything," I said,
thinking that it was eerily close to what Ama had said about my
subconscious.

CHAPTER EIGHT

Knightsbridge Academy seemed like a totally different place the next morning. I felt like I was stocktaking the students and piling them into lists of who was human and who had to be vampire. And it seemed they all knew I now knew the big secret.

Etienne and Mum had returned late that night and, after Etienne and Rune had had it out in Etienne's study as though some kind of world-ending war was occurring, Etienne had imparted the importance of me behaving myself with my new knowledge. It wasn't a threat…per se. I felt totally safe with him. As long as I didn't break the rules. And the rules were 'don't talk about vampires with anyone outside Knightsbridge' and 'just act normal'. I'd asked Etienne when he expected I'd be leaving Knightsbridge and he'd admitted that me exposing their secrets was probably not a foreseeable problem.

So that was my plan. Don't talk about vampires without anyone outside Knightsbridge and just act normal. Though, exactly what was normal when students were compelling others into letting them feed on them in the corridor? When they were shapeshifting and staging fights on the lawns. When kids sprinted past me faster than my eyes could see. When they jumped out of third story windows as a freaking short-cut. When every corner I turned, and every supposedly empty corridor I entered, had kids all-but (or, in some instances) fucking in them.

The larger student populace was undoubtedly still unnaturally – supernaturally – elegant and poised and beautiful, but I saw the… It wasn't monstrosity. It was more like animalistic. And very much inhuman. At least, no human school I'd been to would let those sorts of shenanigans stand.

"So, they told you, then?" Ama asked me when she saw me slow as she came towards me.

I nodded, hesitant and wary and just a lot overwhelmed, to be honest. Grandma Vi and Mia had had a bit more of a talk with me over dinner – a dinner Rune had been suspiciously absent from – and I still wasn't totally convinced I wasn't losing my mind. But despite my trepidation, Ama just laughed and put her arm around me as we walked to class.

"Thank fuck. Right, now that's out of the way, don't go ruining it for Loren. She's quite happy the way she is."

"Loren's…?"

"Mortal, yep. So, she knows it all, but there are things that will shake her compulsion if you're not careful. They told you all the mortals in Knightsbridge are compelled into complacency?"

I nodded slowly. "Except me."

"Except you. Right pickle, I'm sure. *Seigneur* le Rege will be fuming."

"Who?"

"His lordship. Rune's father."

"He's a lord?"

She cocked her head to the side. "He was. Five hundred-odd years ago, before dear old Grandma Vi turned him. I guess,

96

technically, he still is."

I blinked. "I can't believe this isn't some kind of messed up dream."

"Real life, lovely," she said to me. "Do we live up to your little human expectations?" She chuckled.

I shrugged, looking around as a wolf and a large cat shifted in the corridor and launched at each other. "I honestly don't know. Yes?"

"Brilliant. I was worried they were starting to make us too soft. Too lovable."

Yeah, these vampires couldn't really be described as soft or lovable.

"Last week must have been so…weird for everyone. Why didn't you say anything?" I asked.

She shrugged. "Self-preservation 101. It's vamp law. Any non-compelled mortal gets told nothing, shown nothing. In this case, it was supes awkward because you were going to have to find out at some point. No one can live in Knightsbridge and *not* know. But if the great le Reges hadn't done it yet, no one else was going to be the first to do it."

The confusing words from the week before were starting to make sense when Venette walked towards us, her fangs elongating in what was a clear threat.

I nodded to myself. "Right. That's what she meant about 'soon'."

Ama glared at Venette. "Oh, yeah. Don't get me wrong. Torturing mortals is great fun, but there are vamps who enjoy it, and then there are vamps who *enjoy* it. If you know what you mean."

I didn't, but, "No, sure. Totally."

She snorted as she smiled at me. "Totally," she teased, and I nudged her with my hip, feeling like nothing had changed. With her.

I mean, sure, she was a blood-sucking monster who wasn't supposed to exist. She was I didn't know how much stronger than me. Faster. She could have killed me a bunch of different ways before my next blink, probably. And yet... I still felt as comfortable with her as I had the day I'd met her.

And Radu was no different. They were just Radu, the same person I'd started becoming friends with the week before. They were sassy and sarcastic and clearly happy to have me around.

The only good thing that seemed to come out of me finding out the truth about Knightsbridge was that the students paid less attention to me. Like, now they could just be themselves, they'd stopped caring so much about the human stepsister of the le Rege family.

Most of them anyway.

Apart from the occasional random feeding in the hallways, there was a designated building where the vampires fed periodically throughout the day. Loren was on duty – a duty I would apparently be spared because I wasn't *that* kind of mortal in Knightsbridge – and Radu and Ama had popped in quickly while I assured them that I'd be fine just running to my locker to get a forgotten textbook.

Venette stalked up to me, shoved me into my locker, then put her fingers around my throat and lifted my feet of the floor easily. I felt my eyes bug and wondered how long it would take to pass out as my hands wrapped uselessly around her wrist.

"And now, mortal, I get to *play*," she sneered in that way that I was still sure was supposed to be somewhat sexy. But who the hell was she trying to be sexy for now?

"Slither back to Rune," a voice said before Venette was knocked sideways.

I was dropped to the floor, taking huge breaths like my body thought it might not have been given another chance. I looked up and saw Strix standing between me and Venette. She was glaring daggers at him, and he clearly couldn't give two shits about how pissy she was with him. His arrogant confidence was only rivalled by my stepbrother's.

"He will ruin you, Westmeyer," she spat.

"So, he constantly tells me and yet I'm still here," Strix said to Venette, clearly goading her into trying something more on him than simple threats.

He turned to me and held a hand out. After a second of hesitation, I took it and let him help me up. His fingers brushed my throat tenderly as though he was checking for damage. His fingers were surprisingly warm. But then maybe I'd just been reading too many books about the supposed expected temperature of vampires.

"Are you okay?" he asked me gently, concern clear in his grey eyes.

I nodded, noting there was a wariness in me around him. No more or less than I'd felt with Ama and Radu when I'd first seen them that day, but I wasn't getting over it quite as quickly.

"You're going to come between me and this mortal?" Venette asked him.

"Fuck off," Strix told her lazily, as though there wasn't a

world in which she could be a threat to him. There was a humour in his eyes that he was sharing with me. I felt myself smile back at him as Venette did indeed fuck off, hopefully giving up on terrorising me. At least for that day.

Strix's eyes were on me. His fingers were still near my throat, and they skimmed up and over my jaw to brush a strand of hair from my face softly. I watched his tongue dart out and trail over his lips. And those grey eyes told me exactly what he was thinking as he looked at me.

"You finally know."

I scoffed. "Finally? It only took a week."

His eyes were warm. "It was a *long* week."

"It seemed the same length as usual to me."

A smile teased at his lips. "I guess our meeting had more of an impact on me, then."

I bit my lip against a full smile. "I can't tell if you're suave or a total dork," I told him.

"Does it matter? If it's working?" he asked, giving me a smile that I couldn't leave unanswered.

"Who said it's working?" I countered.

His grin grew more rueful as his eyes dropped down and back up to mine again. "Did they tell you…" he started before he licked his lip. "That our hearing is like a lie detector, Lena?"

I felt my heart skip and the way his eyes widened pointedly made me realise what he meant. "You can hear my heartbeat."

He inclined his head. "I can hear your heartbeat," he agreed.

"And what does mine tell you?" I asked.

His grin was both cheeky and sexy. "That it's working."

I pursed my lips. "Maybe last week. But I know what you are

this week, Strix. And I'm just not sure how much I trusted you when I thought you were nothing more than a normal teenage boy."

"Let alone now," he guessed.

I nodded. "Let alone now."

"I'm starting to think I should have asked you out last week."

I smirked and bit my lip coyly. "You think I would have said yes last week?"

"I think it sounds like I had more chance last week."

"You said yourself your little aural lie detector tells you it's still working."

"Which means there's still a chance." It was half-question and half-statement.

I shrugged.

After all, why not? Rune was a vampire and an arse, and I was still hot for him. Strix was, as far as I could tell, just a vampire. If this was home now and I wanted to have some semblance of a dating life, I didn't have a lot of options that didn't include 'and vampire'. So, what could it hurt? If I was still obsessing over Rune, the douche, then I could entertain a romance with a guy who seemed just vampire. Maybe it would even get Venette off my arse about Rune.

"There might still be a chance," I said coyly.

Strix ran a hand over his jaw as he smiled, stepping back a pace. "Okay," he said and sounded genuinely happy. "Cool."

I snorted. "So, you're going for dork, then?"

His smile was gorgeous, and a hint of self-doubt blossomed in it. "Uh, not intentionally. No."

The bell for next lesson rang and we both looked up for some reason. Then we both huffed a laugh.

"I'm this way," Strix said, pointing behind him.

I nodded. "And I'm this way," I said, pointing behind me.

He started walking backwards. "I'll see you later, then?"

"You will. Thanks for… With Venette."

He inclined his head. "My pleasure. I'd say anytime, but hopefully there isn't another one."

We both walked away from each other, backwards while we smiled like goofs. It wasn't so bad, this feeling. Even if I was surrounded by bloodsuckers, maybe that didn't make them all automatically bad.

There were 'good' and 'bad' humans. What was to say there weren't 'good' and 'bad' vampires as well? After all, for the most part, my new family seemed 'good'. Mia, Etienne, and Grandma Vi didn't seem to be just waiting for the moment they could rip out my throat. Maybe they were still good at the game, but I'd not seen any evidence that Etienne was feeding from my mum. I supposed they might have ways of healing a bite, but I certainly hadn't seen any of them do so that morning in the school hallway.

Ama smirked when I met her at the door to our next classroom. "Um, what's with the face?"

I circled it. "This face?" I asked ruefully, and she nodded. "This is just my face. It keeps my insides where they're meant to be."

"No. It's not. This one's *way* goofier." Her grin widened. "Oh, shit. Was someone having a little flirt without me?"

I shrugged, faux-coy. "Maybe."

Ama grinned. "Did he ask you out?"

"No."

She looked me over like she thought she could work it out. "But he's *going* to?"

"I don't know. All he said was that maybe he should have done it last week. He seemed worried the whole vamp thing might have killed his chances."

"And?" she pressed. "What did you say?"

"I told him there was still a chance."

She actually gave a little excited squeal, then she frowned and grabbed my chin to lift my face. "What happened to your neck?"

I rolled my eyes. "Venette wanted to play."

Ama nodded, her eyes narrowing. "I'll play with her if she's not careful."

"Strix came to my rescue."

Ama snorted. "Well, if there's a storybook way to begin a romance, it's saving the damsel in distress."

"Excuse you!" I argued. "I'm no damsel in distress."

Ama gave me a look that reminded me I was now about one wrong move away from being a damsel in distress constantly. "Just make sure you avoid paper cuts, will you?"

"Is it really that bad?" I asked and she looked at me to clarify. "Fledgling vampires and their bloodlust."

Her eyes widened as she realised what I meant. "Oh. Yeah. Pretty much. I mean, imagine your normal human hormones at this age, then times that by about a hundred and add in a predatory instinct that even the oldest of us can't control in the wrong – or right – circumstances. That's pretty much every single vampire that surrounds you right now. And this school, this town, is like ninety percent vampire. If you include the…feeders," she finished, as though 'feeders' wasn't what she was going to say.

"What do you usually call them?" I asked.

She swallowed and had the decency to look guilty. "Cattle. Blood bags." She shrugged. "We're racist, okay?"

I snorted. "Well, at least you know what you are."

"It's hard not to be when we are literally superior. Physically and quite often mentally."

"Being better murderers is hardly an achievement," I pointed out and she inclined her head.

"We are the apex predator. Top of the food chain. At least as far as humans are concerned."

That made me think of something. "Do you have any natural predators?"

"Depends what you consider 'natural'."

"Is there anything above the food chain from vamps?"

She looked at me as we took our seats. Other students were half paying attention to our conversation, but no one seemed to care what I was asking or what Ama was answering.

"By the time you get to vamps, you've got to think of the food chain like a supernatural game of Rock Paper Scissors, right?" she said. "We have the upper hand on some creatures and not others, likewise they have the upper hand on us and not others. And so on. It's confusing and the politics on all that takes like a whole term to cover in the simplest of detail."

"Let me guess, that was last term?" I asked wryly.

She smirked. "Don't worry, they'll cover it again next year."

"Okay," the teacher said as they walked in. "Now that Evangeline has been…enlightened we can get back to the meat of our curriculum. The witch hunts. Who can tell me how many witches actually survived?"

I felt Ama's amusement at my side as I proceeded to sit through a lesson where we weren't just learning about witch trials, but discussing the actual existence of witches in the world.

And that wasn't even the weirdest lesson I had that day.

Like the true sucker for punishment I was, I went for another walk after school. Or maybe, in expert sucker for punishment fashion, I was actually hoping that Rune would decide to torment me. In which case, my jaunt was not in vain.

"Are you afraid, little girl?" Rune's voice suddenly echoed around me in the fog.

Because I knew that for what it was now. It wasn't a dream or my imagination. My brain wasn't trying to punish me for being the weirdo with the hots for her stepbrother. It was actually Rune. Being a total dick.

"Of what?" I challenged him, pretending I didn't know what he was talking about.

"Of the monsters who lurk in the night."

Was I scared? Yes. I'd just found out that those monsters were real and none of them were as nice as Stephanie made them out to be; all of them would kill me without Etienne's protection. And, if vampires were real, what else? School suggested that witches were legit. Was it werewolves I heard howling in these very woods? What about mummies? Ghosts and ghouls?

Yeah. I was terrified, but I was also sick of the bullshit the world had thrown at me.

Mist-Rune swirled around me, then rushed at me through the

fog, solidifying at the last-minute right in front of my face. I held my own as he stared down at me. I knew he'd hear – feel – my heart racing. He could probably tell I had to force my lungs into slow and steady breaths. He could probably read minds too, but it didn't stop me pushing back.

"I've faced worse monsters," I told him, my voice quiet.

It wasn't quiet from terror or embarrassment or shyness. I'd learnt long before the le Reges came into my life that authority and fear and respect were best garnered with a quiet fury. It was more a feeling than a memory now, but it had been burnt into me. Literally. It was a powerful tool, used correctly, particularly for women who were so often accused of hysteria whenever we spoke our minds. And it was clearly a language the le Reges understood.

I watched Rune's eyes darken as he looked me over. "Whatever lies in your past…little Angel, you haven't seen real monsters yet."

I drew myself up, faking courage until I made it. "Nothing hiding out here in the dark can come close to the depravity and cruelty hidden in the depths of humanity."

Our eyes were pinned to each other, so I saw the spark of intrigue as it lit his eyes. He wanted to know what had happened to me. He wanted to know who had hurt me, and how. He wanted to know it all.

Maybe he couldn't read minds.

Or maybe I had to literally think it at him for him to know.

I wasn't all that keen on finding out.

"Where do you think humanity learned it?" he asked me, his voice a purr.

"Did they learn it from you?" I challenged. "Or did you learn it from them?"

He stepped forward, taking my chin in his hands. His lips were too damned close. "I could take everything from you, Angel…" he said, his voice soft and seductive.

I lifted my chin in defiance. "Go ahead and try. See what's left to take, Rune."

He looked me over, his nose bumping mine, brushing my cheek gently. When he finally spoke again, his voice was almost reverent. "Humans always think they're at breaking point, that they've already given – lost – so much that there isn't anything left to lose. It would be my pleasure to show you exactly how much you have left inside you, Angel. How much more can be ripped from you."

That should not have been sexy. It should not have been intriguing. It should have been terrifying and weird and creepy. But I couldn't hear those words, said with such a deep, calm and somehow tender tone of voice, and not be tempted by them.

We were so close that we were breathing the same air. His ice blue eyes pinned mine like he was daring me to either defy him or beg him. I wanted to do both. At the same time. My whole head was a mess and I wondered if it wouldn't be easier to just be compellable and then maybe life would be simpler. Mia had said that lust was easy to compel. Was it as easy to compel away?

My heart pounded and I knew he could hear it. But there was no smug victory in his eyes. He looked at me like he was trying to puzzle something out. Like, at least for this moment, he was as helpless as me after all. Then the moment was gone – or had been my imagination – and he was stepping away, his head cocked to the side.

"Father seems to think I've dragged you into the woods to kill you," he said with a wicked smile. "Grandma Vi might see fit to punish someone if we don't return to the house."

I looked him over, again wondering about the dynamic of the family. So often, Rune seemed to be superior to Etienne; Etienne seemed to defer to his son. While Grandma Vi seemed happy to leave her son and grandson to battle it out for patriarch, she held the sort of authority that told me she was the true head of the household, just as Ama had said. Grandma Vi was clearly very good at delegating and, who knew, probably found enjoyment from watching the men fight among themselves like children.

"Here I thought you weren't the kind to obey anyone."

His eyes caressed my whole body as they travelled over it. "Tell me to ruin you and I would not hesitate to *obey*."

My breath was actually knocked out of me. He said the word in such a way that my whole body tingled and fizzled and burned. The command was on the tip of my tongue, but the knowing looking in Rune's eyes stopped it tumbling the whole way out and I snapped my mouth shut.

He chuckled, deep and dark and deliciously dirty. "Atlas will lead you back," he said simply, the disappeared back into mist.

The raven cried at me, making me jump. He was perched in a tree above, looking down at me with a keen intelligence in his beady, black eyes. His head swivelled from side to side like he was sizing me up, like he was wondering if I was worth the bother. It wasn't the first time, and I doubted it would be the last, that I'd felt spectacularly wanting in the eyes of that bird.

He took off, swooping to a tree behind me. I guessed that was the way back to the manor.

"Atlas," I said, looking him over as I walked. "So, is it Rune's choice you stay home while he's at school, or yours?"

Atlas cawed and I nodded, being able to understand him as much as I had in the holidays when I wasn't even sure he was the same bird.

"No. Great. That's great. You guys must have a really stellar relationship."

His call was more mournful this time and I wondered if their relationship was actually all that stellar.

Watching where I was going, I talked to him more because I had nothing else to do. I also sensed, once again, that he could understand everything I was saying with ease.

"Mia said you'd been around since Rune was born. How does that work, then? Are you a familiar or like some weird spirit made physical? I read a book with those once. A human book. You probably wouldn't know it. It was pretty cool. They had, like, their souls living outside their bodies as tangible creatures they could talk to and stuff. Are you like that? Or is it the familiar thing? *Are* they a thing? I learnt witches were a real thing today. Did you know that? Of course, you did. You've probably met them." I scoffed. "Rune's probably slept with them."

Atlas made a noise that might have been his version of a laugh and my cheeks heated.

"Do not repeat any of this conversation," I warned him. "I don't care who Rune's slept with or who he hasn't. I hate him."

Atlas made a noise that suggested he didn't believe me.

"What do you know? You're a bird," I accused him. "You're a bird who hangs out with vampires. I'm sure that makes you a *real* human expert."

His next caw made me pause and looked up at him again. He was sitting on a branch in line with my eyes. I'd been about to walk straight into it. And I would not have liked to try to explain away that bruise when I got back to the manor.

"Uh, thanks," I said to him, and he bobbed his head before taking off again as though to say, 'hurry up'.

I did hurry up and found the others waiting for my return as though Etienne had actually been worried about my safety.

"What have I told you about wandering too far from home?" he chastised me, like a proper father.

I ducked my head. "Sorry. Atlas was with me."

Etienne looked to the bird, who had perched on one of the statues. "Well, at least one of you sees fit to do this simple request for me."

Atlas cawed in such a way it sounded simultaneously like a 'fuck off' and a 'we both know what Rune's like'. Atlas might not have thought much of me, but I felt like I could get to like him.

CHAPTER NINE

It was just me and Mia left at breakfast after Etienne, Mum and Grandma Vi had needed to be elsewhere.

Rune eventually walked into the dining room in nothing but a pair of low slung trackpants, his hair still tussled from sleep. If his intention had been to be the sexiest thing possible in the whole world and make me crave him more than usual, then I had to say his plan was working.

"Have you forgotten something, brother?" Mia asked him, sharing a look with me like a little sister truly exasperated with her brother's stupid antics.

Rune stood behind his chair and stretched his arms, the unnecessary muscles of his torso and biceps shifting and rippling. Heat pooled between my legs, and I actually crossed them under the table. Rune smirked at me, and I hoped Mia wasn't attuned to my heartbeat. No such luck.

"Stop playing with her, Rune," she snapped at him. "Seriously. She might not be compellable, but she's human." She slid a look to me. "No offence. But it's a biological thing. You don't have to feel bad about it."

I scowled at Rune and found him wearing the cockiest half-smirk as he sat down. "I'm not playing with anyone," he said as he let the servant pour his blood. "I was hot this morning and there's…blood on every last one of my school shirts. I've got nothing to wear until they're cleaned."

"Sure," Mia said, clearly not believing him.

"And just how many injections and protein shakes does that physique require?" I asked him.

His smirk didn't falter. If anything, humour danced even brighter in his eyes as he looked me over. "Oh, Evangeline," he chuckled, dipping his finger in his blood and taking an overly sexual taste of it. "Didn't you hear Mia? It's biological."

"We're built as superior specimens," Mia said, sounding bored and annoyed. "I mean, sure, you can easily want a guy without a six pack and bulging muscles, but a guy with them? Irresistible, right? Apparently, when they were deciding what a 'superior specimen' was, they put a bunch of middle-aged white men who'd lost their figures to age in charge."

I snorted, but it made me think of something. "But you don't sparkle."

They both looked at me in confusion.

"Why the fuck would we sparkle?" Rune asked.

I shrugged. "I heard it's alluring. All glittery and shit."

"Sure, if you like the 'I help out at children's birthday parties and they're all dicks with the craft supplies' look," Mia said, shaking her head. "Who told you that?"

"Remind me to give you a few books," I told her, and she grinned. Then I looked back to Rune. "I dunno. Glitter certainly beats the 'I live in my mum's basement and troll people on the internet while hunting for my Precious' look."

Rune glared at me and leant on the table towards me. "Once

upon a time, pale skin was a sign of upper-class birth."

I leant my chin on my hand to lean toward him with a shit-eating grin. "That might work on you Europeans. In Australia, pale skin is a sign of sickness." I mean, I was exaggerating, but we did exalt those with tans – because they were the ones out in the sunshine, not stuck inside working or studying. We were nothing if not a country who loved our holidays.

"I'm going to be anywhere but here," Mia advised us, picking up her plate and shooting me an apologetic smile. "You two have fun with…whatever this is."

Rune nodded to her. "See you at the car."

Mia gave him what looked like a warning look, but I suspected Rune was just going to ignore it. I was right.

"I suppose one can't expect too much from a country founded by convicts," was Rune's response.

My eyes widened in mock-surprise. "Oh, so you do actually learn about the rest of the world here in your little bubble?"

He smirked like he had me in a corner. "We are separate for our safety only. Even monsters need a haven, Angel."

I nodded. "Then you'll know I come from a free state. No convicts there."

He looked genuinely pissed he hadn't known that. For a second. Then he picked up his blood and sat back in his chair, leaning a hand behind his head to make his bicep bulge again. I saw in his eyes that he could sense my reaction. As he lifted his cup to his mouth, a smile teased at those sensuous lips.

"I'm not really sure what you expect to achieve with this display, Rune," I told him, sitting back in my own chair and acting as nonchalant as possible.

"What display, Angel?" he asked easily.

"You have Venette choking me in the hall because she's so whipped over you. You play with whatever mortal or vamp you see fit. How fragile is your pathetic male ego to have you toying with your *stepsister*? Or is it a vampire thing?" I suggested. I pointed to his face. "Little impotence problem? Fangs don't quite do the job?"

With a snarl, he launched over the table, knocking my seat back onto the floor, and crouched over me. My heart pounded in surprise, but it was more attraction than fear that pulsed in me.

I watched in fascination as his fangs grew slowly, like he was making a point, until they were twice as long as his other teeth. He ran his tongue over the point of one of them. "Do you want me to show you how well they do the job, little Angel?" he asked.

My stomach fluttered along with my heart, and I saw something akin to hesitation – more like surprise – flicker in his eyes, which were now black. Because my reaction was still not fear, despite my head telling me it really should be. No, it was interest. Did I want him to show me how well his fangs did the job? What was wrong with me that I very much did want that? And he seemed to know that. And he hadn't been expecting that.

"Monsieur le Rege," Mortas said, sounding as usual bored by his life in general.

Rune looked up at him. "What?"

"Your uniform is ready, sir."

Rune huffed. "Fine. Have Tiina bring it." He pushed away from me and stood up far more fluidly than I'd ever be able to, looking down at me like there was some pointed message he was giving me. "I need to fuck and feed before being stuck in that prison all day."

Okay, well the message was well received now. I rolled my eyes for good measure. "I mean, if you want to broadcast the fact you only take a few minutes, that's up to you."

Rune snarled and disappeared in mist.

"Very witty, mademoiselle," was Mortas' dry commentary as he walked over. "Do you need a hand off the floor?"

I accepted, but only because I felt like it would annoy Rune.

As Rune drove us to school, Mia said nothing about whatever she thought had happened after she left. She kept her nose in a textbook as though she was very obviously letting us know that she was fine with it as long as she didn't have to know about it. Which was an interesting stance to take. Maybe she thought I was that weak? As a human, I couldn't possibly have resisted the temptation of her brother, so we'd probably fucked all over the remnants of breakfast.

I'd been close, but...

I might have still craved Rune, but I wasn't going to ignore Strix's advances. I'd go so far as to welcome them if they could, even for a moment, distract me from the burning need Rune stoked in me. Especially when it was now painfully obvious that Rune was more than happy to get it off with anyone he thought would annoy me. To use Ama's phrasing; there was being a dick, then there was being a *dick*.

Strix fell into step with me as I was heading outside to meet up with the others. He wasn't alone.

"Having a good day?" he asked me.

I nodded, keeping a close eye on the two with him. "No worse than usual."

He saw where my eyes were. "Orien and Dreven," he said, pointing to his friends.

I nodded. "Hey," I said.

"Hi," they both replied. I couldn't be sure but they, like Atlas, didn't really seem that keen on me.

Something made me look to my left and I saw the flutter of black wings. Surely not. Surely, I'd just been imagining things. Think of the devil and he will appear kind of stuff. Atlas had never been to school before. That I knew of. Had he been following me this whole time? And exactly what was he going to report back to Rune? Because there was no way Atlas was here just because Etienne wanted me watched over. No, Atlas would only be here, I was sure, if Rune had told him to be.

"Lena?" I heard Strix say, and I dragged my eyes back to him and his friends.

"Sorry, brain fog. What were you saying?"

"Just wondered if you'd heard about the party next week?"

I was definitely paying attention now. "I don't think so."

"Oh," was Strix's answer. "Shame."

One of his friends – Dreven? – elbowed him. "Fucking pussy."

I levelled a look on him and scoffed. "Do not use that word like it's a weakness," I warned him. "You're the ones who can't handle a little tap between your legs. You want to try being actually responsible for one and seeing how weak you are."

Dreven smirked. "Fair play," he said, giving me a nod.

But, as they talked and I gave them absent-minded replies, I realised something; I hadn't had a period since I arrived in Knightsbridge. Was it some kind of magical thing? All the better not to tempt the monsters? I could only imagine what a period could do if they'd had to shut the school for a week after the incident with Margot White's sister.

A few nights later, I'd slipped down to the kitchen in the middle of the night for a snack. For creatures that had made a name for themselves being nocturnal, the kitchen was mercifully empty and dark.

"Is your human night vision better than I give you credit for, little Angel?" came Rune's annoyingly seductive voice. "Or are you happy bumbling around in the dark?"

I mean, it wasn't *that* dark.

I turned to face him. "Maybe yours isn't as good as you think it is," was my stupid retort.

Rune smirked at me as he rested his hands on the bench behind me, boxing me in with his body and arms. His nose trailed over mine and I cursed at the knowledge he'd be able to hear my heart fluttering like mad.

"Step away," I warned him.

"Or what?" he purred. "What will you do, little Angel, with your mortal strength? Your mortal body? Hm?"

"I'll bet even a vampire feels a knee to his nuts," I answered.

He laughed and actually took a step back like he needed to look me over better. "It's not your knee you want between my legs, Angel." He cocked his head to the side, so predatory. Like an eagle or a vulture. "Is it?"

I pushed against him, and he let me shove him back into the opposite bench. I kept right on going until my face was as in his as the height difference allowed. My body was pressed against his, but I ignored the way mine felt about that.

"I want nothing to do with whatever unimpressive specimen you keep between your legs that makes you feel like you have to be such a jerk to compensate. You might have the whole of Knightsbridge fooled into worshipping you, but I will not be one of them."

"You seem convinced I have impotence issues," he said, his voice humoured.

But I didn't have a chance to answer him. He picked me up effortlessly, spinning us and placing me on the bench that had been at his back. He yanked me forward by my hips until his pelvis pressed into mine and I could feel him rock hard through the layers of clothes between us.

Yeah, okay. His specimen was fairly impressive by the feel of it. Certainly impressive enough that no one as self-confident as him should feel the need to compensate for anything. Impressive enough that no one at all should feel the need to compensate, but I knew as well as anyone that wasn't how brains worked.

"Do you feel that, little Angel?" he whispered into my ear, pressing against me deeper as his fingers tightened on my hips. I swallowed hard but it seemed he wasn't talking about what was *physically* between us. "That small…tick in your chest when you lie to me?"

My heart thudded almost like it was underlining his words, and I felt him laugh.

"You cannot hide your…desire from me. I know every single beat of your heart, Angel. And even if I didn't…" He breathed in deeply. "I can smell it on you. Your need for me."

I mean, could he blame me? He was like my own personal Kryptonite mixed with my drug of choice, he had his lips against that spot where my ear met my jaw, and he had his massive erection rubbing against my slit! How was I supposed to *not* be aroused at this point? I would defy anyone to be *not* aroused in this situation.

My hand found its way to his chest. I promise my intention had been to push him as far away from me as my meagre human strength was capable. And he did part of the work, pulling back to flash those amused blue eyes at me like he was daring me to do it. Then our eyes locked and his went pitch black. My traitorous heart skipped. My stomach clenched. My clit throbbed. Something swirled around us, and I pulled him to me.

His lips met mine unhesitatingly as he gripped my hips hard and pulled me against him as close as possible. My knee hugged his waist as my arms wound around his neck and our kiss deepened. Our bodies ground against each other with the natural movement of our kiss, and his hands slid up my sides and around my back. One hand kept going until it cupped my neck and the other slid back down until it was gripping the thigh around his body like he was trying to pull me even closer still.

His lips trailed over my cheek, his powerful hand tipping my head to give him better access to my neck. I felt his teeth graze over the sensitive skin and tingles shot through me as my fingers dug into his back and my legs wrapped around him. I breathed heavily and could feel my heart racing. I wanted him so badly. I wanted more so badly.

I felt his hand brush over my breast, his thumb rubbing over my nipple, and I arched into him. A breathy moan escaped my lips and I felt him tense.

His hands went to the bench under me as he stepped his body back, his head dropping in front of my chest. His hair brushed the fabric of my top. He breathed deeply, like he was on the verge of losing control. I wanted to laugh, thinking it funny that this alpha arsehole could get too excited in such a short amount of time with nothing more than some dry humping. As though he sensed my amusement, he tipped his face to mine and I realised that the control he looked close to losing might not have had anything to do with premature ejaculation.

Rune's eyes were black, grey bleeding into the whites, and his skin was ashen.

My hand rose of its own accord and my thumb traced under his eyes, across the darkening tendrils that were appearing there. One side of his lips twisted – whether into a snarl or something else – and I saw his fangs were out.

"Rune…" I breathed.

"Scared yet, little Angel?" he teased, his voice easy but I noticed his body was still tense.

"What happened to showing me exactly what you could do to me, Rune?" I purred.

His lips did snarl now as he shoved away from me. "My father would be…displeased if I killed you."

"Empty threats, Rune," I tutted, sliding off the counter, heading for the door and pretending my body wasn't still begging for more of his touch. "Strix said you enjoyed making them."

Suddenly, Rune had my front against the wall with his front to my back. His slid his hand over me until his fingers were precariously close to dipping between my legs. Said legs opened for him. Slightly.

I felt his smile against my cheek before he said, "My threats are not empty, Angel. There is plenty I could do to you without physically maiming you."

"Like Margot White's sister, I presume? You'll let me maim myself?"

His fingers slid ever so lower, just not low enough, as he breathed a soft chuckle. "By the time I'm through with you, there won't be enough of you left to throw yourself off the tower."

I nodded. "Either touch me or don't, Rune. But if you think you scare me, mind reading is clearly not one of your abilities."

"What will your precious Strix say if he knows I touched you, Angel?"

"I don't know what passes for friendly rivalry around here, but it occurs to me that I'm the one who decides who touches me. Not Strix, and certainly not you."

"My father tasked me with your protection."

I scoffed. "A request you rejected and denied. If you're jealous, Rune, you can just admit it."

His fingers dropped further, and I knew he both felt and heard my heart thud. "Jealous of Salem Westmeyer? Why would I be jealous of Salem Westmeyer?"

"Because," I started as I turned in his arms, "I actually like *him*."

Rune growled, leaning his body into mine. "I don't need you to like me, little Angel. Not when every fibre of your being wants me."

I turned around to run my hand over the still very hard lump in his trousers and those tendrils went stark against his pale skin.

"I'd say I'm not the only one."

He growled, this time in frustration, and disappeared into mist, leaving me standing there alone and so very horny.

CHAPTER TEN

It was probably a good thing that Strix hadn't done any more than talk about asking me out considering I'd kissed Rune again. Or he'd kissed me. Our lips had met, whoever's fault it was.

Then again, given the way people paired off around the school, I doubted casual hookups and multiple partners were that much of an issue in Knightsbridge. In fact, I wasn't sure I'd heard of anyone being in anything resembling a monogamous relationship – except my mum and Etienne – since I'd arrived.

Venette might have thought she and Rune were monogamous – who was to say what kind of fantasy land she lived in – but I at least knew he was hooking up with other people.

And I didn't know why I was giving it so much mental real estate.

Because what did I care either way?

I owed no one anything, and I wasn't going to expect anything from people I barely knew. Strix had been flirty, he'd mentioned asking me out, but was I really so easily influenced by a bit of flattery – or worse, so desperate to avoid thinking about Rune – that I was going to lay a ridiculous crush and wistful hopes on Strix?

That was stupid.

Whatever happened would happen and I wasn't going to feel pre-emptively guilty over something that was, at that time, irrelevant. I may not have had the healthiest of role models when it came to relationships, but I also didn't need to overcompensate for my mother's less advisable life choices.

"I'm not going to take no for an answer anymore," Ama informed me as we sat in the dining room at recess and Radu nodded.

"It is beyond boring now," they agreed.

I smirked. "Sorry, have I evolved from mysterious loner to try-hard hermit already?"

Loren laughed as Radu said, "You're no longer enigmatic, you're just exasperating."

I smiled. "Okay, then. I will come and hang out after school, then."

Ama sighed. "Thank you. That is literally all we've wanted since day one. Radu will even drop you home after, so you don't have to rely on…" she looked behind me and gave a shit-stirring smile to who I assumed was Rune, "him to play chauffer."

I huffed. "I'm sure he'd rather I walked back and got eaten."

Loren waved a dismissive hand. "No one touches a le Rege."

"So people keep saying," I said, turning to sneak a look back at Rune.

When he saw me looking, his eyebrow rose as if to say 'Oh, you think you're going out tonight, are you?'

I frowned at him and turned back to my friends. Because I could comfortably think that they were in fact my friends. They might have been the first real friends I'd ever had, so I could have been wrong about the feeling I had when I was with them, but my motto had always been 'just go with it'.

As an act of defiance, I sent a text message to Mia to let her know that I was going to be hanging with the others after school so wouldn't be getting a ride back with her. Let her tell Rune why I wasn't there. Not that he'd care. But it would annoy him anyway.

When I snuck a look back to Rune again, I saw he was frowning at his phone and hoped Mia had passed on the message.

On the way to the next class, Rune deliberately crashed into my shoulder, and I glared at him. "Original of you," I told him, and he stepped into me, forcing me back into the lockers behind me.

"Have you lost my number, Evangeline?" he asked, and I smirked at him. That made him angrier.

"You heard my plans. Don't pretend you didn't. I didn't need to let you know."

"It's called courtesy," he snarled.

I nodded like the concept was novel. "Courtesy, huh? And what do you call this? If you wanted to hang out with me after school, Erasmus, you could just pull up your big boy pants and ask."

He vibrated with annoyance, and I still smiled in the face of it. I mean, the guy talked a big game, but he was yet to inflict any kind of damage on me at all. Whether he actually heeded his father's wishes or there was some other reason, I didn't care. The result was the same; he clearly wanted to hurt me, but his hands were tied.

"I don't want to…hang out with you," he said, his voice quiet as though he was hoping that no one else would hear him.

I patted his chest condescendingly. "Sure. You keep telling

yourself that."

"I don't," was his vehement reply.

"Good. The feeling's very mutual. I'd rather spend the rest of my life as a feeder than spend an afternoon with *you*."

"Great. I'm sure I can get you on the schedule if that's what you want."

I smirked. "No need for anything quite so drastic. I'd hate you to go to all that bother. I can just keep not hanging out with you. Much simpler."

The bell rang for class, and I slipped easily out from his body.

"Tell our parents that I'll be home in time for dinner, will you?" I asked, faux-sweetly.

He growled and his face wavered for a second. As though that all-precious control was breaking. I had the mad urge to give myself a paper cut and watch what it did to him. If Ama was to be believed, that could be great fun. But I didn't. I just gave him the most saccharine smile I possessed and headed off to class.

I felt Rune behind me, seething. There was a crunch like the destruction of metal, but I refused to give him – or my curiosity – the satisfaction of turning around. However, the next time I passed that locker, it was buckled as though a fist had gone straight through it.

At lunch, I was lying on the slightly damp grass, waiting for the others to come back from feeding, and staring up at the cloudy sky when a body appeared beside me. I looked over and saw Strix lying down next to me.

"Hey," he said with a warm smile.

I smiled back. "Hi."

"How are you?"

I looked back up at the sky. "Fine. How are you?"

"Also, fine. What are you looking at?"

"A spectacular lack of blue and trying to remember what the weather would be like back home by now."

He laughed and I felt his fingers brush against mine between our bodies. "You miss the blinding sun and scorching heat and sandy beaches?" he guessed.

I didn't move my hand. I let it twitch a little, almost like I was playing with his but could be mistaken for nothing more than an innocuous spasm. "What's not to miss? Is it *ever* sleeveless weather here?"

His finger very purposefully rubbed against the back of mine and I bit my lip against another of those goofy smiles. "That wildly depends on how weak your constitution is."

"If this is another pussy quip…" I warned him and he grinned.

"No. It's a human quip, if anything."

"You don't feel the cold?" I asked.

He shrugged. "We don't really feel temperature. At least, not the way they tell us humans do. We feel hot and cold as different sensations, but neither of them really bothers us."

"So, you could walk around all naked at any time of the year, and you'd be fine?"

"Did you want me to walk around naked?" he asked, his voice dipping lower and going more gravelly. It did pleasant things to my body.

"I'm thinking of an answer that isn't yes, but also isn't no," I told him, sparing him a smile.

He chuckled again as his fingers entwined with mine, playing over and through them gently. "Does that mean, if I asked you to come to the party on Friday, you'd come?"

"Do you mean like a date?" I asked, wishing my heart wasn't a dead giveaway for my feelings to these people. It had me at a significant disadvantage.

"I *was* thinking like a date," he said slowly. "But it doesn't have to be if you don't want it to be."

I turned my head to look at him as our hands slid together and held fast. His grey eyes searched mine and I had to concede I liked what I saw in them. I liked the easy rapport I felt with him. He wasn't condescendingly arrogant or mocking or rude. He wasn't Rune. And that was pretty damned attractive.

I nodded. "Yeah. Yes, it could definitely be like a date."

His face broke into a wide smile as he looked back up at the sky. "Cool."

I snorted and he laughed. "Cool," I mimicked.

"See, no. It's cool when I say it. It's just sad when you do," he said and now I laughed.

I sat up, my smile still at my lips as I said, "I don't know. I can be pretty cool," and my eyes fell on Rune across the grass from us.

I didn't know for sure if he'd heard us, but I wouldn't have been surprised.

With his eyes on me, he pulled Venette towards him and sank his fangs into her neck. For a moment, she looked like she was going to object, then she smiled happily and wrapped her hand around the back of his head.

"He really doesn't like you, huh?" Strix said and I saw he was sitting up beside me as well.

I sighed. "Does he like *any* human?"

Strix huffed and squeezed my hand. "Yeah, not so much." Then he lifted said hand and pressed a kiss to the back of it. "I just hope you're safe in that house."

I gave him a look that I hoped told him how much I appreciated the sentiment. "I think so. Rune's had plenty of opportunities to hurt me. Probably more than even I realise. And…" I looked back over to where he was hanging out with his friends. "He never has."

I was almost one hundred percent certain that Rune could hear us. Maybe not if he wasn't concentrating on our particular conversation over the general hubbub that must surround them all constantly. But I didn't doubt that he was concentrating on us. He was just that type. A bully. Overprotective and possessive for no other reason than it was another way of trying to control those around him. Of trying to control me to show me just how uselessly human and worthless I was to him and his world.

Well, not your whole world, Rune.

Because here was a guy who had presumably had a very similar upbringing to Rune, and he wasn't a total jerkwad. I'd made friends with Ama and Radu, who were from that same world as well. Mia was Rune's sister and she treated me like her own flesh and blood…just nicer. I didn't even have anything negative to say about Etienne and Grandma Vi. Although, Etienne was a little absent and I hadn't really spent much time with Grandma Vi. But they were both kind enough.

No. It was just Rune and Venette and their friends. Although, did people like that really have friends? Or were they more followers? Sycophants?

"You know," Strix said slowly. "If you ever want a different ride to and from school, I would be more than happy.”

I looked at him, biting my lip. “You know, that would actually be great.”

He smiled, his eyes bright. “Yeah?”

I nodded. “If you’re offering.”

“I’m offering. Tonight?”

I smiled. “I’m going out with Ama and Radu and Loren, but tomorrow?”

“Want me to pick you up?”

“That would be great, thanks.”

He inclined his head. “Anytime. Say eight?”

“Sounds perfect.” A thought hit me. “Can I ask probably a really naïve and ignorant human question?”

His smile blew me away. It was teasing, but not malicious. “Of course.”

“You guys shapeshift and move really fast. Why do you drive?”

He laughed. “Yeah. Okay. I can see why you’re asking. Lots of reasons, I guess. Protects us from weather we’d rather not get stuck in. Convenience. But, primarily,” He shrugged, “because we can.”

“That is…fair enough.” I smiled. “Okay.”

“Okay,” he agreed.

Ama and the others were heading back. “…would I know why Thorne punched Rune?” Ama was saying.

Radu shrugged. “I didn’t say you did, but you’re usually so quick with a hypothesis.”

Ama sighed like she was thinking. “Rune probably hit Thorne first.” She looked down at Strix and I and I saw the humoured question dancing in her eyes. "Oh, hey, Strix," she said pointedly, obviously looking for an explanation as to why we were sitting on the lawn, holding hands.

He grinned easily up at her, with nothing to hide or pretend. "Ama. How's things?"

"That highly depends on your intentions, good sir," Radu said as they sat down.

Loren and Ama followed suit.

Strix spared me a look. "I won't pretend they're entirely noble," he said with a salacious wink that made my cheeks heat and my heart flutter. "But they're respectable."

Ama's grin was very feline. "Brilliant. It's about time Lena got laid, to be honest."

Judging by the look in Strix's eyes, he was more than willing to take one for the team. My heart hitched again as I realised that I was very willing to consider that as well. If all vampires could smell desire, I wondered just how obvious my scent currently was. I wasn't, like, dripping for him, but I was definitely open to seeing where this could go.

Radu cleared their throat. "Great. So, we've all agreed that Lena's chances of getting laid have just risen exponentially—"

A scream hurtled towards us across the grass, and we all looked to see that Rune had a mortal by the neck and was dangling them over the edge of the roof.

"He won't drop them," Radu said confidently.

"Are you sure?" Loren asked, chewing her lip.

"And risk another Carmen incident?" Ama asked. I wondered if Carmen's last name had been White.

Strix didn't seem to agree. "He wouldn't care if he got the

school shut down for the rest of the damn year."

"Even he would face repercussions," Radu said.

"It's Rune le Rege, do you think he cares?" Strix said. He looked at Loren and I saw her eyes go cloudy. Was that compulsion? "His uncompellable stepsister is sitting right here and he's still more concerned with getting *his* pleasure. I heard Grandma Vi had hamstrung him. But even he can only be tamed for so long before he's going to explode and take the rest of the fucking town with him."

My eyes darted up to where he was still dangling the mortal from the roof. He seemed to let go for a moment, making the mortal drop before catching them properly again. The scream of terror was even louder this time. My heart clenched as I watched, obviously convinced I was about to witness not only the mortal being splattered on the floor at the bottom of the building, but also whatever effect that would have on a school of fledgling vampires.

"He's probably overdue for something deliciously heinous," Radu acknowledged. "What was the last one?"

"After Carmen?" Strix asked and Radu nodded. "Uh, the Quint kid."

"Oh, that's right. They still haven't found all of him, have they?"

That pulled my attention off Rune. I watched the vampires' interaction as they kept discussion Rune's 'accomplishments' with interest. What were they saying about Rune? Ama had called him a monster among monsters and, based on what I'd seen so far, that description seemed scarily apt.

◆ ◆ ◆ ◆

Later that week, I was thinking about the whole getting laid thing. Of course, I was.

Sure, I might not have had a period since I'd arrived in Knightsbridge, but that wasn't any reason not to think about…the risks of sex. Especially sex with a sexually heightened, blood-obsessed supernatural creature.

"Can I ask a question?" I asked.

Ama, Radu and Loren all looked at me expectantly.

"You can ask…" Radu started.

"…but there's no guarantee we'll answer," Ama finished, wiping a bit of blood off her lip. At least, I doubted it was tomato sauce.

I looked around, knowing that ninety-five percent of the people in the whole town could hear me whisper. I closed my eyes, took a deep breath, and told myself not to feel embarrassed or ashamed of something totally natural and normal.

"Protection," I said.

They all blinked.

"Like…a bodyguard?" Radu asked.

"No one would dare touch a le Rege," Loren assured me.

"Even a mortal one," Ama added.

I rolled my eyes. "Like…condoms…" I clarified. "Knightsbridge doesn't even have a chemist, where do you get them?"

They all shared a look, then the one they trained on me was all humoured sympathy.

"And is this an academic question or a practical question?"

133

Ama teased.

My cheeks flushed even though I knew it was silly. "Can we say both?"

Ama leant closer. "We can, but who is making you ask it, I wonder?" She winked and leaned back again.

I sighed. "I just want to be prepared…just in case."

"The mortals in Knightsbridge don't need condoms, Lena," Loren said.

That I couldn't comprehend. "The amount of casual sex that goes down just on school grounds? And you don't use…? That is super irresponsible."

All three of them laughed.

"Vampires don't have diseases to pass to mortals," Radu explained.

"And no vampire and mortal coupling has ever conceived a child," Loren said with a shrug.

I blinked. "Seriously?"

Ama nodded. "Seriously. Sex with a vampire is the safest sex a mortal can have. No risk of disease or pregnancy. You can do it anywhere and any way. All the benefits and none of the downsides."

Loren nodded knowingly. "There is the risk of death."

"But once we're past fledgling, the risk is less," Radu said.

"Which doesn't help me at all!" I reminded them.

"With either of them," Ama added with a salacious wink and I frowned at her.

Radu pursed their lips. "Good point."

"If he really likes you, then he's unlikely to even bite you the first time," Ama said matter-of-fact.

I blinked again. "Excuse me? Bite me? During…?"

Ama rolled her eyes. "Duh. Vampires. Blood equals sex, sex equals blood. Yadda, yadda."

"Even with…" I leaned forwards and dropped my voice lower, "vampires and vampires?"

Ama nodded. "Blood is blood."

"Except dead blood," Radu added.

Ama shuddered. "Dead blood will only do for so long."

"But other than dead blood, blood is sexy," Loren said.

I looked at her and wondered just how compelled she was. Then again, maybe it wasn't so much compulsion as it was just different kinks.

CHAPTER ELEVEN

Strix picked me up on Friday night for our date and I was glad that Rune was inexplicably absent. I didn't care where he was, I was just glad to be free of the judgement and the snide commentary I'd dealt with for the last few days.

Strix had been a little more attentive. Nothing that implied that night was any more than a first date. But he, Orien and Dreven sat with us at lunch a couple of times. He held my hand now and then. Occasionally, he kissed my cheek. He picked me up for school and dropped me home again. He even took Mia one morning because Rune had annoyed her.

Rune had watched us get into Strix's car, leaning against the front door with his arms crossed and Atlas sitting on his shoulder. Strix seemed to find it funny, but I appreciated that his immediate thought – that he gave away – was that Rune was jealous.

"Your brother seems to be taking the whole protection thing overly seriously," he'd said.

"Dad threatened to have Grandma Vi kill him if Lena gets hurt," Mia had answered. "Grandma Vi seems overly amenable to the idea."

I looked back at Mia in question, and she shrugged. I hadn't heard that, and I wasn't sure if she was telling me that 'it is what it is' or if her shrug was a 'you're welcome for me coming up with something plausible'.

Even Mia wasn't around when Strix's car crunched up the driveway to the manor, but Mum and Etienne were.

"Is he nice?" Mum asked and I could hear the excitement in her at the idea of 'romance'.

"Salem comes from a very respectable family," Etienne told her, and I noticed that didn't really answer her question. "His great-grandmother is on the council. Word is that he's a strong contender for her replacement one day." Still not an answer.

"Yes," I told her with a terse smile. "He's nice." They still hovered. "You know, you don't have to wait with me."

Mum put her hand on my shoulder. "I know, darling. But it's your first date."

I rolled my eyes. "No one needs to know that, and you've probably just told the whole town. So thanks, I guess. That's not embarrassing at all."

Etienne chuckled like a doting father and Mum tittered along with him.

"We should never be embarrassed by our firsts," he told me.

"Easy for you to say when yours are all…what? Half a century ago?"

He took Mum's hand, and they made goo-goo eyes at each other. "Hopefully not all of them."

Ugh. Gag me. I did not need to know what kind of firsts he had left and what role my mum could play in those. Strix's car thankfully saved any chance I might find out as it pulled to a stop in front of us.

"Evening, le seigneur," Strix said as he got out. He nodded to

Mum. "La dame."

From the little foreign languages I understood, that could be French. But did that mean we were near France? Or just that Etienne's family were French? The accents certainly didn't instantly scream even French-like, so who knew.

Etienne met Strix halfway to us and shook his hand. "Salem. Good to see you. You have a date with my daughter?"

Strix nodded, a wide smile on his face. "Yes, I do. I hope that's okay."

Etienne laughed, but the crinkle to his eyes seemed tight. Or maybe it was just me. "Of course. Of course. I hope you two have a good night." Something seemed to pass between them.

Strix gave a single nod. "She's safe with me," he said, and Etienne finally let go of his hand and stepped back.

"Of course, she is. Why wouldn't she be?" he gave a warm chuckle that Mum went along with.

"If that will be all, we'll be going," I said as I went to Strix's passenger door.

"Don't be home too late, Evangeline," Etienne said carefully.

I turned to him, halfway in the car. "Don't worry. I'd hate to have you think I was being murdered again."

His eyes widened imperceptibly, but he just schooled his expression then nodded again. I got into the car. Strix took what felt like far too long to say his goodbyes before climbing into the driver's seat.

"He's not my father," I told him as we drove away. "You don't need to brown nose him."

"Brown nose?"

"Suck up to."

Strix nodded. "I'll remember that."

"If this has any chance of working, the only one you need to brown nose is me."

He threw me a grin and I cursed my poor choice of words. "If you want my head between your legs, Lena, you only have to ask."

Oh, boy.

Heat flooded me and I was sure he could tell. So, I flippantly answered. "All right. I'll let you know."

He laughed as we continued onto the party.

Despite the Knightsbridge vampires not knowing much about the mortal world outside of their textbooks, their parties were scarily similar. This one was at someone's house on the edge of a lake in the middle of the forest. Music played loudly. A bonfire raged outside. And drinks flowed freely. Somehow, though, I felt like there was probably less chance of it being busted up by parents or the cops. Namely, because I hadn't seen a single police officer since I arrived. Not that I, admittedly, had spent much time in the town proper yet but I'd driven through it quite a few times. Twice a day at least.

Strix and I danced and drank and hung out with his friends. Ama and Radu hadn't been invited and, as far as I could tell, any other mortal there wasn't a guest but a snack. I tried not to dwell on that. Certainly, none of the others seemed to look at me and wonder if it was worth tasting me, so I felt safe enough. Still, by the time the vampires were obviously getting drunk and rowdy, Strix pulled me inside and found an empty bedroom.

"Hopeful?" I teased him and he smiled.

"Protective," was his answer.

I nodded as I went to the window and looked out below us. "Rethinking the sense in bringing a mortal to a vampire party with a bunch of drunk fledglings?"

He huffed a laugh and came to stand behind me. "Maybe. Maybe I thought some one-on-one time would be nice. This is a date after all, isn't it?"

I leant back against him, and he wrapped his arms around me. "It is."

"Unless you prefer groups?" he teased, and I laughed.

I span in his arms. "Maybe not on our first date," I said and was gratified when he took it as the joke it was intended.

"So you have rules for a first date?" he asked.

I nodded. "Some."

"Like what?" He took a step closer as he looked down at me. "Could I, for example, kiss you?"

I bit my lip, then hurriedly let go. "If you wanted."

After a heartbeat – in which mine fluttered like crazy – Strix closed the gap and, when his lips claimed mine, I still felt the smile on them. It was soft and cautious, just like his kiss. It wasn't embers sparking into a blazing passion. It was…nice, but it wasn't curl your toes, grab them close and hold on for dear life.

I leant my forehead to his. "Please tell me you're worried you'll break me?" I begged.

"Why?" he asked, all cheek. "Does my superhuman strength turn you on?"

I smirked. "More like your hesitation turns me off."

He nodded. "Ah."

"Might I remind you, you asked me out and you kissed me. You didn't have to do either of them if you didn't want to."

An ugly thought hit me, and I shoved away from him.

"Oh my, God. I'm so stupid," I whispered.

Because what if this whole thing was a ridiculously elaborate ruse? Their animosity. Strix's kindness. They had eternity stretching out before them. Who knew how long their long games actually were?

"What? Why?" Strix asked.

"Did Rune put you up to this?" I accused.

His face got uglier than the thought running through my head. "Rune fucking le Rege? Why would I ever do anything for that cocky beatless bloodstain?"

"Beatless?" was the part of that my brain decided to focus on.

The tilt to Strix's lips wasn't pleasant. "Beatless. As in his heart doesn't beat."

What? "Doesn't beat? He's dead?" How had I not noticed?

Strix cocked his head like he wasn't agreeing, but also wasn't disagreeing. "Even an undead vamp isn't *really* dead." He took my hand and placed it on his chest where I felt the thump of a steady pulse. "Our hearts beat. We live. But some of us – like le Rege – are so fucking monster that their hearts stop."

"But how is he…?"

"No one knows. And he's not the only one. But no heart beats within his chest. One poetic nutter, who thought they were prophetic, said it lives outside him. But then she jumped off the roof of the main building."

Carmen. Margot White's older sister, no doubt.

"But I don't want to talk about your stepbrother tonight, Lena." He stepped close to me again and his hands gripped my waist. "And I don't think you want to either."

I bit my lip, my thoughts on things that were certainly, thankfully, not Rune anymore.

"What did you have in mind?" I asked him.

His grin was all sexy and devilish and it made my whole body hum. "Showing you that I'm not worried about breaking you."

He picked me up, wrapping my legs around his waist, and kissed me hard as he climbed onto the bed and lay me down onto it. I smiled against his lips as our kiss deepened. His fingers slipped between my legs, and I arched into him as he rubbed over my clit. I know I moaned against him.

As his lips trailed over my cheek and down my neck, I ran my hand over his cock, and I felt him shudder. Then he was suddenly over the other side of the room, breathing heavily. His irises were black, those dark tendrils curled down his face, and his fangs were bared.

"Fuck," he muttered. "Sorry."

I sat up and shook my head. "Uh. No. Don't be." It was more question than anything because I wasn't sure if he should be sorry or not.

"Just… Give me a second."

I smirked. "Did you get a little bit too excited, Strix?" I teased and I saw him relax just slightly as he huffed a rough mostly-humourless laugh.

"Just a little bit."

I bit my lip as I looked him over. "How close did you come?"

"Me cumming to soon would be the least of our worries," he answered, and I nodded, guessing as much. "Maybe this was a bad idea."

I nodded again as I wrapped my arms around my legs. "That's

why you were hesitant?" I asked.

"Yeah," he said slowly. "I don't want to hurt you, Lena."

I gave a single nod. "Are you likely to?"

"I want you. I'm attracted to you. Like, a lot. I was arrogant enough to think that I could control it. I don't know a single fledgling who can control the urge to feed when things get…heated with a mortal."

I knew a single fledgling who could. At least, I knew one who worried about their control to the point they felt the need to put himself on the other side of the room. Rune had gone dark last time I'd kissed him, but he'd also just taken a breath. Had I not slipped off the bench that night, I had no doubt that we would have kept going. How far, I didn't know, but I had a feeling it would have gone the whole way.

"I shouldn't have let myself believe I could," he continued. "I shouldn't have risked you like that."

"Practise makes perfect?" I suggested and he finally seemed to properly relax as he smiled. His vampire face receded, and I unwrapped myself. "I know you won't hurt me."

He stalked over to me. "How do you know that?" he asked me.

I shrugged. "Because you just proved you wouldn't. You chose not to."

Strix crawled back over me, coaxing my back into the bed under me. "It's not always a choice, Lena," he said gently, his voice dropping into that sexy quality.

I wrapped my arms around his shoulders and my leg around his hip. "Isn't it?"

$$\blacklozenge\ \blacklozenge\ \blacklozenge\ \blacklozenge$$

After the party, Strix dropped me home again and I snuck in to hear raised voices coming from Etienne's study. Not really thinking about logistics after a few drinks, I crept over and hovered outside.

"Of course, she's not pregnant!" Rune said snidely. "You are chasing a myth, Father."

"Your mother–"

"Was not pregnant when you forced Grandma Vi to turn her!" he hissed, vehemently.

"You are finally admitting you were born, then?" Grandma Vi asked, her voice just as snide and all-knowing as Rune's.

"It is impossible for our two kinds to procreate," was Rune's answer and I was sure Grandma Vi was just as cognizant as me that it wasn't actually an agreement on Rune's part.

"You don't know that," Etienne said, his voice small.

"No," Rune admitted, almost like a taunt. "But neither do you."

There was silence a moment. I imagined the two men facing off against each other, fuelled by hate and rage.

Then Rune said evenly, "You may as well come in now, Evangeline."

I cleared my throat and stepped into the doorway. "I didn't mean–"

"Of course, you didn't." All Rune had for me was contempt. Not that I was surprised, but it seemed excessive even for him.

"How did you know–?"

Rune huffed. "Your heart has a very…unique signature."

"I heard a mortal heart, nothing more," Grandma Vi said, and I had a feeling she was stirring shit. I wasn't going to risk Rune's reaction if I encouraged her, though.

"I'm sorry," I said.

"Take her back to her room, Erasmus," Etienne said dismissively. "She could obviously do with a good sleep."

I was going to argue, but then realised that I wasn't being chastised for coming home a little drunk, so I was going to take the win and be grateful.

Rune grumbled until Grandma Vi glared daggers at him and he huffed and directed me out.

Halfway up the stairs, I said, "I'm sure this is fast enough. Go fuck and feed a servant and you can probably convince your dad that you did your duty."

Rune growled but said nothing until we got to my door, then he pushed me against the wall beside it. He seemed to take a deep breath, which only served to make him angrier.

"Did you enjoy your *date*?" Rune asked snidely, saying the word as though it was something dirty.

I glared at him. "Do you have no one else in this town to torment? Doesn't your harpy queen demand her own date on a Friday night?"

His lips rippled, giving me the exact response I'd been hoping for. "I don't date, least of all Venette."

"I'd tell her just how little she means to you, buy she's so arrogantly deluded about what she is to you that she'd probably kill me for the insult," I said flippantly.

"No one touches a le Rege."

"I'm not a le Rege, Rune. Or have you forgotten that?"

"No one touches you."

I snorted. "I mean, Strix does."

He pressed into me, his leg slipping between my leg tantalisingly, as pissed off as I'd ever seen him.

"You do so love your empty threats, don't you, Rune?" I said, my eyes warm as I dared him to do any one of the things that he was clearly dying to do to me.

My slightly drunk brain thought of something.

"The shrine room…" I started.

"What about it?" Rune asked, sounding bored again.

"You never told me what happened to them all."

"I didn't, did I?"

I sighed. "Just tell me, will he kill her?"

"Only if he has to. Or wants to."

I frowned at him. "You think you're better than us? All immortal, unending, sitting in your manors with your lordships and your secret towns where all the humans are just cattle to you. You're not better than me!"

He was standing in front of me in the blink of an eye. "I *am* better than you. *We* are better than you. And yet my father insists on mingling the bloodlines. Thinks one of his human wives must finally fall pregnant and birth the fabled dhampir."

There was a lot to get my head around in that statement. I wasn't sure what to lead with.

"But why *my* mother?"

"Because he thinks he fell in love with her. It would have been better for everyone if this one didn't already have her own progeny."

I glared at him. "Then why not kill me and compel away the

memory of me? Make her forget me and you can all have your weird little perfect family without me?"

Rune looked me over condescendingly. "There are many things our kind can compel away. A mother's undying love is not one of those. My father has tried that before with…" He paused as though underlining his next words, "deadly results."

"So, I'm stuck here while your dad tries to breed…" I was still trying to wrap my head around it. "He just wants to get my mum pregnant?"

"When – if – we have the baby, we'll be done with you both."

I looked him over and wondered what the hell vampire kids went through for him to be this… He was so full of hate and anger. But then, maybe that was just vampires in general. It wasn't like I'd had a lot of experience.

"Is that why you hate me?" I heard myself ask him.

His glare turned slightly questioning. "What?"

"Because humans are inferior? Worthless?"

He sniffed, his nose curling. "I hate you because *you* are worthless."

Ugh. He could be as sexy as he wanted, but I was not going to let myself pine over a guy who treated me like less than the dirt on the soul of his shoe. Clearly, whatever had happened that night in the woods and again just the other night, one of us had been high on something. Because there was no way in this frozen hell on earth that I would ever kiss him again.

Still, my hand found its way to his chest, and I realised that Strix was right. I'd been too caught up in the moment the other night to realise, but there was no heartbeat in Rune's chest. At the realisation, *my* heart thumped hard. His eyes were pinned to mine, scathing hatred burning on those icy depths.

"Scared *now*, Angel?" he sneered.

But fear wasn't what spread through me. Against my wishes, it was something closer to pity.

"What happened?" I asked, my voice a mere whisper.

"Didn't they tell you I'm a monster?" he seethed.

"Ama's words were 'monster among monsters'."

He huffed a humourless laugh. "She's not wrong."

"Does it hurt?"

"I've been this way for almost eighteen years. I don't remember anything else." He snapped his mouth shut as something flashed in his eyes. Something that made him look more like he was just a normal nineteen-year-old guy with pain in his past. It was only there for a split second, but I still saw it.

"Why did it stop?" I asked.

"No one knows for sure. Those who insisted I was redeemable blamed my mother's departure, though they gave up that pretext after a while. Those who knew better than to make flimsy, unnecessary excuses knew my mother left after. All I remember is overwhelming emptiness. It has been that way ever since."

"You're…empty?" I said slowly.

He looked down at me and, for a brief moment, I wondered if he was about to disagree. Or if he wanted to. Wanted it to be different. "I have no other description for the gaping chasm in the place my soul should reside. They call me monster, my little Angel, because I am a monster. Where most vampires have a sliver of what you mortals call 'humanity', a vampire whose heart no longer beats has none."

"Will it ever start again?" I was thinking of him – of anyone in that situation – but I was sure he took my words the wrong way.

"Why don't you worry less about what I'm capable of feeling for you and focus on someone who could actually ever care about you?" he sneered.

I shoved him, not that it made any impact other than make him sway imperceptibly. "I don't give a shit about what you could or couldn't feel for me," I told him, and I felt like every word was truth. "I am indeed quite happy focussing on a guy who might care about me. Thank you. Not that I need your permission or approval. Believe it or not, Erasmus, I try to be what we mortals call a 'decent human being'. I'm capable of sympathy and empathy, even for creatures – monsters – who I despise. Even those who certainly don't deserve it!"

He swayed towards me, and I held my ground. "You think your fire – your defiance – angers me, Angel? Annoys me? Does anything other than arouse me? You think fighting back is going to make any difference? I always get what I want."

"You can't compel me, Rune," I reminded him. "I won't throw myself off a building for you. I won't debase myself for you. I won't let you feed from me. You can't hurt me."

"Can't I?" he whispered, and a thrill ran through me. By the flash in his eyes, I knew he was very aware it was still not fear. "I suppose not. But you will beg me, Angel." His nose trailed over mine as his lips made their way to my ear. "Before the year is out, you will beg me to touch you, to fuck you…to taste you."

I leant my lips to his ear, pressing my body against his. "No, Rune. I won't."

When I pushed against him, he let me slip into my room and

close the door in his face.

After I'd showered, sobered up a little, and got into bed for the night, it wasn't Strix I thought of as I touched myself.

CHAPTER TWELVE

The next week, Rune was back to ignoring me unless he and Venette were…? I don't know, showing me what I was missing out on? As though either of them still believed it bothered me that she got to touch him, to kiss him, to feel his fangs and I didn't.

I 'retaliated' by going about my life however I felt. If that meant walking through school with Strix's arm over my shoulders, then that's what I'd do. If it meant kissing him wherever we happened to be, not really bothering about who might or might not have witnessed it. Then I did that.

Ama refused to believe that my interest in Strix had nothing to do with Rune.

I rolled my eyes at her as we strolled through the streets of town. "It honestly has nothing to do with him," I told her for what felt like the millionth time.

"So, neither of you are trying to make the other jealous?" she asked.

I shook my head. "No. He's enjoying his life. I'm enjoying mine."

She snorted. "Oh, I believe you're enjoying yours. And I won't begrudge you when it's a guy like Strix. But I don't buy that Rune's enjoying his."

"He's maiming mortals and fucking Venette at every opportunity. How is he not enjoying it?"

"Except he's not actually fucking her, is he?"

Wasn't he? "You didn't disagree that he's maiming mortals."

Ama shrugged. "Rune would have to be dead to not be maiming mortals. That's just a given. It probably has very little bearing on his enjoyment of his life."

I smiled at her flippancy, even knowing she was probably not wrong.

"You know we can smell desire, right?" she asked.

I nodded. Wary. "Ye-es…?"

"And you know that I know you're hot for Rune–"

"I'm not–" I started then stopped at the look she gave me. "I don't like him."

"You don't have to like him to want him, honey," she said with a smirk. "No. My point is, and I could be wrong, but I'm sure I've noticed a hint of desire off him."

"Aren't vampires in general just constantly wanting to bury their fangs – both literal and metaphorical – in someone?"

"Well, yeah," she conceded. "I guess so."

I nodded. "So, there's nothing between me and Rune."

She laughed and I looked at her. "That is not what your heart just said."

Said heart betrayed me again and she looked at me pointedly. I sighed. "We've…hooked up a couple of times. I guess."

"You guess? You either did or didn't, honey. Which is it?"

"We did. We… Before we knew we were stepsiblings."

"Uh huh…" she coaxed, and I knew she didn't believe me.

"*And* after."

"There you go!" she said happily, and I couldn't help smiling at her.

"But it was an accident!" I argued. "I mean, after. It was… We didn't plan it, it just kind of happened. We were arguing and then… One thing led to another."

"Oh, by the blood. That's even better!" she crowed.

"Am I gross?"

"Gross?" she asked. "Uh, no. It's what we call human."

"Mia said much the same, but I have no inclination to jump anyone else's bones."

"Strix included?" she asked, waggling her eyebrows.

I frowned. "No. Between Strix and…Rune. But no one… Do you know what? Shut up."

She laughed. "Cannot do," she said with a wild grin. "This is hilarious."

"It's not hilarious. It's annoying."

She shrugged. "Just channel all that lust for Rune into Strix and you won't feel so bad about it." Her amusement died as she looked me over. "What are you worried about? That they'll come to blows over you?"

That actually hadn't occurred to me. "Would they?"

"Depends how much Rune insists his father wants him to protect you, and what he decides 'protection' means. Big, bad Strix could very well fall under threat if Rune's thinking with his smaller head."

I shoved her companionably and she laughed again.

"What? Let me enjoy this. I have never seen Rune le Rege ruffled."

"And, as far as I can tell, you still haven't," I pointed out.

She huffed. "Pfft. If he's kissed you, then he's ruffled. Rune's not the kind of guy to kiss someone 'by accident'. That just doesn't happen. He is methodical and precise."

"He didn't kiss me first. I kissed him," I accidentally said out loud.

She frowned. "You kissed him?"

I nodded. "I know. I know. Stupid, uninhibited human with no control over themselves. But, in my defence, he gave back as good as he got."

She was looking at me weirdly and I didn't know why.

"What?"

She shook her head. "I don't know. I just hope Strix knows what he's getting into."

"Rune had absolutely no say or bearing on what Strix is or isn't…getting himself into," I said lamely, and she snorted.

"Smooth."

I rolled my eyes as we got into her car, and she drove me back to the manor.

Rune was waiting for me, a scowl on his face that turned to amused condescension as Ama pulled up. My heart hitched and I really hoped she didn't notice. She totally did.

"Oh, yeah. No bearing," Ama laughed, and I glared at her. She held up her hands in mock-innocence. "No bearing. I am fully supportive."

"I'll see you tomorrow," I told her as I climbed out.

Rune's body crowded mine as I passed him. "I'm driving you tomorrow."

I paused to look at him, knowing full well that Ama hadn't driven away and was watching us. Rather, was listening to us.

Rune would obviously have known as well and he seemed to care as little as I did.

"I'm not sure you get a say," I told him.

He took a step forward and boxed me against the door frame. "I'm not sure you're in a position to argue with me." He didn't take his eyes off my face as he said, "Go home, Amaris. Before I lose my patience and remind you what we do to trespassers."

The ghost of a smile lit his lips as though she'd answered him. Knowing Ama, it wasn't very complimentary. But I heard her car leaving and it wasn't until the crunch of gravel had faded from my hearing that Rune's hand alighted on my waist.

"You tell him he's not welcome on my property, or I will do it for you."

"You don't get to choose who I spend time with or when."

A sinfully wicked grin sparked across his face, making him more beautiful than even usual. "If he sets one foot on this property again, I will tell my father that you're feeding him. I might not get the pleasure of ending him, but at least he'll rethink looking at you twice after Father is done with him."

"If you're jealous, Rune—"

"Then, what?" he asked snidely.

"Then get the fuck over it," I told him, saccharine sweetly.

He clearly didn't like that answer, but he did let me slip away from him and up to my room. I did tell Strix that I was getting a ride the next day, I just didn't tell him who with. The next morning when I got into the car with him, Rune's silent gloating was annoying enough that the first thing I did when I got to school was kiss Strix. Whether Rune felt anything about that or not, I didn't care, but I wasn't going to let him completely dictate my life.

Rune and I then both spent the day blissfully ignoring each other.

"So, are you coming out this afternoon?" Ama asked at lunch, looking at my hand holding Strix's where it hung over my shoulder.

I gave her a look that told her to shut it. She could disbelieve my relationship with Strix as much as she wanted, but that wasn't going to change the fact that I didn't want to be with Rune. Rune was off-limits and, even if he wasn't off-limits, he was an arse and not at all interested. And neither was I. So, it was perfect.

"Maybe," I told her, all coyness a total sham. "What do you have planned?"

As we all walked across the quad, I saw Rune watching Strix and I carefully, and Ama's words were drowned out.

Despite what I'd just been telling myself, I pictured it; Rune's arm around my shoulder as we walked through school. Him pushing me against the lockers to kiss me fiercely until the rest of the world disappeared.

Annoyingly, Rune looked at me like he knew what I was thinking. I was almost stupid enough to believe he was thinking the same thing.

I cleared my throat. "I'll meet you at the café at about five?" I suggested.

Ama nodded. "Sounds good. How do you plan to get there?" There was a hint of playful teasing in her voice, like she knew what the alternative was, and I just looked at Strix.

"Do you mind driving me?" I asked him.

He shook his head, obviously understanding what I was implying and what I was actually asking; do you want to hang out first? "Not at all. I'd love to."

After school, I walked right past Rune's car and over to Strix's.

Strix opened the door for me, his eyes behind me as a rueful smirk rippled at his lips. "You've pissed him off."

"I couldn't care less," I told him.

Just before I got into the car, Strix pulled me to him and kissed me hard. We both smiled before pulling away and I looked into his eyes. I knew it was probably bad that it felt like we'd only done that to piss Rune off more and that was probably not a great reason. But, at the same time, I also felt like if we were doing it together then maybe it wasn't the only reason.

As Strix pulled out of the school grounds, he said, "I've got a plan."

I nodded. "Do you?"

He smiled. "I do. Trust me?"

I looked him over. "Should I not?"

He laughed and I noted it wasn't an answer. "You'll love it."

Strix woke me with a gentle kiss, and I looked around, realising I must have fallen asleep on the drive up the winding roads.

We were parked on a mountain top, surrounded by nothing but snow and a few trees. Below us there was only fog, but above the tree we were parked under was bright, dazzling sunlight. I hadn't seen sun like that for months. I'd almost forgotten it existed.

"Okay," I said carefully. "Why did you bring me up here?"

Strix grinned as he helped me out of the car. "Come with me."

He was walking straight for the sunlight. Panic gripped me but nervous laughter threatened.

"What are you doing?"

"Proving we're not all monsters," he answered, and he took his last steps into the light.

He blinked against the brilliance.

"Are you okay?"

He nodded. "It's like…an allergy. All vampires have it, but to varying degrees. Some of us can handle sunlight with only mild discomfort. Others can't stand it."

"And they're the ones we get the whole burn to dust in the sun thing from?"

He nodded. "Yes."

I looked him over and realised that his intention hadn't been wrong. Looking at him standing in the middle of the streaming sunlight, I did feel like he couldn't possibly be the monster that so many books and movies had tried telling me he was. Which was ridiculous, because I was learning that no one book or movie or show seemed to get everything right.

Strix standing in sunlight with very little effect was about as much a guarantee that he wasn't a monster as Ama telling me Rune *was* a monster. It was no different to any other rumour in any human school, because I didn't know for sure that being able to withstand sunlight automatically made them less monster. All I had was the assurances and beliefs of the people I spoke to, and they could be just as prejudiced as pop culture had made me.

But I told myself to stop overthinking it and just go with it. I didn't feel wary around Strix so what did it matter if he was 'monster' or not? If he wasn't a risk to me, then I didn't really care how monstrous he was.

I went over to him and lay my hands on his chest. "And is that all you had planned while we were up here?" I asked him coyly and he smirked.

"Why? What were you thinking?" he replied and, in answer, I just kissed him.

Strix had me back down and to the café right on five where he kissed me goodbye and said he'd see us all at school the next day.

"So, I hear Strix took you up the mountain," Ama said as she ate a chip. I didn't totally know what the deal with 'human' food and blood was, but vampires seemed to need both. Or maybe they just liked both.

I nodded. "He did. Is that weird? You say that like it's weird."

She and Radu shared a look.

"It's not weird…" Radu started. "It's just a little odd. Why did he do it?"

I shrugged. "Something about showing me you're not all monsters."

Another shared look.

"What?" I asked, putting my fork down. "You clearly both know something. Or think something. What is it?"

Ama tried playing it cool. "No. I'm sure it's nothing."

"It doesn't look like nothing," I pointed out.

She took a sip of her drink before answering. "I'm just not really sure why he'd feel the need to prove it like that," she said slowly.

"What's wrong with proving it like that?"

Radu looked thoughtful. "Well… I mean…" They scratched their head absently. "We're not really in the habit of proving we're not monsters, for starters."

"Like, who was he comparing himself to?" Ama added, like it was a silly afterthought.

"Maybe he just really likes her?" Radu suggested.

Ama nodded. "No. Of course. Maybe he does. I'm sure that's it."

"You two are making no sense," I told them.

They shared yet another look, then sighed.

"Okay," Ama said. "So, there's one reason he might have it and it's…not a great reason."

I frowned. "Okay…?"

"He was comparing himself to Rune."

I blinked, huffing a nervous laugh. "What? That's ridiculous."

Ama nodded. "Yeah, but…"

I burst. "If you guys share one more look without explaining yourselves, I'm going to…take my cake and go home." Because that was pretty much the only threat I could actually see through in this situation.

Radu smirked. "It's hard to explain without you knowing our world better. Our politics. If Strix was comparing himself to Rune, then he's…"

"Getting possessive," Ama said.

"Not in a good way," Radu added.

"He sees Rune as a threat."

I snorted. "Rune's not a threat to Strix."

Their eyes slid to each other, then Ama held up her hands.

"Sorry! Rune is, though. Strix might not see it as anything more than familial–"

"Good, because it's not," I reminded her.

She gave me a look that suggested I might have forgotten who I was talking to, and I pressed my lips shut before I argued so hard that I could only be guilty. "But it's not a great idea for him to be setting up for a war against Rune regardless."

"It's a sure-fire way to *make* a war," Radu said.

"Okay," I said. "But you also said maybe he just likes me a lot? And I'm human, so presumably making sure I know you're not all monsters is…a good thing?" I suggested awkwardly.

Radu shrugged. "It's totally possible."

"We do like conspiracy gossip," Ama conceded.

"That could be all we're doing," Radu acknowledged.

"It's been very known to happen."

"We just want you to be careful with Strix. Don't…rush into anything, okay?"

I nodded as I reached into my bag to get my wallet and caught one of my books at the totally wrong angle.

"Ow," I hissed.

"You okay?" Ama asked, then I saw her eyes go black.

Next to her, Radu's vamp face was getting stronger as well. My eyes did a quick scan of the café, and I realised it was full of our school peers. Fledglings. Panic thundered through me, but I told myself it would be fine.

I pulled my arm out of my bag too quickly and snagged it on something else that dug in even harder. I felt the heat of the blood well up. In all honesty, it felt a bit like my body was overreacting just a little.

"Lena…" Radu said slowly as their fangs elongated.

"Shit," Ama breathed, hers already out, as the whole café turned to me.

The room was suddenly deadly silent. I heard something like cutlery clatter onto a table or the floor. Expectation swirled. I felt very much like the hapless little mouse while the owl hovered. There was a very pregnant pause in which I felt the first instance of real fear since Mum and I arrived.

These people were predators, and I was their prey. No matter how we tried to dress it up and play at friends or like I belonged as much as them.

Just as I was sure the whole café was about to lunge at me, I felt hands on me, and I was whisked outside so fast I felt like I left my stomach behind. I was thrown in a car and then we were racing through the streets.

I felt bile rise and put a hand to my mouth to stop the retching.

"Don't fucking hurl in my car," came a recognisable voice, full of even more anger than I think I'd ever heard.

I glared at him. In answer he picked up my hand and frowned at me.

"You fucking idiot," Rune snarled, his eyes dropping to my hand. There was no sign of his vampire face save for a darker blue in his irises.

I pushed him off me and he deigned to return his hand to the steering wheel. "Don't 'idiot' me!" I snapped at him, my heart thundering at the near miss.

"Then don't earn it," he said. "Were you not warned? Over and over again. Knightsbridge isn't a fucking joke, Angel. We are old-school here. That means little contact with the outside world.

We don't bother with domestication beyond what is necessary to function when we leave. Blood is life. You can't just bleed here and expect to survive."

"I don't see you diving over the car to drink me dry," I huffed.

"You have no idea how much I want to," he said, his voice dangerously low.

Time to change the subject. "How were you there in time? Were you spying on me? Was Atlas?"

His jaw twitched like the truth was worse than any lie he could come up with. Finally, he admitted, "It was luck. I was across the street. I…smelled your blood and acted on instinct. Be lucky I was close enough this time."

"Or what?"

He threw the car off the road, and we actually span to a hard stop. He looked at me with utter fury. "Or you would be dead!" he yelled.

"Wouldn't you prefer that?"

"I save your life, and this is the thanks I get? Some sullen child who fails to appreciate how fucking frail she is?"

"Child?" I huffed. "You're barely two years older than me, Rune. You think you're *so* mature just because you were born immortal?"

"Vampires are never like mortal children, Angel," he said carefully. "We are born with the memories, the knowledge, the mentality, the…acumen of our ancestors in our blood, regardless of what age we are born. It batters and breaks against our consciousness in every waking moment. I am no mere nineteen-year-old. My whole being is skewed by the legacy of the blood in my veins. And it is the same for all of us. For Mia and Ama and

Radu, even Strix. I call you child because that is what you are to us. You are ignorant and naïve, and this latest incident makes me debate the sense in convincing my father to just lock you up or all his plans will be for nothing."

"You care as little for your father's plans as you do about me," I said. But my heart pounded as though it was asking me how much I believed that. "Why did you really save me?"

He snarled at me. "If you crash my car, I'll kill you myself."

Then he disappeared in a cloud of mist and left me sitting there wondering what in the hell had just happened.

My phone buzzed and I saw a missed call from Ama. It was quickly followed by a text apologising profusely. I took a deep breath as I leant my head back against the headrest. I didn't really blame Ama and Radu's reaction. They'd both warned me about something as little as a paper cut and I'd stupidly just assumed they were exaggerating. But I also knew that if they really wanted to hurt me then they easily could have numerous times.

I shot off a quick reply telling them it was okay, and I forgave them but would talk to them about it later. Then I awkwardly climbed into the driver's seat and headed back to the manor, making sure there was no way Rune could even claim the tiniest rock had flicked up and damaged his precious car.

Chapter Thirteen

A week passed and there was no sign that Strix was getting possessive. No sign that Ama and Radu's musings had been anything other than conspiracy gossip after all. And they conceded as much, between profuse apologies for almost eating me.

It didn't matter how much I told them not to worry about it, they still clearly felt bad about it. Which I appreciated. The thing I didn't appreciate was the fact that they seemed to be grateful to Rune for 'saving' me from them. I wouldn't say they were pulling a Venette and worshipping the ground he walked on, but they were ever so less snide about him.

Strix had been understandably concerned when he heard what had happened, but thankfully didn't seem to let that make him think any better of Rune. I was a bit ashamed that I'd ever thought that he'd only asked me out because Rune had put him up to it. Whatever was between them – because it obviously predated my arrival – there was clearly no way that Strix would do anything for Rune. Rune held charisma over the majority of the school, but not Strix.

Not that Strix overtly stood up to Rune. I noticed it was all behind his back, against Venette or one of their other sycophants.

Just not Rune's closest two. I'd heard their names were Thorn and Marcellus and whoever they were to Rune, Strix avoided them at all costs as well.

The next Saturday, as I walked past the lounge room that had been put aside for the kids' use, I saw Mia was watching something. I didn't recognise it or any of the actors in it.

"What are you watching?" I asked her.

She looked back at me with a smile. "Eternal Academy."

On the screen there was a kind of dorky girl with an exaggerated semi-future-librarian look going on. She ran into this hot guy who clearly had as much effect on the girl as he was supposed to have on the viewers. I felt myself edging around the couch and sitting beside Mia as the two characters had a very confusing interaction on screen.

"What's it about?" I asked.

"So that's Minka. She's new to the academy. She was born a vampire, but they tried dampening her powers by giving her hunter blood and raising her human. Then she *died* and came back as the first vamp-hunter hybrid. And that's Damien. He's a vampire prince."

I nodded. "Okay." The same actor who played Minka came on with a black wig. "Who's that, then? Future self?"

"No, that's Stasie. She's Minka's secret twin. She thinks she going to marry Damien. But he doesn't want her. He wants Minka."

"Riiight," I said slowly, trying to put it all together in my head.

While we watched together, Mia gave me the rundown between dialogue on the basic premise for the plot and, but the time she was done and that episode was finished, I was officially hooked.

"So, this in vamp TV?" I asked as she navigated to the next episode; number three. It looked like she'd just started.

"Yeah. It's my favourite series. Bit different to the books, though. Season four drops next month so we have to make sure you're caught up."

I smiled at her. "Who said I was enjoying it?"

"Lie detector, remember?" she said with a grin.

A couple of episodes later, things took a turn for our heroes.

"You guys have zombies?" I squeaked and Mia laughed.

"Zombies aren't real, Lena," she chastised, and I rolled my eyes.

"Oh, sorry. Vampires and witches are real, but not zombies. Of course."

Mia indicated the very zombie-like creatures on the screen. "They're the Wretched."

"And exactly how do they differ?"

She shifted in her seat. "They're vampires. Of a sort. The Wretched are probably where humans get their myths about us being undead. They're not really undead, but they're closer than us."

I remembered Strix saying something about the undead among them at the party the other week. "I was going to ask if they were the ones who kill when they feed." I'd read that book, too. "But I get the feeling Rune's definitely done that at least once."

Mia nodded. "At least once. It's difficult not to when we're young. We went through a *lot* of nurses as kids."

Human nannies. That kind of made sense, I guessed. "So, are these Wretched guys just fiction or real, too?"

"Oh, they're very real. I was kind of surprised when they added them to the series, to be honest. They weren't in the books. The majority of us never meet one, but they kill indiscriminately and if there was anything that scared a vampire, it would be the Wretched. Wretched are what happens when a turned vamp tries turning a human. They don't turn…right."

I didn't know exactly what that meant, but it didn't sound good. "So, what? They're faster, stronger, deadlier?" I asked.

She shook her head. "Not really. They're just…insane. They have no fear. Very little sense of self-preservation aside from the drive to feed, which makes them unhesitating in their attacks and relentless, and therefore often more successful than they should be. Thankfully, they can't turn anyone. They just…kill."

Which is exactly what the Wretched on the screen were doing. Or trying to do. They managed to kill off a whole bunch of extras before one of the main characters pulled the rest of the central cast together to make a stand.

"Geez. They're powerful," I mused.

Mia snorted. "They tamed them down for this."

I blinked as I watched one Wretched rip a werewolf in half. "That's tame?"

She nodded. "They didn't want to make it too real. You know? The main characters have to prevail. Gives us a sense of hope."

"This all still screams fantasy to me," I said in awe.

She smirked. "They've made changes to real life."

I nodded. "Yeah. This isn't the real life I'm used to."

She grinned at me. "You love it. Although, I could do without Altair, to be honest." She shuddered. "I don't get what people see about Hunter love interests. Like, slumming much? I just don't see the appeal."

"No? Who does appeal?" I teased. "Damien or Anton?"

She gave me a small, awkward smile. "I'm a wolfie."

"A wolfie?"

"Shifter groupie," she explained, looking a little embarrassed. "The animal's kind of sexy, you know?"

I gave her a knowing smile. "Sure. Why not?"

We watched a few more episodes before it was time to meet the others for dinner.

"What have you girls been up to?" Etienne asked as Mia and I walked in chatting about my theories for the rest of the season.

"I introduced Lena to Eternal Academy," Mia said.

Etienne rolled his eyes. "You and your romance shows," he said, but his tone was fond as he took Mum's hand. "Are you enjoying it, Evangeline?"

I nodded, my eyes darting to Rune as he walked in and took his seat across from me. "It's fun. I think I spend more time asking Mia what they've fictionalised though. It's really confusing."

"Ignorance in our world will do that," Rune said.

Etienne clicked his tongue at him. "Evangeline's ignorance is not her fault, and she's obviously doing her best to learn. Isn't that all we can ever ask of anyone?"

Rune rolled his eyes and Grandma Vi smacked him upside the head with a frown. "I'd like to see you survive in the human world as long as she's survived yours, boy," she said, and Rune glared at her.

"I do fine in the human world."

"You fuck and you feed. That is hardly surviving," Grandma Vi said, then she turned her attention to me with a very sincere interest. "Who's your favourite, dear?"

I smiled awkwardly. "Uh. Clichéd I know, but I like Damien."

Grandma Vi nodded. "You know, I had a Damien back in my day?"

"Mother," Etienne sighed, and I saw Mum pat his hand as though to say 'hush, let her pass on her stories to the children'.

Grandma Vi spared him a condescending look. "I did. Back when we still had the remnants of monarchies and there were still princes."

"Weren't you a princess?" Mia asked her and I saw the look of ridicule on Rune's face, like his sister was stupid for getting excited about the idea of princesses.

Grandma Vi gave me a cheeky smirk that told me she wasn't giving up her secrets easily. "Was I? It all kind of fades together after a while."

Rune's ridicule was aural as he snorted. "As if you don't spend plenty of time in your archive reliving it all. I've seen your plethora of journals, old woman. You've forgotten about as much as I have."

"Less, I would wager," was Grandma Vi's quick answer and Rune's ridicule turned warm humour as they shared a look.

"My point stands," Rune said. "You don't need to play vague, doddering old lady for Evangeline. She's smarter than to fall for that."

"A compliment, Erasmus?" I quipped and his eyes flew to mine. "Are you ill?"

The whole table erupted in laughter, and I felt a very smug satisfaction at the annoyance rippling off him.

"Isn't this nice?" Etienne said gaily. "The whole family

together and getting along." He looked to Mum. They gazed into each other's eyes like they were still as enamoured with each other as the day they met. It was both heart-warming and a bit gross.

"It's like they really are siblings."

Suddenly, I breathed in heavily just as I took a sip of my drink and started coughing violently.

"Lena!" Mia said. "Are you okay?"

I nodded. But my eyes slid to Rune, and I was very much not okay because he was looking at me like he knew what I'd been thinking to almost choke on my drink; there was no way in hell that Rune and I were familial. I didn't know what we were, and I didn't want us to be anything, but it was very definitely not familial. Our parents' marriage meant nothing to us. As far as I knew, it meant nothing to anyone else either. Rune and I were not and never would be like siblings.

But neither of said anything. I knew we were both thinking it. I didn't know if anyone else noticed as talk continued on around us. Mia regaled the elders with stories of school and other shows or books she was currently into, and what her friends thought about them. Grandma Vi told us about her favourite stories from when she was a fledgling. And Rune and I just glared at each other. Or rather, I tried to avoid looking at him, failed only to find his amusement still fixated on me, then I'd glare at him and try avoiding him again. Rinse and repeat.

Later that night, Mia knocked on my door. "Here. I found that book I wanted to give you. Thought you might be ready for it after our binge session."

I smiled at her as she came in and dropped it on my bed. "Thanks."

She nodded. "No worries. Can't wait to see what you think."

"Did you want to do a swap?"

She grinned. "Sure. What have you got for me?"

"Do you want faeries, or do you want to see what humans think of vampires?"

"What are faeries?"

I deflated. "Do not tell me that, of all the supernatural creatures who actually exist, fae are not one of them?" I told her.

She shrugged. "Not sure what to tell you. I have no idea what you're talking about."

I sighed. "Ugh. Fine. Ruin all my fun."

She laughed. "Oh, I like the sound of that, then. Give me one of those!"

I nodded as I headed for the bookshelf. "Can do." I got one book for her, saying, "This is only book one, mind. There's five. At least there was. There might be more by now. I guess I have no way to know for sure."

She took it with a smile. "Compare tomorrow?"

I nodded. "Sounds good."

She hurried out, clutching the book to her chest like it was indeed something precious. Rune and I might be the very antithesis of siblings but at least I felt a genuine sisterly bond with Mia. One that was just growing the more we talked and hung out. I didn't think we'd necessarily be the bestest of best friends or start hanging out together in town or at school or anything, but I really enjoyed spending time with her and wanted to get to know her better.

After she left, I was up reading long into the night.

How could I not?

It wasn't Eternal Academy, but Mia had found a book that I knew was her way of trying to say that she knew how weird everything was but maybe this would help. Because it was an old fairytale about the so-called fabled dhampir. The most interesting thing about it was that there was quite a large preface in which the translator went to pains to explain the mythology of the dhampir, the arguments among vampire mythology scholars – yep, they had those – and the fact that there was absolutely no proof outside about three stories that the notion of a dhampir was even something anyone thought about before a few hundred years earlier.

That was what fascinated me the most.

I was a total newbie to mythology. I had only barely just begun to stick my toe in those waters, but I knew enough to recognise that a lot of myths had very similar stories in different cultures. Like humanity shared a common subconscious, that our fears and beliefs manifested in similar ways throughout time and location. From what the preface said about the dhampir, that was not the case.

There were literally three stories that were believed to date back to prehistorical times, from a total of three vampire cultures. Three out of the innumerable cultures that vampires had. From what I could understand by reading between the lines, vampires had as many cultures as humans. The same way humanity had spread through the globe and grown, so had vampires. It made me wonder just how many there were in the world. Especially if they could, for the most part, walk around and blend in with humans if they needed or wanted to.

It also made me wonder just how ridiculous Etienne's quest

was. Why did he believe the dhampir was real? Why did he believe he could be the one to father it? Did vampires have scientists who had spent years trying to create a hybrid in laboratories and labelled it impossible? Or was it one of those things that were already fact and didn't need science to draw a line under it?

I couldn't even begin to come up with any answers, but Mia and I had a great time speculating the next day when we debriefed.

CHAPTER FOURTEEN

The next weekend, I woke as we pulled up to the manor's gates and stretched. With no idea how much time actually passed between the airport and the manor, I had no idea if our parents would have arrived at their destination or still be en route.

Looking around the car, I saw Mia on her phone and Rune looking bored out the window as Atlas swooped past.

"No one slept?" I ask no one in particular. "Just me? Great?"

"Oh, that's a mortal thing," Mia said, still focussing on her phone screen.

"A mortal thing?"

She nodded. "Means no mortal unaccompanied by an immortal can get into Knightsbridge. The wards put you to sleep, and you only wake up when you get through the wards. The last thing we want is hunters getting into our sanctuaries."

"Hunters?" I asked, realising yet again that my brain had seemed to pick the wrong thing in a statement to focus on because I'd definitely been under the impression that hunters existed after my crash course in vampire media the last week.

"The witches who spelled Knights–"

"These are not your secrets to tell, Mia," Rune said. His voice was low, but the warning was somehow more terrifying for it.

"Especially not to mortals immune to compulsion."

"Rune, I…" she started.

But her brother dissipated to mist and out through the open window.

Mia huffed and slouched in her seat. "I hate when he does that."

"He does that often?" I asked, not really needing the answer because I was well aware, but feeling like she could do with talking.

She looked out the window like he was in the mist running alongside the car. He easily could have been, but I doubted he was.

"Rune is single-handedly the best avoider I know. Conversations. Relationships. Work. School. Father's displeasure. He both gets away with whatever he wants and doesn't get in trouble for anything because he just… Fft." She waved her hand towards the door in a wave-like motion I assumed was meant to be Rune in mist-form.

"Anyway," she continued more jovially. "What are your plans with the parents away and me out for the weekend?"

"You're not home tonight?" I asked.

"Nope. I'm staying at Liliana's for the weekend. Matthew Bain's coming over to…" She stopped and looked at me.

I nodded resignedly. "You're going to fuck and feed."

"Uh, yeah. Yes, we are." She seemed to be asking if that was okay.

I shrugged. "I guess he thinks he's fine with it, and I know you do better with more than just dead blood."

I knew that the other families had in-house feeders but, as far as I knew, Etienne had got rid of them when we moved in under some kind of misguided attempt to show us humans weren't just food under his roof or something. So, the only live blood Mia and Rune had, as far as I knew, was at school. Besides, I wasn't going to judge kinks.

"You're not seeing Strix tonight?" she asked, obviously hoping the answer was a resounding yes.

I smiled. "We didn't make plans."

"Ama and Radu?"

I shrugged. "I was kind of looking forward to a quiet night in."

She nodded. "You know, they say vampires have old souls, but I think yours is even older than Grandma Vi."

"Was that supposed to be a compliment?" I laughed as the car rolled to a stop outside the front door.

"You can take that however you like," she told me cheekily. "Okay, I gotta go get ready. I'll see Sunday night?"

I nodded. "Have a good weekend."

She grinned happily. "Thank you. I will. You enjoy yours, too."

"I will."

She headed up to her room and I stood in the entrance hall for a moment.

"Can I interest you in dinner, Mademoiselle le Rege?" Mortas asked, stepping into the hall with me. "It is ready when you are."

My heart thundered and I tried to hide how much he'd surprised me. "Yes. Thanks."

He followed me into the dining room, pulling my chair out for me. "I suspect it will just be you tonight, mademoiselle."

I nodded. "Not surprising."

"Can I put on some music? Bring in a television? Your book?"

I looked him over and actually appreciated him for what shouldn't have been the first time. I had to admit that Mortas had always looked out for me in whatever way he, in his position, could. He was kind and thoughtful and legitimately saw me as a rightful member of the household. It didn't seem to matter to him that I was human or Etienne's stepdaughter. He was bound to me the same way he was to Mia.

"I can get it, thanks," I told him with a smile.

But he snapped his fingers to one of the servants along the wall who was gone and back before I had time to object. Mortas took my book from him and passed it to me.

I inclined my head. "Thank you. That wasn't necessary, though."

"It is rare, Miss Basset, that we can truly care for those in our charge. Allow me this one indulgence."

I bit my lip against a smile because I didn't want him thinking I was laughing at him. Especially not when he'd used my real name for once and I took that as the compliment it was supposed to be. "All right. Just this once, mind."

A sliver of a smile ghosted his face, then he gave me a short bow and set to having the rest of the servants fawn all over me for the next two hours. I sat and ate and drank in not only the lap of luxury but also in utter contented laziness. I sat at the table, taking my leisurely time, until I'd finished my book and I was pretty sure I might burst from the amount I'd consumed.

"Everything to your satisfaction, miss?" Mortas asked me.

I nodded. "Very. Thank you. That was lovely. It was nice to just have some time to relax and not think."

"If you've finished, can I return your book to the library?"

I shook my head. "Thank you, but I'll take it back and find another one. Mia showed me where she keeps all her favourites, but I've also found some other ones I want to make my way through."

He inclined his head. "Wonderful, miss. If you don't need us then, we shall retire for the night. But please just sing out if you want for anything."

"I will. Thank you, Mortas."

His bow was ever so deeper this time, then he and the other servants slipped from the room.

I made my way to the library, the walk making me feel less full again. With nowhere to be, no one to talk to, and nothing else to do, I took my time in the library as well. Just perusing the shelves and looking over the artefacts that the family had collected over the years. It was like a museum of curiosities. I supposed to them it was little more than the clutter I'd accumulated in my room even in such a short amount of time. But, to me, it was history and stories and knowledge.

"Isn't it past time that little mortals should be abed?" I heard and turned to see Rune leaning against a bookshelf across from me. His arms were crossed, and his hair hung over his eyes.

"Isn't it past time for self-righteous arseholes to be feeding and fucking anywhere else but here?" I suggested.

A wicked grin crept over his face, making the shadows fall across it strangely. It was both intimidating and devastatingly beautiful.

"Jealous, Angel?" he purred. "Is that what he's off doing tonight? Leaving you home to pine?"

My chest hitched and I frowned. "I don't owe anyone anything. Nor do they owe me."

He chuckled and it made heat pool between my legs. "Is he honestly that shit? Is that what you tell yourself to settle for him leaving you unsatisfied?"

"And what do you tell yourself?" I countered. "What do you tell yourself that has you at home on a Friday night, Rune? Does no one in this town *satisfy* you?"

He moved in the blink of an eye, suddenly standing directly in front of me. "You think of me whenever you're with him," Rune told me, his nose all-but running over mine.

My heart hitched in my chest, but I kept my face neutral. "Do I?"

I saw the smirk in his eyes before he leant forward so his lips brushed my ear as he purred, "My hands where his grip your body. My lips as he kisses you. My teeth grazing your skin. Me, not him, deep inside you."

"Bold of you to assume I've slept with him."

"Haven't you?"

"No."

He pushed me and my back hit the bookshelf behind me as he stepped as far into my space as he could get. He was as dark as he ever got. His skin ashen. The veins under his black eyes stark. Danger swirling around him like a warning I would never heed.

Those eyes burned into mine like he was demanding the truth. "No?"

I could only shake my head.

What did it say about me that I wasn't afraid of him? Of this man – this creature – who could rip out my throat with more finesse than I ripped open a chocolate bar. Venette and her harpies terrified me. With the others, I was wary. Ama and Radu I trusted, but knew the smallest slip could cause an accident. With Strix, I was wary of the effect lust could have on a fledgling vampire. But not with Rune.

Rune made me feel reckless.

I didn't care if he could kill me quicker than I could draw breath. I'd wanted him since the moment I'd first laid eyes on him, and I wasn't sure anything could ever change that.

"Why not?" Rune asked, his voice deep and low.

"Why not, what?"

"Why haven't you fucked him?"

This Rune made me feel not just reckless but bold.

"Because it's not him I want," I told him.

I saw the understanding in Rune's eyes. His irises might have been black, but they still conveyed as much meaning as when they were blue. "What?" he said slowly.

I arched my body towards his. "Is that what you want to hear?" I asked him, my voice lowering impressively seductively.

Rune twitched like he was trying to control himself.

I didn't want him to control himself.

I was done with him controlling himself.

I wanted to know I wasn't the only one who felt this… This thing between us. This pull. This draw. This aching chasm of desire and need that had seemed to fill me since the first day I'd met him in the woods.

We were standing next to the desk. From the corner of my eye, the letter opener glinted at me like it was beckoning to me. I knew from experience that wasn't any modern letter opener. It was sharp. I grabbed it and dragged it across the skin of my inner arm. It was only deep enough to sting. Deep enough to sting…and to bleed.

At the sight of my blood, Rune took a stumbled step backwards. We stared at each other, both breathing hard. I'd thought his vampire face was out in full force? It turned out I'd never really seen a vampire face in full force.

In the space of a heartbeat, his skin was grey, even the whites of his eyes were black, the veins under his eyes were thick and dark, seeming to spread across his cheeks and down his jaw, his fangs were sharp and long, and his top lip curled in a silent hiss.

"You want me to say you've invaded my filthiest fantasies?" I continued, me now walking towards him. "That I lie awake, imagining you stealing into my bed and ruining me, night after night. That I see you, even like this, and all I want is to scream for you, to *bleed* for you. Is that what you want me to say?"

"Is any of that true?" His voice was less than the broken rustling of leaves along the sidewalk in autumn.

I licked my lip before telling him, "All of it."

His jaw clenched. I saw one fang pierce his bottom lip, not that he paid it or the thin rivulet of blood running down his chin any mind. His hands balled into fists at his sides. He took a deep breath in, blinked agonisingly slowly, then surprised me.

"Run," Rune whispered, and I couldn't tell if it was a command or a warning.

I felt my eyes widen.

"Run, Lena," he almost begged.

So, run I did.

As I left the library, I heard him roar and the sound of

something breaking. Lots of things breaking actually. A lot of big things. And I'd thought his father had a temper. It seemed Ama had been right about Rune le Rege; he truly was a monster among monsters.

Not knowing what I was doing or where I was going, I headed up the stairs. I passed one or two surprised servants, but they didn't seem to think it necessary to ask me what had happened. I sorely doubted it was the first time a human had run from the library while one of their masters was having a tantrum in it.

I couldn't tell if the beating of my heart was exertion, adrenalin, the possibility of being pursued, or excitement. Probably all of it. I wasn't sure that Rune *would* pursue me, but there was surprisingly little noise coming from downstairs all of a sudden.

As my hand lighted on the handle of my bedroom door, Rune's body crashed into mine. With a speed and dexterity no human could ever hope for, he got my door open, whirled us inside, and closed and locked it behind us. He pushed me against it as he stared down at me, all hunter. And I was his prey.

But the tingle that ran through me wasn't fear.

It was excitement.

It was anticipation.

It was desire.

His hands were splayed on the door on either side of my head, but a knee was between my legs like that was all he needed to keep me there. I wondered if he knew it would take as little as a single look.

He breathed long and deep, but I didn't think exertion was to blame. He wasn't fighting for breath. He was fighting for control.

My hand rose slowly, like I was trying not to startle him, and cupped his cheek gently. Unthinkingly, I'd used the hand belonging to the bleeding arm. Rune nuzzled into my hand, his eyes closed as he breathed deeply.

"It's true then," I said softly.

"What's true?"

"Lust. Blood. Control. It's all connected, isn't it?"

"Not always." As he stepped even closer, one hand dropped and his fingers brushed my hip lightly. "For example," he breathed into my ear as the back of his fingers ran up my side, "blood can be a powerful aphrodisiac." His fingers brushed back down my side as he continued, "But, like humans, we have other turn ons." His hand grasped my hip tightly, "Control, meanwhile," and pressed me into the door behind me, "is relative." He dragged his nose over my jaw. "Were you anyone else, I wouldn't require…control."

My hands clutched his tee, trying to pull the immovable mountain he was closer as I leant my head against his shoulder. "Why?" I dared ask.

He took both my wrists in his hands and slowly raised them until he held them above my head as he looked into my eyes. "Because if I break you, I won't get to play with you again."

He reached up and licked the cut on my arm that I'd made with the letter opener, and I felt more than heard his carnal groan as he pressed a kiss to the very same spot. A slight tremor ran through him and the arms holding me tight seemed to tense as though the alternative was to fully tremble.

He hung his head and breathed deeply.

"What?" I asked, my heart tripping over itself. "What's

wrong?"

"My father forbade me from playing with you," he said, and I heard the humour in his voice. His head still hanging, he looked up at me through his eyelashes. "But I so desperately want to play with you, little Angel."

Play.

There was nothing more here than the physical. But I was okay with that. Rune was a bully, a narcissist. All I wanted was his body, and all he wanted was mine.

I arched my body into his and demanded, "Then play with me, Rune."

He stretched his neck as he breathed deeply once more and, when he was looking at me again, his face had softened just enough that his fangs were gone. And that was where the soft ended.

Rune took one of my arms and threw me across the room, aiming me perfectly to land among the safety of the million pillows on my bed. Before I'd bounced once, he was lying over me and claimed my lips with his. I wrapped my arms around his shoulders as my leg hugged his hip.

"You've bled for me, Angel," he whispered against my lips. "Now, I'm going to make you scream."

Rune kissed his way down my body, ripping my clothes off me as he went. His lips, his hands on me, were warm and strong and sure, especially when his finger gripped my arse as he licked over my clit slowly. My back arched off the bed and my hands fisted the sheets under me. I felt his smile against the inside of my leg and then he stopped teasing.

His tongue was relentless. Sucking. Licking. Probing. He

made me cum twice before he allowed my insistent hands pull him back up my body. My lips went to his eagerly, tasting me on him and not caring at all. My hands ran over him madly, trying to find purchase on his clothes to just get them off him.

Finally, he acquiesced and helped me get him naked. As he pulled back to undo his jeans, he looked down at me with such need dripping from his dark eyes that my whole body shivered in excited anticipation. I had never felt more wanted than he made me feel in that moment. Once he was naked, my whole body reached for him and brought him back to it. Before he was fully lying over me, he slid into me, and my fingers dug into his back as I took him in.

There was nothing soft or gentle or remotely tender about the time he spent in my bed that night. He slammed into me over and over again, wringing absolute pleasure from me again and again. No human I had ever been with – like I'd been with anyone not human before – had such stamina. Not only did he take far longer before he finished, but he was ready again in moments.

I think he finished something like four times before I fell asleep against him. Sometime later, I woke still in his arms. He either woke as well or hadn't slept, and we went another two times before I slid into full unconsciousness for the night.

When I woke the next morning, he was gone but I was sure his scent still lingered. The satisfied ache between my legs and the sting of the cut on my arm told me I certainly hadn't imagined it.

Chapter Fifteen

Having slept with Rune the night before, I couldn't in good conscience keep seeing Strix. I was sure the vampires wouldn't have any qualms about having multiple hook-ups on the go, but I could barely even think of looking at Strix when I had the memory of Rune so deeply ingrained in my soul.

It seemed better to put a stop to anything before I found myself in more of a pickle than I was already in.

I just didn't know how I was going to go about that. It wasn't like Strix and I were strictly dating, so I couldn't just break up with him. And messaging him out of the blue all like 'I think I'm rushing into things' would be a bit weird if things for him were purely casual. Which, to be totally honest, was more than likely given the way everyone else in Knightsbridge behaved.

So, I waited until school went back on Monday. I waited until he mentioned hanging out again and I could only bite my lip and hope that he didn't know what I'd spent the weekend – yes, the whole weekend with the *whole* house to ourselves – doing with Rune.

"I was thinking dinner on Saturday?" Strix said to me, and my steps faltered as he reached to put a hand around my shoulders. "What?" he asked.

I paused and looked at him. "Uh... I..." I took a deep breath. "If it's as friends, definitely yes," I said slowly. "I really enjoy hanging out with you, but I really don't think I'm ready for more than friends right now. Not yet. It's...all been a lot these last few months. And I just need to kind of get my head around it all."

To my surprise, Strix smiled. "I totally understand."

I breathed a sigh of relief. "You do?"

He nodded. "Yeah. I should have given you some more time to get used to everything. I can imagine it's been a big change."

I smiled at him. "It has, yeah. I don't think I really processed it all. So, I just... I need–"

"Some time," he finished for me, and I nodded.

"Some time," I agreed.

"Lena, you can have all the time you want. I'm happy to wait until you're ready."

I put my hand on his arm before we continued walking. "Thanks."

"No problem. Hey, do you want a ride home tonight?"

"Sure. That would be great. Thanks."

On the way home, Strix, Ama, Radu and I all stopped by the café for a bit before Strix drove me back.

"I hope you're aware this proves just how much I like you that I'm risking the wrath of the le Reges by driving you back," he teased, and I laughed.

"I will vouch for you. I'll tell them I insisted. I'll tell them I was barfing everywhere and would have died if you hadn't driven me home."

Strix laughed as well. "Well, go big or go home, eh?"

I was still smiling as I walked into the manor, the sound of

Strix's car cruising back up the driveway. Rune was waiting for me outside my bedroom door.

He snarled at me. "Was our weekend together not enough for you, Angel?" he hissed. "Did you need more?" I could tell what he thought about the quality of that 'more'.

"*What* is your problem with him?"

"What *isn't* my problem with him?" was his retort. "He's arrogant, doesn't know his place, and is just a general piece of shit. He's dumb, sloppy, and weak. The only reason he was interested in you was to piss me off."

"Oh, and I see it didn't work at all," I said sarcastically as I pushed my way into my room.

"He pisses me off by existing," Rune said, following me and closing the door before I could argue. "Pissing me off by flirting with you comes under the general concept of existing."

"If you had such strong feelings about him, why didn't you stop me hanging out with him in the first place?" I snapped.

"Would you have listened?" he snarled.

I flailed my arms. "Maybe. If you weren't such a dick!"

He smirked. "I might be a dick, but you'd prefer mine to his."

I rolled my eyes. "There's no lying to you vamps, so I'm not even going to bother trying. But know that, just because I wanted you, it doesn't mean I'll give in to it again."

"You're choosing him over me?"

I bristled. "I'm not choosing *anyone*," I said indignantly. "And, if I *was*, that is my choice, not yours."

"But you've decided that wanting the monster is unacceptable so you're going to settle for the lap dog?" he scoffed.

"God, your ego!" I huffed. "No. I haven't 'decided' anything of the sort. For your information, I told Strix I thought I was rushing into dating. I told him I wanted to just be friends for a while before anything else happened. So, no. I'm not settling for anyone. I don't have to *settle* for someone else to just not want to do whatever it is you think we're doing."

"I thought you weren't going to lie to me, little Angel," he said, his eyes full of black fury.

"I'm not lying to you, Rune. Do I still want your body? Sure. Of course, I do. I don't want to want it, but I'm concerningly obsessed with it. To the point I'm sure I should probably seek professional help. But that doesn't mean I can't exercise my own willpower. I'm not compellable, remember? You can't make me do anything."

He growled as he took a step towards me. "The fun lies in you giving in to me, little Angel. None of this would be half as satisfying if I just forced you into it. I get what I want every time you weaken. Every time you kiss me. Every time you touch me. Every time your heartbeat trips because you just *thought* of me. My touch. My kiss. My taste." He took my chin in his hands and made me look into his eyes. "Every time you try to force your breathing steady, and you think that will hide your heartbeat from me."

My eyes narrowed at him. "Are you so very obsessed with my heartbeat because you don't have one of you own?"

A devilishly sexy half-smile played at his lips, and I saw his fangs growing. "My heart may not skip when I see you, little Angel. But my cock stiffens for you. My fingers itch to touch you. My lips need to kiss you. My fangs ache to…taste you. I have no simple human reaction to you, Lena, but every single one of my predatory instincts become very difficult to ignore."

"Then just kill me and let's put us all out of our misery."

He smirked. "It's not you I want to kill, Angel."

I frowned. "Then who?"

"Anyone who touches you instead of me."

The heartbeat he seemed so obsessed with fluttered traitorously, but it didn't make him even more insufferably smug. His fingers loosened their grip on my chin and brushed down my throat to slide around my neck under my ear.

"You have no idea how much I want to kill him. I scented you on him. Him on you. I saw him kiss the hand he held like it was such a simple, intimate thing. It was all Thorne could do to convince me how very…stupid it would be."

I remembered Ama and Radu talking about Thorne punching Rune. Had that been why?

Another flutter, mirrored deeper down. "But you hate me."

"I can hate something and still not want anyone else to have it."

"Thing. Of course. Because humans aren't even people to you." As weird as that sounded, but we both knew what I meant.

"Some*one*," he said softly, like it pained him to correct himself but that didn't change the fact that it was the word he should have used. Would have used if he wasn't being his usual arsehole self.

"What do you think this is, Rune?" I asked him.

"Physical," was his answer and I nodded. He seemed to think a clarification was necessary. "Since the moment I met you in the woods, I was drawn to you, Angel. I wanted you with a need even stronger than my need for blood. I didn't know who you were then. Maybe I did, and I just didn't want to. Because my father

191

warned me what he would do to me if I…played with my new human stepsister. He would not risk his plans just so I could take pleasure in destroying you. I resented you and your mother, seeing you as nothing more than the manifestation of his ridiculous obsession. And the more we clash, the more I crave you, the more I resent you. Something– Someone I *need* with a strength I can't control but have been told not to touch. And I so want to touch you, Angel…"

"Is this where I tell you to ruin me?" I asked, humour warming my eyes. "Or do you just disobey everyone now?"

His eyebrow crooked in amusement and question. "I thought you weren't giving in again?"

His gaze was so intense that I was having trouble breathing deeply enough. I didn't bother trying to hide it this time. "Touch me, Rune."

"Are you choosing me?" he asked, his lips teasing across mine.

"Is that what this is? You or him? I can't just have what I want?"

"You can have what you want, little Angel. Knowing what you want, I might even go so far as to beg you to let me give it to you. But I want to hear you beg first."

"I'm not going to beg you, Rune."

"Then just admit it."

"Admit what?"

"Admit that this – you and me – is all you think about."

"And why would I do that?"

"Because…" he whispered. "Then I'd know I'm not the only one."

My answer was to pull him close and kiss him hard, but he seemed to take that as my acknowledgement that I felt the same. I didn't even mind, because I did feel the same. After all, that had been the reason I put a stop to my relationship with Strix before it got to a point I couldn't stop it so easily.

The way Rune touched me.

The way he kissed me.

The way he knew exactly how to ruin me in the best possible way.

The next day at school, the screaming could be heard across the campus. It was so dramatic that birds took off from the trees in droves. It wasn't fear or pain. It was pure, unadulterated, animalistic fury. My own fear skittered up my spine and made goosebumps chase across my skin in a really bad way.

Loren and I were waiting for Ama and Radu to come back from feeding and we shared a look. It was a look that only mortals could give each other, no matter whether they were compelled or not. Fight or flight was heavily engaged. Around the campus, I could see other mortals pause as well, all looking around like they were just double checking that they weren't the one currently in the firing line.

"Who do you think that was?" I asked.

Loren bit her lip nervously. "It sounded female. Higher pitched than the males. Less vibration though the core of the earth kind of stuff."

Something niggled at me and sent my panic into overdrive.

Then Ama and Radu appeared in a blur from the feeding building.

"Oh, my blood," Radu said excitedly. "You are never going to guess what happened." They were bouncing on the soles of their feet.

Loren and I shared a look before turning back to the vampires. "What?" I asked.

Ama narrowed her eyes on me. "Anything you want to share with the club before we proceed."

I know she and Radu heard my heart thud. I saw it in the way their heads cocked to the side in interest. That birdlike predation of theirs.

"What the fuck did you do?" Ama breathed.

I shrugged. "I didn't do anything." Even I felt the lie in my heartbeat. "Don't tell me that was—"

"Oh, it was."

"Why?" I asked.

Radu smirked. "Can you really not guess?"

Oh, I could guess. But I didn't want to look even more guilty by immediately coming up with the right answer. "Her family are marrying her off to some Bela Lugosi looking dude?" I guessed and they all looked at me blankly.

"Who?"

I shook my head. "Never mind."

"What's going on?" Loren asked, obviously having no idea what we were talking about.

Ama looked at me pointedly. "Care to shed some light?"

I shook my head again. "Not particularly."

Ama rolled her eyes, but humour tugged at the corner of her

lips. "Rune just rejected Venette."

"What?" both Loren and I cried, and Ama nodded.

"Oh, yes." She and Radu sat down. "Rune just gave Venette her marching orders. They're over."

"As over as two people who were never really together can be, anyway," Radu added.

Loren's mouth actually dropped open in a little 'o'. Radu leaned over and close it for her.

"I think we all know why," Ama said, her eyes telling me I had some serious explaining to do.

I scoffed. "If you think Rune would end things with anyone because of me, you're insane."

Ama's head cocked again, and she frowned. "Truth. At least your truth. Well, that sucks. I totally thought you guys had, like, spent the weekend engaged in some seriously degrading, mind-blowing sex and he was totally whipped for you now."

Both Ama and Radu's eyes darted to mine and I knew they'd heard. I held up my hands, knowing it was futile to lie to them. "Half of that might be partially true. But that is *not* an explanation as to why he got rid of Venette."

Radu pursed their lips. "She's right, though. Depressingly."

Ama chewed her nail. "So, you're not like suddenly together or anything?"

I actually laughed. "Oh, my God. No! I hate him. And even if I didn't, he has made it very clear he doesn't date."

Radu deflated a little. "Well, boring. I thought we had it nailed for sure this time."

Ama shrugged. "Makes for a good story, though."

Radu pointed at her. "It does. Love it. We can always pretend it's true."

I rolled my eyes. "Or we could not."

"Is that why Strix is a little extra pissy today? Did you dump him, too?" Radu asked and Ama's mouth dropped open this time.

"You what?"

I sighed. "I didn't dump him. We weren't dating. I just told him I felt like I was rushing into things. I'm new here. I'm new to the whole vampires exist thing. I thought it would be better to get to know everyone better before I started dating. Is that a crime?"

Ama nodded. "Uh, yes. When you didn't tell us about it."

"And the timing. You're really going to try telling us it had nothing to do with the raging lady boner you have for your stepbrother?" Radu asked.

I looked around. "Can you not broadcast it, please?" I hissed. "It's embarrassing enough you guys know now. I'd rather just be the idiot human."

"Rather than the idiot human who fell for Rune le Rege and got said human heart absolutely massacred," Ama said matter-of-fact.

I batted her. "Shut up. No one fell for anyone. Am I not allowed to be single or unattached or whatever you guys call yourselves?"

Radu nodded. "No. You can. But we get to call bullshit on that."

I smirked. "Believe what you want."

"Thank you. I shall."

"It doesn't make it true."

"That is not what Venette and Strix are going to think if they compare notes."

Ama pointed at them like it was a good point. "But are they likely to compare notes? Strix hates Rune."

"HATES him," Radu agreed.

"And anyone associated with him."

"LOATHES," Radu said.

"So, they'll have to wait for the rumour mill to circulate which could take a while. I mean, everyone's going to know about Venette being dumped, but Strix isn't the brightest bulb. He might just think Rune got bored."

Radu nodded again. "It's happened about a million times."

"Just to Venette even."

"To say nothing of all the others."

They both looked at me.

"You should be right for a while," was Ama's pronouncement.

Oddly enough, it wasn't all that comforting.

Something woke me in the dead of night.

I sat up and saw the fog curling through and around the big velvet curtains at the window, spilling across the carpet. I felt the smile tug at my lips, but wouldn't give him the satisfaction of seeing it. The mist crawled up the end of the bed, solidifying into Rune as it – he – crept up my body. The curtains of the bed closed around us as Rune climbed on top of me and guided me back into my pillows.

As his lips found mine, my body wrapped around him as though we'd been made for each other. His hand ran over me firmly, coaxing my leg higher around his hip as he pressed against me, hard and needy.

There were no words in the dark. We kissed and we touched until we were both naked and I straddled him, taking him in slowly and gently until he slid to the hilt. He lay back and watched me ride him, a thumb on my clit.

This wasn't the frenzied, hate-fuelled marathon of our first time. This was something we would never speak of in the deep, dark night, let alone in the dazzling – more like drizzling – light of day.

I wouldn't kid myself that I even liked Rune, but my body craved him like it had never craved anyone or anything before. I needed his hands on me. I needed his lips on mine. I needed him inside me. Something was pulling us together that I didn't even want to try to understand. I needed him – and only him – to bring me to the pinnacle of pleasure and let me crash to pieces around him. Pieces only he could put together again. I needed to be the one to do that for him.

And, like we would never speak about the way we came together in the solitude and safety of the dead of night, we would never speak of the way we both knew he felt it, too.

CHAPTER SIXTEEN

Mia bounded into my room on Saturday after lunch with a wide smile.

"Can I help you?" I asked her, with a wide smile of my own. "Do you need book five already?"

She nodded. "Yes. But I also wanted to know if you want to watch a vampire horror with me?"

I was intrigued. "A vampire horror. What does that entail? A world without humans?"

She laughed. "No. Well, actually they did do that one. But no. This one has a much more realistic portrayal of the Wretched. It's just released, and I've been dying to watch it. But we'll need to watch from number one for it to make sense."

Something hit me. "How do you get this stuff?"

She blinked. "What do you mean?"

"Like new shows and movies and stuff."

"The internet…?" she said like she wasn't sure if I'd heard of it and, if not, where I'd been for my whole life.

I frowned. "But I can't get anything outside Knightsbridge. It's like I can't even access the real world. Like some uber specialised firewall."

Mia sighed and rolled her eyes. "Really?"

"Really what?"

"Standard issue mortal access. That's shit. I'll talk to Rune. We may be able to convince him to break the controls on your things. I can't believe they did that."

Now I was blinking. "What do you mean Rune could break them?"

She waved a dismissive hand. "Rune is mad skilled with technology. Didn't you know?"

I frowned. "No. Why would I know that?"

She shrugged. "I dunno. You guys talk and stuff. Don't you?"

I shook my head. "Not really."

"Huh." She seemed legitimately surprised by that. "Like, not at all?"

I shook my head again. "Does insulting each other count?"

"That's weird. He never shuts up around me."

"You're his sister," I reminded her and, for a split second, I felt like she knew the number one, blazing reason I would never think of myself as Rune's sister.

Mia looked me over carefully, then huffed. "Ah well. I don't know. What do you think about this movie, then?"

"How many are there?"

"Four."

I looked at the time. "Have we got time for four movies?" I asked her.

She scoffed. "Have we…?" she laughed. "Oh, Lena. You crack me up."

She came over, grabbed my hand and dragged me to the kids' lounge. While we were settling in, Mortas arrived with a little trolley of popcorn and snacks and drinks.

"I planned ahead this time," Mia told me, pride evident in her voice.

"Thanks."

She wriggled against me. "I like having sister time. You're much better company than Rune. Honestly, I watched two with him and he spent the whole time laughing at me because I had the audacity to be scared. It's a horror movie. I was eleven. Of course, I was scared!"

I didn't know why, but it weirdly warmed my heart to hear that vampires got scared, too. Well, some of them. I couldn't imagine Rune being scared of anything. But there was something ever so comforting to know that there was, indeed, something akin to what mortals called humanity in these creatures.

We got through the first two before we took a break for some Eternal Academy as a bit of a palate cleanser, then dinner. A dinner Rune didn't attend. Mia excitedly told the others that we were having a girls' night and still had two more movies to go.

Mum beamed at me, and I knew what was running through her head; she was thinking that I finally had all the things she'd never been able to give me before. It wasn't just about going to a decent school – although, I maintained that was subjective – but it was also the fact that she felt we were all a 'real family' now. Whatever 'real family' actually meant. She'd be happy because I wouldn't be lonely anymore. Sure, she didn't have to work anymore, but she was still barely more present than she'd been before. I just knew better where she was now. Or, at least, who she was with.

"Are you sure a horror movie marathon is such a good idea?" Etienne said, in that kindly way parents had when they wanted to support your life choices but were subtly suggesting those very choices might be a bit shit.

Mia grinned. "Of course, it is. If I'm not safe with my big sister, where am I safe?"

Okay, so my heart warmed significantly on hearing that, and I had to look down at my dinner to hide the wide, goofy smile that was threatening to spread across my face. I'd never been a sister before, let alone a big sister. There was something really nice about it. I couldn't put my finger on what it was, but it made me really happy.

When I felt like I finally had control over myself, I looked back up and happened to catch Grandma Vi looking at me. Her eyes shone knowingly, a tug at the corner of her lips and I felt like she was proud of me. She was happy to have me. She'd recognised the effect Mia's words had on me and she appreciated my reaction. She gave me a slight nod, then I turned back to Mia's conversation.

The dessert plates were barely empty when Mia was plucking at my arm. "Come on. Come on," she said eagerly. Time for three."

I gave the rest of the family a smile as I let her pull me out of the room and back to the lounge to get back to our marathon.

Each movie was getting steadily gorier and darker. Which, I guess was to be expected from a franchise. They couldn't very well just plod along at the same levels and expect to hold people's interest. Still, it meant that by the time we were hitting play on the fourth one, Mia and I were practically hugging each other for comfort.

These Wretched were not like the Wretched in Eternal

Academy. These ones were hands down freaking terrifying. And the worst part? When it was painfully obvious that the love interest was going to become one. For plot furtherance and all that, naturally.

"What are you two watching?" Rune asked as he dropped onto the couch next to me just after we finally started the fourth one.

I pretended I felt nothing about that, but I was sure neither of them would have believed me. I just had to hope that Mia was too heavily invested in the movie.

"Return of Wretched," she said.

"Part Four," I added.

Rune sighed. "Seriously? Three was bad enough."

Mia and I both jumped as a Wretched burst through a cupboard door and Rune laughed. An actual, head back, belly kind of laugh. I told myself my heart reacted to the jump scare and not his laugh.

"Wow," he whistled. "Really? How lame are you two? That wasn't scary at all."

"How about you leave us to it, then?" Mia suggested none too politely.

Rune wriggled like he was settling in. "Oh, no," he chuckled. "This, I have to see. How far do you think you're going to get?"

"We'll have you know," I told him, "that we have watched the other three today already."

Mia nodded before she jumped again and buried her face in my shoulder. "Yeah. We'll easily make it through the whole thing."

Rune crossed his arms. "Okay. But I'm not going anywhere."

"You don't believe me?" Mia asked, still in my shoulder.

"I mean, to get the whole way through it, you kind of have to have your eyes on the screen, *Teemie*."

She sat up quickly, glaring at him over me. "Shut up, *Razz*. Does Father know why you missed dinner?"

"No," Rune admitted. "But neither do you."

"What *were* you doing?"

"None of your damned business."

"Don't you have better things to do than interrupt girls' night?"

"As a matter of fact, no. Interrupting girls' night is officially at the top of my list of things to do tonight. Every night, in fact."

Mia sighed. "Fine. But no more talking."

Rune huffed a rough laugh and settled even deeper into the couch beside me. His legs bumped mine and I spent too many seconds wondering if it would be more telling to leave it there or move it away. By the time I realised it had been too long, I just left it there.

By the end of the movie, Mia was asleep, and my heart was still thundering.

"Scared *now*, mortal?" Rune asked, his voice low and tantalising, and I knew he was listening to my heartbeat.

I huffed. "No more or less than after any human horror movie."

He nodded slowly. "Sure. You're not at all affected by it."

"No, I'm not. Which is why I'm going to bed."

I got up, but then saw how dark the room was, and the hallway beyond it, and paused. Rune chuckled as he got up and stood behind me.

"I thought you weren't scared of the creatures that lurk in the dark, Angel?" he whispered and my whole body responded, almost forgetting the fear still lancing through me.

"I'm not. I was just wondering if we should get Mia to bed."

"She'll wake up soon. If not, it won't be the first night she spends on the couch. I'm amazed she lasted that long."

I nodded, trying desperately to think of any excuse to put off going to bed until maybe Mia was awake again and we could walk together. I couldn't think of anything, and my heart just raced faster because of it.

"Aren't you going to bed, then?" Rune asked.

Wasn't I? "Yes."

His fingers teased my side. "Let me walk you to your room, Angel. I will keep you safe from whatever hides in the dark."

I batted his hand away. "The only thing in the dark I'm worried about is you being annoying." Because I was a strong, independent, modern woman and I could walk through a dark house after watching a horror movie. See if I couldn't.

I started walking to my room, and Rune followed along.

"I can manage," I told him as we headed down the hallway.

"Father would be so displeased if you were hurt because I wasn't diligent enough," he said. The sarcasm was strong. Sexy and strong.

I rolled my eyes. "Sure. Use your father as an excuse."

He pressed me against the wall. "*I* would be disappointed if you were hurt because of my lack of due diligence," he said, his nose trailing over my cheek. "How else would we play again?"

My heart thudded and I felt his amused breath against my lips.

"Why fight, little Angel?" he asked seductively. "We both know you'd rather welcome me into your bed than be alone.

Horror movie or no."

I breathed out deeply, knowing it was yet another futile attempt to try to control my heartbeat around him. "What happened with Venette?" I asked and I felt him tense.

"What?"

I took a deep breath in. "What happened with Venette?"

He pulled back to look at me. "Why do you think anything happened with Venette?"

"Because you told her it was over, and then she literally scared the birds from the trees."

"How do you know that?"

"Was it supposed to be a secret?"

He snarled. "I got bored of her."

"Convenient you don't have a heartbeat. Must make lying so much easier."

"Why would you think I was lying?" he asked.

"I tell you I ended things with Strix, then you tell me you and I are all you think about, and the next day Venette's screaming down the heavens themselves. Mighty big coincidence, wouldn't you say?"

"What do you want me to say, Angel? Do you want me to tell you I threw away something easy and meaningless for you?"

"If it's the truth."

"Why?"

"Because then I'd know I wasn't the only one," I said, using his words against him from the other night, knowing in my heart that it was true; I liked Strix, but I was never going to *like* like him. It wasn't totally meaningless, really, but it didn't mean anything either.

His eyes widened as he looked down at me. I was over being scared of monsters in the dark. All I wanted was him. I didn't even know why I wanted him, but I did. I certainly didn't like him, but I needed him.

"I think you know what this is, Angel," he said softly.

"And what exactly are we, Rune?" I asked, wanting him to say it.

"You are an angel, and I am a demon. What we are seems only fitting."

"That's hardly an answer."

His fingers teased the possibility of squeezing my throat. "We have the power to destroy whole worlds, little Angel."

"How?"

"Because, as much as I despise you, I would destroy any world for you."

My heart thumped once. Twice. Three times. Then I wrapped my arms around him and kissed him hard. He spun us into my room, closing the door behind us, and didn't stop until we were lying in a jumble of clothes and sheets on my bed. Almost as though we had to make up for words that could almost be considered sweet, we went hard and fast. He showed me no mercy and I didn't want any.

It was hard and dirty, and filled a need in me that I didn't even know I'd had until Rune.

CHAPTER SEVENTEEN

I wouldn't in a million years ever think the words 'dating' and 'Rune' anywhere near each other, but a definite enemies-with-benefits situation was going on between us.

At school, nothing changed. Rune drove the three of us in then he and I spent the day ignoring each other. He seemed particularly callous to the mortal students, but as far as I knew he wasn't hooking up with any of them or anyone else. Maybe he still was, but he'd never been shy about it before.

Strix and I were being friends. We talked and laughed and hung out. Just there was way less bodily contact now. Part of me felt a little bit bad that I'd probably given him some hope we could be more again when I was ready, and I didn't plan to ever be ready, but I also tried not to lead him on. That way, I could hope that whatever spark we'd had – or not had as the case may be – could fizzle out naturally and we'd both kind of just forget about whether I'd ever be ready or not.

But, at home…

Things were decidedly not the same.

Rune came to my room almost every night. We'd fallen into a pattern of, before he left, showering together in my ensuite while he seemed to go to pains to leave me jonesing for my next hit.

If the rest of the household knew what we were doing, they were pleading ignorance and pretending it wasn't happening. I didn't know if he waited until they were all asleep or, knowing vampires, they'd probably sound proofed all the rooms for added privacy. I could only imagine what it would be like living with other people when your hearing was so heightened.

So, during the day, I went about my life. Including hiding out in the library and reading everything I could get my hands on in the mythological scholarship section. Which is where I was that weekend.

"Evangeline," I heard Grandma Vi's voice and looked up to see her. "I would speak to you."

I smiled and nodded. "Uh, of course. What about?"

"Let us walk, child."

I was a little confused about the sudden interest she was paying me, but I wasn't going to sniff at a chance to get to know her better. So, I nodded and got up to follow her. She took us outside and made for the hedge maze that I had decidedly been avoiding; I'd seen that film as well.

"You seem to have settled in well," she said as she navigated through the paths.

I nodded. "I guess so. Yeah."

"I heard you went out with Salem Westmeyer."

I swallowed. "Uh. Yeah. A couple of times. We're just friends now. Again."

"I see. Did you not get along?"

I shrugged. "I guess there just wasn't any…spark."

"Life is too short to waste on a lack of spark, Evangeline."

"Even for an immortal being?"

She smiled softly. "Especially for an immortal being. You made the right choice."

"It doesn't always feel that way."

"Why not? Is there someone else?"

Damn, my heart! She was going to have heard it. "Sort of, but also no," I said carefully, trying not to lie but also wanting to be open to this whole bonding thing.

"I see," she said again. "Anyone I know?"

"Don't you know everyone in town?"

She slid me a cunning look. "Avoidance. Clever. I wonder if you would really play me for such a fool."

My step faltered as I was struck by the surety she knew. There was a very 'do you think I honestly don't know what goes on under my roof' vibe to her.

"Not at all, Grandma Vi. I just mean that it's probable you do know them."

"You are hesitant to tell me."

I nodded. "I'm nearly eighteen. Of course, I'm hesitant to tell you," I said with a smile.

She returned it. "I see. My question is why, dear? Do you think I would be displeased? Are you embarrassed? And if so, because they are objectionable or because they do not return your feelings?"

What was it about – the majority of – this family to make me feel so welcome and relaxed and normal? Here I was, having a conversation about boys with Grandma Vi like I knew plenty of teenagers did with their grandparents. Despite all the conflict Rune made me feel on an hourly basis, I still felt like I had finally found my home in every other way.

"I can say with certainty that he returns my feelings." Assuming, of course, that hate annoyance and lust were the feelings we were talking about. "He's definitely…objectionable. And I honestly don't know if you'd be displeased or not."

"In what way is he objectionable?"

"He's rude. Brash. Annoying. Arrogant. Conceited. A total arse. And just such a dick."

"And yet you ended things with the Westmeyer child for him?"

My cheeks went red, and I felt her chuckle.

"Oh. He's attractive as well," she deduced.

I nodded. "He's *very* attractive. Criminally so."

"Lust is a fickle creature," she conceded. "Much like love, it can hit us harder than we expect and completely out of the blue. Were you not you, I would ask if he compelled you. But then, if you were not you, I wouldn't care if he had."

"Is that a very backhanded way of saying you care?" I asked, feeling like teasing her wouldn't be totally wrong.

I was rewarded with a rough chuckle. "If it was backhanded, then it was delivered poorly, and I apologise. That we have not had the proper time to get to know each other is my failing, Evangeline. But I would have you know that you are as important to me as those who claim my blood. I wish you to be happy and safe in more than just your physical state."

I gave her a nod. "Thanks."

We came to a dead end with a bench at the end and she indicated I sit. I didn't know where we were in the maze. I'd seen it from my window but there was no way I'd ever be able to memorise the winding paths. It never looked the same to me anyway.

She sat down next to me, looking at me far more intently than I had ever seen before. "What does your world know about mates, child?"

I blinked, confused by the change in subject. "Uh. Like friends?"

She rolled her eyes. "Australians," she bemoaned.

I grimaced apologetically. "Do you mean from a fantasy book?" I asked.

She looked even less impressed. "Everything with you mortals is 'like a fantasy book'. You know the myths of the world were around long before your 'fantasy books'? They merely came along and mixed everything up."

I was contrite on behalf of the whole of humanity. "Sorry?"

She waved a hand at me. "You are hardly to blame for being a product of your upbringing and your kind. But I speak not of fantasy books, Evangeline. I speak of real fated mates. Lovers written in the stars. So preordained by the very cosmos that nothing can sunder them. Destined for a love the likes of which only a handful will ever experience."

My stomach bottomed out, but I was spared having to formulate an answer because we were rudely interrupted.

Rune huffed as he appeared around a corner. "What nonsense are you spouting now?"

Grandma Vi stood, grabbed the front of his shirt and picked him off the floor effortlessly. "Watch how you speak to me, Erasmus," she warned, her tone icy. "Unlike your father, I don't 'spout nonsense'."

She practically threw him on the floor, and he scrabbled to get his feet under him with any semblance of dignity. He shot me a look that clearly told me to keep any humorous thoughts about that to myself. I did, but only because I was still reeling from what Grandma Vi had said.

"Say that again," I said to her.

"Fated mates," was her response as she sat back down next to me, and Rune huffed like it was the biggest crock of shit he'd ever heard. She glared at him. "How much do you know?"

I shrugged. "Nothing."

"Because there's nothing to know," Rune said, derisively. "Fated mates are as real as Father's dhampir."

"How sure about that are you?" Grandma Vi asked him carefully and I felt a deeper meaning in her words.

Rune looked at her like she'd gone mad. "How sure are you that you want to continue this conversation? Because it sounds an awful lot to me like you're trying to tell her that fated mates exist."

"Perhaps I am."

"For what purpose? You think she has one?" He was derisive, but that wasn't going to put Grandma Vi off.

"I think you *both* have one," she said pointedly, and my heart tried to drop out of my arse.

"What?" Rune and I both said, because there was really only one way to take Grandma Vi's words. But it was an awful lot to get my head around and it was steadfastly refusing to get on board.

She looked between us. "Please tell me you're not that stupid," she said, as though she thought we hadn't understood.

"Please tell me *you're* not that stupid," was Rune's reply and Grandma Vi hissed at him. "Fated mates don't exist."

"No one asked you to be part of this conversation, Erasmus," she reminded him. "I asked for a moment with Evangeline, and it was you who decided to interrupt."

"Perhaps it was lucky I did if only to spare her from filling her head with insanity."

"Is it insane?" she asked. "You think I don't know how you spend your nights, boy? You think I don't know why?"

"The why is no great secret," Rune said dismissively. "Even you were young once."

"If you think it has been a while since I last felt the pleasures of the flesh, then you are stupider than I thought you were."

"You think because I take advantage of easy sex that it means fate has stepped in?"

"I think because you were expressly forbidden from touching her and have done so anyway that you are not fully in control of your actions."

"I'm a fledgling, Grandma Vi. Of course, I'm not fully in control of my actions."

Now Grandma Vi scoffed. "You have had better control since you were five than a vampire twenty times that age. Do not patronise me. You know I am no doddering elder slowly losing my wits. Were you not so heavily in denial, you would know I'm right."

Rune huffed as he turned to leave. "Are you *sure* you don't spout nonsense?"

"Whether you believe it or not, do not breathe a word of it to your father," she said scathingly, as though worried Rune was about to run to Etienne and do just that.

"Why not?" Rune asked, obviously thinking she was making a big deal out of nothing, and he was just placating her.

"Because if he even *thinks* it could be possible, then his quest will be all that matters. He will not wait for proof. He will not see or listen to reason. He will kill her."

My heart clattered in my chest and Rune's eyes darted to me like he was checking on me. I could have mistaken real concern in his eyes, but then he was back to bored indifference and amused condescension.

"Why would he kill her?" Rune asked.

"A vampire with a *human* fated mate?" Grandma said gently and I could see I wasn't the only one who didn't understand what she was getting at. She rolled her eyes and was clearly done with gentle in the face of our obliviousness. "He will not suffer being the *grand*father of the fabled dhampir."

Rune had looked like he might be starting to consider her words, now he was done. "The dhampir is impossible. It's less than a myth. I will not have this conversation again."

"Someone has to, Erasmus," Grandma Vi said earnestly. "Because Evangeline's life depends on it."

Rune flung his arm up in a dismissive motion. "No. They don't. Father charged me with protecting her and, if that means against him as well then, I'll do what it takes. But you will not convince me that he'll believe in fated mates or concern himself that she and I will create some mythological creature."

"He believes in one. Why not the other?"

"Because there is only so much insanity even he can hold onto, surely."

"Why do you think it's true?" I asked quietly and they both looked to me, almost like they'd forgotten I was there for a moment.

Grandma Vi's eyes softened as she took me in. "You are new to Knightsbridge, dear one. You don't know Erasmus the way we do–"

"It's irrelevant–" he started, but she cut him off.

"It is not irrelevant, child," she snapped at him. "Your heart stopped beating shortly before your second birthday. It froze. Through none of our history has a beatless vampire had the capacity for love or kindness or compassion."

I snorted despite myself because that sounded exactly like the Rune I knew. Although…did it? They both looked at me and I gave them a guilty, apologetic shrug. Rune glared, but in the kind of way that he knew what I was thinking and couldn't really disagree with my assessment.

Grandma Vi's eyes were cunning as she continued. "Yet, I have seen Erasmus with you. You may not see kindness and compassion, but neither did you see the havoc he wrought before you came to us. His *restraint* is kindness and compassion in itself."

Rune scoffed. "And love? Are you going to claim me capable of that as well?"

Suddenly, Grandma Vi had pulled me to standing and was behind me. Her hand was on my throat. As were her fangs. Rune's reaction was palpable. His eyes went pitch black, his face was streaked with those dark tendrils, his fangs appeared, and he hissed at her threateningly.

As my heart pounded at the shock of it all, I felt Grandma Vi chuckle before she let me go. "And what would you call that then, child?" she asked him, so horrifically politely she could have been talking about the weather.

Rune seemed to be fighting to rid himself of his vampire face. Finally, he shook it free and piercing ice blue eyes fixed on her. "You said yourself, at no point in our history has a beatless been able to love."

Grandma Vi. "You said *yourself*, that at no point in our history have there been fated mates."

"You are just proving my point for me," Rune told her, exasperatedly.

While they continued talking – arguing – my mind was whirring. I wasn't any more convinced about this fated mates business than Rune. But I'd have said the same thing about vampires a few months ago. Who was I to dismiss Grandma Vi's words? I didn't have to believe them to consider them. To not immediately dismiss them as frivolous.

I was sure I didn't want it to be true, but I wasn't going to deny that there was something compelling about Grandma Vi's certainty. In the months I'd known her, she didn't strike me as a conspiracy nut. She was calm and calculated and intellectual. She must have seen – or known – something that I didn't if she believed not only fated mates were possible, but that I was Rune's and he was mine.

When Rune stole into my room that night, we didn't talk about fated mates or what we could be to each other. It was much like any other night, every other night; he arrived, we came together wordlessly, he rocked my world, then he left much the same way as he came.

Only there was something different about that night.

Rune didn't leave right away. In fact, he didn't leave at all. Not until the wan light of dawn was stealing around my curtains.

CHAPTER EIGHTEEN

Rune and I continued not talking about the concept of fated mates, and Grandma Vi seemed to think better of bringing it up again. But I kept thinking about it. Never knowing if I thought it could be real or not.

Sometimes, I'd almost convinced myself that there was no other option for Rune and me; it was a convenient explanation for the way I felt about him given that I very much didn't want to feel that way about him. Other times, I was sure she must be making things up; surely you couldn't have a fated mate and not know for certain that's what was happening.

A morning after another night where Rune had stayed, sleeping with me tucked against his body, I was wandering the halls, trying not to think about the concept of fated mates and what it would mean if it was true. Because that was the main problem. I didn't know what it meant. Did I just give up my life?

I knew I was overthinking things again. Fixating on a possible problem that might never have an answer in favour of trying to fix a very real problem. The kind of very real problem like me having causal sex with Rune and Grandma Vi knowing all about it.

So I wasn't watching where I was going, just kind of nodding along to whatever Ama said when Strix bumped into me as we passed in the hall. A look of something I did not like passed over his face. I didn't know what it was, but it actually scared me.

"Shit," Ama muttered, and I looked at her.

"What?"

"I hoped if he didn't get close enough to you, he wouldn't notice."

"Wouldn't notice what?" I asked.

She looked around like she was worried that someone would hear her answer. "Have you been fucking Rune again?"

I choked on some spit and stared at her through teary eyes. "What? Why…? How…?"

Her eyes were rueful, but her mouth was hard. "It's not like super noticeable…" she started. "But if you get close enough to you, you can smell him. On you. Your skin. You. Rune's scent is all over you."

I batted her. "Okay. I get it. Thanks. You didn't want to tell me?"

She shrugged. "It's only occasionally. Like so rare and so faint that I didn't think it mattered."

"And? Does it matter now?"

"Uh, based on Strix's face just now? Little bit."

"Shit," I echoed her sentiment. "Do you think he's got a reason to talk to Venette now?"

She gave me a sidelong glance. "I think it's very possible that he's got a reason to have a little chat with Venette, yes."

I groaned. Ama also groaned as we got to the back door to the main building, and she saw the cloudless, blue sky outside.

"Great. The sun's out," she huffed. "Go find Loren and chill on the lawns 'til I'm done. You should be fine until then. No self-respecting vamp is going to bother even with torturing a mortal outside on a day like today."

I gave her rather a sarcastic smile. "Gee. Thanks so much for those words of encouragement."

"Take the luck as you get it. I'll be as quick as I can."

I sighed, nodded, then headed out to the spot on the lawn we usually occupied when the weather was its usual overcast.

I found Loren lying back on the grass, a contented smile on her face. "I know they all hate this, but it is nice."

I squinted up at the bright sunlight, feeling the warmth on my face for the first time in months that didn't involve a trek further up the mountain and through the wards. "Does it happen often?"

"We get about four, ten at the most, days like this a year," she said as I sat down with her. "Rumour is, the witches threw it in as a screw you to the vamps. But honestly, so few of them are like proper allergic to the sun anymore that it's kind of moot."

It didn't stop them all walking around with parasols or hats with the collars of their blazers up around their necks. Some had their blazers full-on over their heads to protect them from the sun's rays as they hurried between the buildings. The only ones sitting on the lawns, enjoying the sun were the mortals. And there were not very many of us.

But we all enjoyed it for the hour we had of lunch. It was actually kind of nice chatting with Loren without the others. She was always so quiet when they were around. I wondered if it was part of her compulsion. Some in-built subservience. Not that I would ever ask anyone out loud.

Suddenly, Loren shrieked, and my back was in the grass, and

Strix was the one pressing me into it. My heart thundered and my head felt like it was bruising after hitting the ground so hard.

But I forced myself to hold my own, at least on the outside. "What can I do for you?" I asked him, acting like everything was pleasant and he wasn't exuding serious danger to my person.

"You think you can choose him over me?" he snarled.

I blinked as though I had no idea what he was talking about. "I didn't choose anyone over you," I lied, feeling like this conversation was sounding very similar to one I'd already had with a different guy.

But then I thought, it actually wasn't a lie at all. I didn't *choose* Rune. I felt an overwhelming draw to him, no matter what my personal preference was. I needed him. I certainly didn't want him.

"We'll see how much use you are to him as one of us…" Strix said.

He bared his fangs, and they were making right for my jugular. I squeezed my eyes shut as I felt the tips graze the skin of my neck. I vaguely remembered fantasising about being in this exact position and being a little excited about it. There was absolutely nothing exciting about it just then.

Strix's fangs pressed against my skin but, just before they broke it, he was lifted off me and flung so far that he crashed through a window on the tower. A couple of hundred metres away, at least.

I looked over to my saviour and found Rune scowling bloody murder down at me.

But that wasn't what had my attention.

Rune's face, as annoyingly perfect as it was, was blistering and charring and burning, like severe degree burning you saw in hospital shows. His jaw was set as though against pain, but if he was in pain that was the only sign.

I sat up quickly. "Rune!"

"Do not move," he said, his voice low.

"Le Rege!" came Strix's booming voice as he appeared at the window his body had just destroyed.

Rune grabbed me. "This will not be pleasant," he warned me.

Then he wrapped his arms around me and the weirdest feeling came over me. Time and space lost all meaning. The next thing I knew, I was tumbling to the floor of someone's bedroom and Rune was solidifying from mist as he stumbled back and fell in a chair.

As my stomach was deciding whether it was going to hurl or not, I looked around. The room seemed old and largely unused, but clean. Embers burned in the hearth and…

Rune's laboured breathing made me turn and focus on him. If he was healing, it was agonisingly slow. I hurried over to him and dropped to his side.

"What's wrong? What can I do?" I asked.

He shook his head and tried to push me away, but I put my hand on his leg.

"Rune?"

"You have done enough, little Angel," he snapped.

Anger thundered in my ears as I stood and moved away from him. "You could have just let him bite me."

"No one touches a le Rege," he said, like that was all there was to it.

"I'm not a le Rege! You can't all just change my name because it suits you, then just plan to throw me away when we're of no use to you again."

He stood up swiftly and was in front of me in the blink of an eye. "I will never be done with you, Lena," he said, his voice so full of venom for such a sentiment.

"You should have just let Strix turn me. Then I wouldn't be such a mortal burden to you anymore."

"No fangs but my own will take you, Angel. No lips but mine will taste you. And if any blood will turn you, it will be mine." He took a step closer to me. "You are mine."

"Just because you say so?"

"Because you are. You know it's true."

I mean, he wasn't wrong. I didn't want there to be, but there was something in me that refused to disagree or to fight it. I wouldn't go so far as to agree with Grandma Vi's theory, but there was definitely something more between us than just simple lust. I knew, like I knew my name or the grass was green or snow was white, that I was his. Whether I wanted to be or not, I was.

Not that I'd admit such a thing out loud. "You're not healing," was how I changed the subject.

"I will be fine. I just need fresh blood."

"Then take it," I told him.

He looked down at me like he'd never seen me before.

"What?" I asked. "You said yours would be the only fangs, the only lips, the only blood, yadda, yadda. Well, prove it."

His eyes were overtaken by black. "You would offer it to me so freely?"

It was crunch time now. Go big or go home. "I'm yours, Rune. There is nothing I am that is not yours. My blood. My body.

Everything."

He seemed to sway towards me, and I put a finger to his chest to pause him. He looked at me expectantly.

"But I do not offer it freely."

He took a step back. "What do you want in return?" he asked. "Money? Help with your homework? Eternal youth?" The sarcasm in his voice suggested that deals like that were commonplace when a mortal offered their blood.

I shook my head as I took off my blazer and dropped it on a nearby chair. "No. What I want, I doubt anyone has ever asked of you before."

"Do you intend to tell me? At this rate, I'll heal before you get around to it."

Given how little his burning had lessened, I got that to be the insult it was intended.

I undid my tie and my top button. "All I want," I said as I kept undoing shirt buttons, "is for you to admit," I pulled my shirt open, exposing my bra and bare torso, and watched the lust heat his eyes, "that you are as powerless as me in this."

"I don't need your blood that badly."

"But how badly do you *want* it? You don't have to say the words. Accept my offering, and that will be all the admission I need."

I could see the fight playing in him. He wanted it, but did he want to keep his superiority more?

"I told you I'd bleed for you, Rune," I said slowly. "It's yours. All you need to do is claim it."

He breathed deeply for the space of one heartbeat. Two. I could see him fighting for control. A fight he seemed to be losing based on the full vampire face before me. Painfully slowly, he closed the gap between us. His hand went to my waist, a soft touch that slowly tightened until he had the control to push me against the table.

"How much does it hurt?" I asked him.

"The burn or what you're asking of me?"

"Either. Both."

"It is almost unbearable." He ran his tongue over his elongating fang. "If I do this," he said, his black eyes pinning mine, "I can't take it back."

"Good."

Rune wrapped one arm around me. "Are you sure, Lena?"

"Are you not?"

He seemed to hiss in frustration, then he bent his face to my neck and plunged his fangs into me. My skin gave up the barest hint of resistance. My hand tightened on his arm at the sting, then all I felt was…

Warmth flooded me. My heartbeat was strong and steady. Everything in me zinged and tingled and I wanted more than just Rune's fangs in me.

He pulled away slowly to look at me, a single rivulet of my blood slipping over his lip. His perfectly healed lip. His tongue darted out to catch it. I watched as the rest of his face finished healing to his usual porcelain perfection.

"Was it…okay?" I asked when he didn't speak.

A smirk lit his lips. "Okay? To me, your blood is…impeccable. Like a finely aged wine, drunk while eating decadent chocolate. Rich. Bold. Intoxicating."

"Was it…enough?"

The smirk deepened. "I'm not quite so obsessed by you that I don't know how to pace myself."

He lifted me up onto the table as slid his hands firmly up my thighs as he kissed me deeply. As I'd expected – fantasised – his fang nicked my lip and we both tasted blood. He leant his forehead to mine and his eyes were totally black. My hands dropped to his belt as his fingers ran between my legs.

"Not *quite* so obsessed?" I asked.

He sighed as he gently stroked over my clit. "Not quite," he seemed to agree.

"That implies you're at least a little obsessed with me."

"So, it does."

My heart skipped a beat. "You're not disagreeing with me."

His shook his head, still leaning it against mine, then nuzzled my nose with his. "I prefer not to lie to you outright."

I wasn't sure either of us wanted him to be any clearer than that. What had started out as pure carnal lust had morphed into something way more complicated. I didn't want to know about it, so I planned to ignore it for now.

So, I wrapped my arms around his shoulders and reminded him, "I've bled for you, Rune. Isn't it time I screamed for you, too?"

I felt rather than saw the wicked smirk at his lips as they claimed mine again.

He did make me scream. Him on top. Me on top. From behind.

Rune brought my back up to his front as he thrust deep into me. His face dipped to my shoulder, and I felt the tip of his fang graze over my skin. Goosebumps chased across my skin, my chest fluttered and sparked, and my hand gripped his where it lay over my stomach.

Another graze, like he was teasing me, asking me.

I reached my hand back to cradle his head, titling mine in unspoken consent. An unspoken offer. No. More demand. Entreaty.

Still, he seemed to hesitate to sink his fangs into me, even as he still thrust into me strong and steadily.

"Am I not good enough for a fuck and feed, Rune?" I asked, only half-teasing. I was also half-worried.

He wrapped his arms around me tightly. "You are…too good. This, Angel?" he said as his lips trailed over my cheek. "This would be more than a simple fuck and feed. Are you sure you're ready?"

I wanted to ask him what made it different, but I wasn't sure either of us were ready for anything like that to be put into words. There had already been enough of those words between us for one day.

"I'm ready," I told him.

When his fangs broke my skin this time, it did feel different. I couldn't put into words how or why it was different. It just was. Like there was some kind of new connection between us, or perhaps one that was finally being acknowledged. Recognised and accepted without the need for making it permanent with words.

We spent the rest of that night in his room, and I was sure I wasn't the only one who knew everything had changed because of it.

CHAPTER NINETEEN

There was no pretending or ignoring what had happened the day before; the whole school knew that Strix had attacked me, Rune had saved me, and then we'd disappeared for the rest of the day.

Ama and Radu blew my phone up all night with questions and theories.

Questions and theories that were obviously doing the rounds because the whole family seemed to know what had happened the next morning when I walked into the dining room minutes before Rune. The whole family minus Mum, since she wasn't there. That potentially boded not well.

"I trust you are well, Evangeline?" Etienne said, a calculating look in his eyes.

I swallowed hard. "I am."

"Would that I could punish the Westmeyer boy, but your mortality has my hands tied."

I nodded as I sat down. "I see."

"Erasmus," I heard Etienne say and my eyes shot up to Rune with embarrassing speed. "When did you plan to tell me that you were disobeying a direct order from your sire?"

"Uh, never," Rune said as he sat down across from me. "You wanted me to protect her. I protected her." His tone screamed 'what more do you want from me?'

"I also asked you not to touch her."

"She is sitting right here," I huffed pointedly. "And, as she is uncompellable, perhaps you can get off your racist, misogynistic, undead horse and accept that maybe Rune isn't the only one to blame?"

Mia failed to completely hide her laugh and even Grandma Vi's eyes sparkled in approval.

"Whoever is to blame," Etienne said slowly, "know that I will not suffer anything to go wrong."

Rune scoffed. "Don't worry, Father. I'm not going to get carried away and kill her. Your experiment is safe from my interference."

Etienne stood. "Be sure you don't. And the next time, I give you an order Erasmus, I expect you to not only obey it, but do so without so much melodrama."

Rune rolled his eyes. "Of course, Father."

Etienne nodded, then swept from the room.

"Eat up," Grandma Vi said. "I suspect there's a shitstorm waiting for you at school."

Mia barked a laugh, slapping a hand over her mouth, but her eyes were bright.

"You're taking pleasure in this," Rune accused Grandma Vi.

"Of course, I am, child. Your father is pissed yet there's nothing he can do, and you have finally shaken up this boring little town."

"Grandma Vi!" Mia chastised and Grandma Vi shrugged.

"What? Just because I've lived nearly one and half millennia, I can't like a little drama?"

We ate in mostly silence, interspersed with Rune muttering whenever he thought Grandma Vi or Mia were going to say something, then the three of us piled into the car.

As we drove to school, Rune took my hand. I could almost feel Mia's smile from the back seat.

"Don't say anything," he warned her, as though he could feel it, too.

I glanced over and saw him looking in the rear-view mirror.

"I didn't say anything," Mia answered, but her tone was all humoured. "Since you brought it up—"

"I didn't."

"Are you dating now?"

Rune growled. "I don't answer to you."

"No. But, as you're holding Lena's hand, I'm going to go ahead and say you answer to her. So, she probably wants to know."

I bit my lip against a smile. "She doesn't need to know."

"Doesn't she?" Mia pressed. "Because the whole school is going to be asking."

I snuck a look at Rune, who was clearly furious.

"Lena is mine," he told Mia. "Whoever has a problem with that has me to deal with."

"And how are you planning on telling them this?" Mia asked.

Rune's answer was to walk into school holding my hand. People noticed that well enough, but then he decided to slip that arm around my shoulders and hold me close. That made people stop in their tracks as they passed, before Rune glared at them and they hurried on again.

But the kicker was when we got to my locker. Rune didn't just kiss me like any 'boyfriend' – if that word could be applied. No. He took my hand gently, pressing a kiss to the inside of my wrist, then he equally gently sank his fangs into me. All the while, his eyes were pinned to mine.

I didn't know a lot of vampire etiquette and politics, obviously. But by the gasps of people around us, it meant something. Were I to take a wild guess, I'd guess it was a very visceral announcement to the school – town, world – at large that I was his.

Grandma Vi was making more of an effort to hang out with me, to talk to me. Whether she was trying to subtly convince me that fated mates were actually real – and it had to be real subtle because she barely mentioned it – or she was impressed I'd snapped at Etienne, I didn't know. But I enjoyed the time I spent with her.

"Did she mention mates again?" Rune asked when I met him in his room that night, a knowing smirk glinting in his eyes.

We were lying on his bed, just together.

"Have you thought about it more?" I asked, turning my head to him. "Is it true, do you think?"

He turned his to me. "Fated mates?"

I nodded.

"It's not supposed to be. But Grandma Vi is anything but shrewd and keenly intelligent. If she thinks they do exist…" He breathed out. "Then maybe they do."

"You don't sound convinced."

"I don't know that I am. But…"

"But, what?" I pressed when he didn't continue.

He looked back up at the ceiling. "But I don't know what else explains…the way I feel about you. The depth and unrelenting force of my feelings for you. From the moment we met, I couldn't ignore them. Fated mates would be a perfect explanation. But perhaps it would be too convenient an explanation."

"What does it mean? Fated mates?" I asked.

"I don't know. The first stories are so old that they're lost to legend. Certainly, none of the stories have a human and vampire coupling. They're always both vampires."

I shivered and I know he felt it.

As though he was avoiding anything that could even vaguely stray into suggestions of me being turned, he said, "But I don't know of a single instance where it's happened in real life."

"I didn't know of a single instance of vampires happening in real life until recently," I pointed out.

He huffed what could have been a small laugh. "I don't know any vampire with what is basically a familiar either."

"So, you're coming around to the idea?" I didn't know that I was, but he knew more about the myths of his world than me.

He smirked at me. "I don't know. I don't think so, but there's a very strong part of me that is willing to consider it. Like it knows there might be truth to it, but how the hell can it be true?"

"That's exactly the same way I felt when you told me vampires existed," I told him.

He looked at me, his tongue dragging over his bottom lip. "Someone had to tell you."

"So, you did it for my own good?" I sassed.

He smiled as he rolled on top of me. "I did it because I wanted to play with you."

"But you were forbidden from playing with me," I reminded him, giving him a rueful smirk.

His eyes were soft as he looked into mine, but I saw the return smile in them. "Yes, I was. But you know as well as anyone that I'm not very good at doing what I'm told."

"If Grandma Vi is right, you can always blame Fate."

He chuckled as he nuzzled his nose with mine. "I might blame her anyway."

"It's not like I asked for this, either," I said.

He nodded, his nose bumping mine. "I know. Though, I'm not sure it makes this…obsession any better if it's some larger cosmic power."

"I'm well aware you don't really like me for me."

I felt his chuckle vibrate through our chests. "I don't know that I really like you at all."

"The feeling is mutual, I promise."

His face was too close to see his lips, but his smile shone brightly in his eyes. "So, you're not about to demand monogamy or a ring or want to move all your shit into my room?" he teased.

I shook my head. "Yeah. Not so much. I have no overwhelming desire to plan our lives out or name our children."

Something darkened in his eyes, but it was the black I was so used to seeing now. "If we could have children…"

I swallowed hard. "If I was a vampire, would it be possible?"

Wry humour lit his eyes now. "You want to have my kids so badly you're ready to ditch your humanity?"

I batted him playfully and he rolled off me with a cry, acting like a killing blow. I laughed and he smiled at me. "No. I don't even know that I want to date you. I'm just curious about how it all works."

He shrugged. "Two vampires, whether one or both are turned or born, can breed children. Yes. How else did my father have me and my siblings."

I blinked. "Siblings? Plural?" I asked.

He nodded. "Plural." He gave me a sideways glance. "In my defence, that one's not really a family secret so, strictly speaking, I haven't broken any laws."

"How many siblings do you have?"

He rested his arms behind his head. "There are seventeen of us."

"Seventeen? Your dad's been pretty busy."

Rune laughed. "You'd have thought his obsession with siring the dhampir would take up all his energy, huh? Man's so convinced he's destined for it because he's so fertile." He snorted. "The council once entertained the idea that he was building an army. They didn't like that idea."

Like many of my conversations these days, there was so much to unpack. But I focussed on, "Where are they all?"

"Hm?"

"Your siblings?"

"You'll have met a few of them at the wedding, but they could hardly tell you who they were then. They're travelling or working or living their lives anywhere else but Knightsbridge."

"Are you and Mia the youngest?"

He shook his head. "No. Not at all. Last I heard, the youngest was four. He lives with his mother. I haven't met him yet."

"When do you stop ageing?" I asked.

"What do you mean?"

"I mean, you look like a nineteen-year-old guy. But your dad. Grandma Vi. They slowed down at some point, right?"

He nodded. "Right. It kicks in slowly. There's no like, on your twenty-first birthday that's it or anything. Like puberty, it just kind of happens. As far as the biology books say, by the time we're in our mid-twenties, our bodies ageing has slowed as much as it will." He turned his head to me again. "Are you worried you'll be old and grey, and I'll still be in my prime."

I smiled and he returned it. "Who says I'll want anything to do with you when I'm wise and mature?"

"We're fated mates, Angel," he purred, dragging me onto his body and wrapping his arms around me. "We're destined for eternity."

"Are we though?"

He shrugged. "Fuck knows. But that's what the stories say."

I laughed. "Why don't we just see how long it takes us to argue again?"

He nodded, his smile deep and warm in his eyes. "I think I can work with that."

But it got me thinking. Did fated mates exist? And was that the reason I couldn't stay away from Rune? Why I seemed to hate him and need him in the same breath? I'm not sure if it made these complicated feelings better or worse. But, in that moment, I didn't want to push them – or him – away. There was something bright happening between Rune and me that I couldn't help but lean into. Whether it was fate or something far simpler, I wanted to see where it took us.

But not just that.

If Grandma Vi was right about fated mates, could she be right about the fabled dhampir as well?

A week passed. Two. And I fell into a new normal for the second time that year. I still wouldn't have called what Rune and I were doing 'dating', but the whole of Knightsbridge knew I was his.

But no one dared touch a le Rege, let alone a le Rege claimed by Rune himself. I felt like it should have made me wary that the whole town full of vampires were scared of what Rune would do to them if they so much as looked at me wrong. I wondered if maybe things were finally going my way. If I was finally living the life I was supposed to be.

It didn't take long for me to realise that those things were not going my way.

I'd been waiting so long I'd fallen into complacency. But this must have been those consequences I'd been expecting that first morning I woke up in Knightsbridge. All of it, really. Vampires. Rune. Venette. And now Strix.

Good things just didn't happen to me.

Of course, I'd find myself just handed the lap of luxury on a gold plate and then it would all go to shit. At least, if things *were* going to go to shit, I may as well go all out and get myself killed over it. I never did do anything by half.

Because, as I was wandering between main streets in town that afternoon, I felt hands on me and then everything went black.

$$\blacklozenge \; \blacklozenge \; \blacklozenge \; \blacklozenge$$

When I came to, Strix was pacing agitatedly, and I was shivering. I was lying in snow next to a huge lake that was still covered in ice. I sat up carefully and watched Strix.

"What are you doing?" I asked him.

He turned to me sharply, like he was surprised to hear my voice. "Enjoy your nap?"

I frowned. "Not particularly."

His head cocked like he was listening to something. Or maybe for something. Then he smiled. But there was nothing pleasant about it. It was thin and crooked and showed way too much fang.

"Lover boy is on his way, Lena," he said and my stomach fluttered while my heart thudded. "But can he save you in time?"

I knew then that Strix had planned this. Planned it to the minute. He hauled me off the ground none too gently, heedless of how much strength he used.

"I've wanted to do this since the day you stepped foot on campus. If I can't have you, no one can," he sneered.

"RUNE!" I yelled, then Strix's fangs pierced my neck, and I screamed in pain.

Strix pressed an arm to my lips. It was slippery and there was a metallic tang I did not like. Then his fangs ripped from my neck, causing me to cry out again, and everything went fuzzy.

Strix threw my ragdoll-like body at the lake, discarded and unneeded anymore. My body crashed through the layer of ice on top, knocking the wind out of me. I felt like I was sinking in slow motion, the freezing chill of the water permeating every single cell of my body. My blood trailed through the water, marking the path as I sank.

I knew my brain was shutting down from the cold as well as the blood loss, and still all I thought was that all that wasted blood could have gone to such a better use. Nourishing Etienne or Mia or Grandma Vi or Ama or Radu or…Rune…

My Rune.

CHAPTER TWENTY

RUNE

"If I can't have you, no one can," Strix's voice echoed around me.

I whirled, trying to pinpoint where it was coming from.

"RUNE!" Lena yelled, then screamed in pain.

I was going to kill the fucker.

It was bad enough he'd ever been allowed to touch my Angel. But I'd been stupid then and denied the call of her soul to mine. She'd been free to take whatever comforts from whoever she wanted. But not anymore. She was mine now and he hadn't just dared to touch her; he'd tasted her.

I ran, following the sounds of her screams. In my rush, branches whipped across my cheeks, my arms. I paid them no attention as Lena screamed again and I pushed myself faster.

Had my heart still beaten, it would have broken to hear her pain.

As I came to a stop at a ridge, the lake spread below me. I scanned quickly and saw, just in time, as Strix threw Lena at the water. It was still cold enough up here for snow and ice. Her body cracked the frozen surface and, had I a god, I would have prayed to them that she hadn't broken anything with the force. Her body sank and my immediate concern was Strix.

"Choices, choices, Rune," he taunted me. "Do you have time to kill me *and* save her?"

I wasn't going to bother asking him why he'd done it. It was clear he was obsessed with her. I knew the feeling. I liked to think that, if she chose someone else over me, I wouldn't have decided no one else could have her. But in reality, I knew I'd never let anyone else have her.

It felt suddenly prudent to find myself some gods so I could pray to them that she never chose anyone else over me.

Caution, Atlas told me.

I frowned. *I will kill him.*

Atlas was oddly quiet. It was as close to permission and approval as he had ever been when it came to anything about Lena.

Okay. Killing him, it is, I said to Atlas.

I had nothing to say to Strix. There were no words for the anger and frustration and absolute pain I intended to rain down on him. Him and his cocky arrogance. Anger, the type and strength I had never felt before, filled me. Leaping off the ridge, I saw slight hesitance in him, and I sailed towards him. My feet had barely hit the ground when I pushed forwards, aiming my shoulder for his stomach. Snow kicked up behind me, then there was a satisfying crunch as my shoulder found his ribs.

We fell in a pile of snow and flailing limbs as we scrambled to get the upper hand. There was no way in hell I was giving him the upper hand. He would pay for touching my Angel. Pay for hurting her. Pay for tasting her.

Rune... I heard Atlas' concern and blocked him out as I roared my fury at Strix.

My cry echoed off the mountains around us, shaking the trees.

"She's dead either way," Strix said with a grin, and I saw utter madness in his eyes.

"It's like you want me to kill you," I growled. "It would be my pleasure."

After a quick scuffle, I had him pinned to the ground. My fangs bared I plunged them into his neck, ripping his throat out of him. There was still some kind of amused victory in his dying eyes as he looked up at me. Weaker vampires than him had come back from such a wound, though, and I had to be sure. One hand pinning his head to the ground, the other stabbed into his chest and ripped the still-beating heart straight out of it.

Strix's body convulsed like it was trying to follow its heart and his lungs gurgled as blood pooled in places it really had no business being. When his body finally stilled and turned to grey, I noticed his eyes. Still so cocky. Like he knew something I didn't.

Lena.

With Strix's death still echoing in my ears, I dove into the lake. I felt nothing as I searched for her. For the first time in months, I couldn't hear her heart. I couldn't smell her under water. I tasted her everywhere and knew she was bleeding out. My vision was blurred at best. I could feel Atlas' agitation from the surface and told him he was not helping my mounting panic. But finally, I felt movement. Telling myself they weren't death throes, I shot to her, grabbed her limp body in my arms and propelled us to the surface.

Completely unnecessarily, I gasped as we broke free. Nothing inside me cracked when she didn't do the same. But the concave place my heart should have beat seemed to crumble ever so slightly more inward on itself.

"Fucking humans," I muttered, ignoring the way my voice shook. "What the hell are you supposed to do with them again?"

Atlas cried and I felt the images tumble through my head. Nodding, I leant over her and started the compressions against her chest. Then I stopped and leant down to breathe into her mouth. As soon as our lips met, I recoiled. A new surge of anger flooded me. He hadn't just tasted her…

He tried blooding her, I said in disgust.

Then you must save her.

I glared at the bird. *Thanks. The thought hadn't occurred to me,* I said snidely as I leant down to breathe into her.

It took too long. I could feel her essence dribbling away. She was too cold. She'd lost so much blood. And I had never once tried saving anyone. What in the hell did I think I could achieve?

I felt a soothing reassurance from Atlas and spared him my appreciation while I continued trying to save Lena.

Eventually, she took the smallest breath on her own and I felt – and heard – her heart beating feebly again. She was clinging to life, but was it enough? Had Strix damaged her beyond what time or magic could repair? I was loathe to call in a hunter or a witch to help; it would take too long, and they may decide to destroy her anyway if Strix had fucked up. I wasn't risking blooding her myself to hasten her healing only for that to be the time I found out that I'd been turned after all.

Get her warm. Get her safe. There will be time to worry when it's necessary, Atlas said and, as I dissolved Lena and I into mist, I tried to believe it wasn't necessary yet.

The doors of the manor crashed open as I solidified in front of them and dropped to my knees with Lena's limp body in my arms, frigid water still streaming off both of us. Atlas shrieked, his call echoing through the whole house. It was like some death knell and I hoped it wasn't an omen.

"Rune?" I heard Mia's voice, then, "Rune!" as she ran down the stairs to me. "No. Lena. What happened?" she asked me.

I looked into my sister's face, but I felt nothing. I thought nothing. I was numb. Even the day my heart stopped beating, I hadn't felt such all-consuming numbness. The only thing trying to push its way through now was anger and hunger and the desire to burn the whole world to ash, feeding until I bled it all dry. I briefly wondered if this was how the Wretched felt.

"Rune?" Mia said, shaking me. "Rune, what happened?"

"Erasmus?" I heard Grandma Vi's voice and I looked at her sharply.

This was all her doing. If she hadn't been hounding us all about her fated mate bullshit, then this wouldn't have happened.

"What's going on?" Father said as he walked in with Lena's mother.

"Lena!" Julie cried. "What's…? Oh, my baby!"

She threw herself into Father's shoulder and sobbed loudly.

"What happened, Erasmus?" Father asked me, clearly as angry about the fact that someone dared to touch a le Rege as he was that his stepdaughter was on the brink of death in his son's arms.

"Salem Westmeyer is dead," I said, my voice hoarse and sounding like it couldn't have possibly come from my throat.

"Strix?" Mia said, confusion furrowing her brow.

"You killed him?" Father asked and I nodded. "By the blood, why?"

"He tried to kill…Lena," I answered.

I saw father's ire rise. "You killed a vampire over a mortal plaything?"

Julie stumbled back from Etienne in shock. "You're talking about my daughter, Etienne," she said, her voice more forceful than her fragile mortal frame would have suggested.

Father actually looked chastened, and I believed he did love her, in his way. "We have laws, my love," he said softly, kindly, like that would make a difference to a grieving mother. "Mortals are fleeting, they are–"

"Worthless?" Julie suggested and Father looked honestly sorry for it.

"It is the way it is."

"He won't see a tribunal," Grandma Vi proclaimed.

"How?" Mia asked.

"They will overlook his transgressions in light of the circumstances."

Father scoffed. "Just because she is a le Rege doesn't make her any less mortal."

Grandma Vi shook her head. "Those are not the circumstances, Etienne."

"What possible other motive could he have had?"

"Lena is his fated mate."

It felt like silence had descended over the entire world as the whole family turned to look at first Grandma Vi, then to me with Lena still cradled in my arms.

"Fated mates?" Father asked.

"Look at the boy," Grandma Vi said gently. "He is broken at the mere thought of losing her. He is a shell. Had his heart beaten these last eighteen years, then it would not beat now. No vampire, no matter how deep the love, has ever been that broken by a mortal's…mortality. It is built into us to accept their lives are but a blink of the eye to us. We love them and enjoy them in the time we have, but they leave us. Unless we turn them, and we all know that's incredibly rare."

"You believe this?" Father said. I couldn't tell if he was shrugging off her superstitions of weighing up the truth of it.

"You believe in the dhampir, Etienne," Grandma Vi said snidely. "Without a single shred of proof. I give you proof that your son's mate lies in front of him, and you dare scorn my beliefs?"

I snuck a look at my father and saw that he was giving more consideration to her words now. He knew as well as I that his sire was no fool. After all, she had lived considerably longer than almost any of our kind. Save Acheron.

"His obsession does not make it true," Father scoffed.

Grandma Vi gave him a withering glare that suggested he seriously rethink his stance on how much obsession counted for making something true.

"Never in our history—" he started.

"Never in *your* history," she said firmly, and we all looked at her gobsmacked.

"What?" I whispered and she threw me a glance that could only have been apologetic.

"I wanted you to believe it first. I wanted you to feel it. To know it."

"Before what?" my father asked.

"Before I told you I had seen it. Before I told you my mother had seen it before me. Before I told you that the women in my family have kept these secrets for thousands of years.”

“Why?” Julie breathed, though I didn’t know how much of it she really understood.

“Because the council do not believe what they cannot see. They do not believe what they cannot test. And those who are lucky enough to have and find their fated mate deserve more than a lifetime of experiments. They deserve the privacy to live their lives in peace.”

“What kind of experiments?” Mia asked.

Granma Vi’s eyes darkened. “There is a story that one pair were found. By hunters. They believed a fated mate made them stronger. The hunters couldn’t allow this. They tried to find a way to sunder them.”

“Did they?”

Grandma Vi shrugged. “I don’t know more than the story. Perhaps it had been given a happy ending? Perhaps the pair survived. Perhaps the hunters in question were actually wiped out. The truth has been long lost to the annals of time.”

I felt my anger rising, but my eyes were on my father. He finally believed my grandsire’s words. He believed that Lena was my mate.

“And my son is now a pair.” I heard the sharp calculation in his tone, and I remembered the conversation with Grandma Vi.

I gently placed Lena on the floor and stood up, prepared to protect her at all costs. I’d already killed one vampire. What was two? He was only the man who had given me life. But if he took Lena from me, then he may as well be taking that life right back. And I would take his before that happened.

“Do not touch her,” I growled, heedless of the trepidation on

Julie's face.

Father's eyes narrowed. "She is human, Erasmus."

I shook myself out, picturing the ways I could incapacitate him before he even moved. I'd always been stronger than him. Even since birth. It was one argument that supported my status as born. The other was just that he was weak.

"And?" I asked pointedly. "Are you threatened?"

He hissed, knowing that was a threat in and of itself.

"Threatened?" Julie asked, her motherly love overriding any compulsion my father had laid on her to make her complacent to our behaviour. "Why would he be threatened?"

Father snarled at me. "Watch yourself, Erasmus…" he said carefully.

"She is no threat," I told him, equally as carefully. "I, however, am. Touch her and I will ensure you never get your precious dhampir."

Father wavered. I could see he was torn. His self-preservation fighting his burning need. "You love her?" he finally asked, surprising me.

I blinked, but answered him honestly. "I can't not love her," I told him, and I saw Julie's eyes crinkle in joy. I ignored her display of emotion. "Whether we are truly mates or not–"

"You–"

"Are not arguing about the truth now," I answered Grandma Vi's interruption. "Whether we are or not, I love her. She is mine."

"And you killed the Westmeyer child for her?" Father said slowly.

"He was going to kill her."

Father looked me over and I saw something in his eyes I had

never seen before. Something I only recognised with some primal part of myself. It was vaguely paternal. It was almost as though, despite the circumstances and disappointment of my birth, he was capable of feeling something for me other than pride for the kind of vampire I had become.

"Get her to bed," Father said.

Disgusted I hadn't thought of it sooner, I picked her back up and transported us upstairs in a cloud of mist. I was pulling the covers over her in my bed when the family traipsed in and took their places around the room like we were setting up for some perverted movie poster or something.

Mia brought a chair over and I sank onto it beside the bed. She put her hand on my back and moved over to stand by Grandma Vi.

Vampires were nothing if not prepared to wait for extended periods of time. For anything. Barring an unfortunate or intentional accident, we had eternity stretching out in front of each of us. I had never been an impatient creature, but the time I sat by Lena's side and there was no change seemed to stretch to eternity itself.

Patience, came Atlas' voice.

Do not speak to me of patience, I snapped at him, feeling something in his mind. *How much did you know?*

You don't want to know the answer to that.

I looked up at him. *How much did you know? Did you know she was my mate?*

I did.

Why didn't you tell me?

I couldn't.

Why not?

They wouldn't let me.

I frowned. *Who?*

You had to walk the path yourself.

Who, Atlas? I tried again.

He shook out his feathers with a mournful cry and said no more. I dropped my head again but, understandably, the family took his agitation to be a sign of my distress under the circumstances.

"She will wake, Erasmus," Grandma Vi said.

I shook my head where it hung. "You don't know that."

"She is your mate, Erasmus," she insisted. "She will not die. She cannot die."

"Tell that to the fates," I barked harshly as my fury snapped to her.

She didn't deserve it, but she allowed my defiance under the current circumstances. Had my mate not been lying near dead by my side, I would have felt the sharp sting of my grandsire's fangs before I'd finished my sentence.

"Mates were supposed to be a myth," Father said, his voice still wonderous about it, even now. Even after he clearly believed.

Grandma Vi huffed. "A myth," she scoffed. "*We*, dear boy, are supposed to be a myth. Fated mates are but once in a lifetime. Once in a millennia. There is no power in this universe that can sunder fated mates."

"And yet mine lies on the brink of death," I snapped.

"There is a solution," Grandma Vi said gently. "But you must be the one to do it."

I shook my head. "It might not work."

"And she may die either way."

"You seem determined she cannot die."

"You seem determined not to believe me."

I hung my head again. "Better it be by another's hand than mine."

Grandma Vi said nothing more and we all went back to hovering in silence, never-ending waiting, uncertainty in the face of a demon our kind rarely had to deal with.

I knew not how much time passed. Minutes. Hours. Months. I refused to leave her side unless she breathed her last. I wouldn't insult her by doing what needed to be done even in front of her unliving body.

Finally, "Rune?" came her voice. Weak, but hers.

I lifted my head and saw her watching me like she wasn't sure I was really there.

For the first time in almost eighteen years, my heart started beating once more.

But what was she?

CHAPTER TWENTY-ONE

My heat still beat steadily in my chest.

That didn't tell me anything.

Rune had told me a vampire's heart kept beating unless something stopped it, and that didn't have to mean they were dead. I'd felt his own lack of a heartbeat. The fuzziness of my mind wondered how circulation worked if the heart didn't beat, but I didn't know enough about biology, let alone vampire biology, to come up with an answer.

I looked around and saw my family, such as it was. But at that moment, it was the most wonderful family in the world, eclectic as it may have been.

Mum sat on a chaise, Etienne with his hand on her shoulder as they spoke quietly to each other. Grandma Vi sat in a chair by a vanity table with Mia at her side. And on a chair by my side was Rune, his arms leaning on the bed and his head hanging in what could have been mistaken for despair.

"Rune?" I whispered, my throat feeling dry.

He looked up at me and it was the first time since I'd met him that he didn't look impeccably put together. His hair hung around his face, his eyes were haggard and dark, but not like his vampire face dark, and his clothes were rumpled as though he hadn't changed in days.

"Lena?" he answered, his voice as soft as mine. His eyes cleared of the weariness as he took me in. "Lena. Angel!" He took my hand and squeezed it tightly.

"Evie!" Mum cried and then she was hurrying to sit on the other side of me, looking no better than Rune. As though, she too had sat there and just waited for me to wake.

"How long—?" I started.

"A few days," Grandma Vi said, getting up and standing at the foot of the bed. "You gave us all quite the scare."

I noticed that Etienne hadn't moved. His eyes were wide as he took me in. I wasn't sure if he was scared of me. For me. Or perhaps was just in disbelief. I was in a bit of disbelief myself.

My memories were hazy. I could remember Strix biting me. I could taste his blood in my mouth. The cold of the water as I sank.

"Am I…?" I asked slowly, quite sure I didn't want the answer.

Grandma Vi shook her head. "No. He didn't take enough blood. And the water's chill slowed your pulse, so his blood was ineffective by the time it reached your heart."

I nodded, not sure why that felt disappointing. It wasn't like I wanted to be a vampire either.

"Come," Grandma Vi announced to the room at large. "Erasmus and Evangeline should be given some privacy. I'm sure they have much to discuss."

Despite his tiredness, Rune had enough energy to frown at her. "Do not start, old woman," he warned her.

She merely smiled at him and ushered everyone else out. When they were gone, Rune helped me to some water and to sit up more comfortably. My whole body ached, and I felt a bandage on my neck where Strix's fangs had ripped through me.

"What do we need to talk about?" I asked him, feeling some amusement of my own.

"Grandma Vi no doubt thinks I have…some admissions to make to you, Angel," he said slowly as he came and sat next to me, facing me like he couldn't bare to take his eyes off me for a moment.

I felt my eyebrow rise. "Admissions? That sounds serious. Am I going to want to be a little more recovered for this?"

The light smirk at his lips didn't meet his eyes. "I need you. I love you, Angel," he said softly.

I chewed my lip for a moment before answering. "Do you love me or is it whatever preternatural draw this is between us?"

He smirked. "I don't know. My heart started beating again when you woke, and I didn't want to live without you. Is that love? Or something else?"

"And how do we know the difference?" I added and he nodded.

"Indeed."

I looked at him and wondered. What did I feel for him? And why? Grandma Vi was convinced we were mates and…there was something in me sure she was right. If so, could I trust my feelings? Did I really feel so deeply for him or was fate just telling me I did? Telling me to? Was fate just a convenient excuse to not have to think all this through?

I put my hand on his chest, and he lay his over it. The beat was steady under his skin. Steady if slow. It was so weird after so many times touching him and it being silently absent. On one hand, it was like he wasn't him anymore. On the other, I felt like he was finally really him.

"What do you want to do, Angel?" he asked me.

"I don't know. I don't even know what our options are."

"They are whatever we want them to be."

"Are you suggesting we date? Or continue on? Or…?"

"I can only tell you what I'd like. The decision is up to you."

I cracked a small smile. "And are you going to tell me what that is?"

"I want to be with you, Angel. I want us to have eternity together. I want to spend the rest of time knowing you and loving you."

Eternity.

For that, I had to be turned. I had to become a vampire. We couldn't have eternity if I remained a human.

"You want me to turn." It wasn't really a question.

"You are my mate, Angel," he said, his voice constricted. "Why should we not have forever?"

In theory, I agreed. And it's not like I didn't want that. But…

I nodded. "I'm not saying never, Rune. I'm just saying not yet."

He searched my eyes. "You don't trust me."

Maybe a little, but that wasn't the most important thing.

"I don't trust *us*. Yet. It's like I know in the depths of my soul that we're meant to be together forever, but that's not enough for me to change who I am. Last week, we still hated each other as much as…"

"Loved each other," he finished for me.

I nodded again. "Yeah. It might sound silly or overly romantic or just naive in the grand scheme – in hundreds of years, I'll probably look back and wonder why the hell I waited – but I don't want to be turned until we're…" I tried to think of the right word, but couldn't find it.

He took my hand. "I understand. Cosmic pull isn't exactly enough to make you abandon your humanity." I'd have thought he was pissed off, except for the rueful glint in his eyes.

"You don't mind?"

He shrugged. "It's not my choice."

"That doesn't mean you don't have an opinion."

"I am suddenly far too aware of your mortality. Your fragility. Someone has already tried to take you from me once, and I'm scared it will happen again. I'm scared I won't be fast enough or strong enough again. But…"

"Are you still worried about the whole born versus turned thing?"

The glint in his eye warmed as one corner of his lips tipped up. "You put the pieces together." It wasn't a question.

"I remember the argument where Grandma Vi asked you if you were admitting you were born, and I got the impression Etienne thinks you were turned. And I had a pretty graphic discussion with Mia about the whole ability to turn thing, and the consequences when it fails."

Rune nodded slowly as his thumb traced circles on my hand. "I don't even know if I can turn you."

I wasn't exactly looking forward to the repercussions if he tried and failed either.

"Does it have to be you?"

He sighed. "There's no rule that says I must. There aren't any rules for fated mates, none outside mythology books. But it's the done thing. If a love is strong enough to consider a turning, and the vamp in question is born, then it's expected. Some of them even have grand rituals, much like a wedding."

I took a moment to unpack all that. "Is there a way to know for sure?"

"I mention a wedding and that gets your attention?" he teased dryly.

I bit my lip against a smile. "It does actually sound kinda nice, but I was more concerned with potentially going zombie bride."

"There are rumours of a witch who can tell the difference between a born and turned vamp, but there are so few of us who honestly don't know that it's not something our kind has bothered with."

"Do you really not know?" I asked him.

He sighed again. "My father is adamant my mother was pregnant before Grandma Vi turned her. As much as I believe his obsession over siring the fabled dhampir has him taking leave of his senses, it gives me pause for thought. Especially now. Before you, I refused to believe or acknowledge one way or another because it annoyed everyone around me. Was Father close to siring the dhampir and ruined it for himself, or was I conceived after and his quest is futile? Either way, he lost. Now, I'm terrified my father is right and I was turned. If so, I lose."

"Then we wait. We wait and we find out for sure."

His eyes pinned mine. "And if I was turned?"

"I'd prefer you to be the one to turn me, Rune. But if you can't?" I shrugged. "I'm sure Grandma Vi or Mia would be happy to do it for us."

"And what do you want to do in the meantime?" he asked.

"Are you asking me out?" I teased and a cheeky smirk lit his eyes.

"I feel like dating is almost a step back for us now, but I understand wanting to…do this right."

"Right?"

He shrugged again. "From the start. A certain way. Just because we're fated to a love the likes very few could ever even hope for doesn't mean we have to rush into anything. We have forever, after all."

"So, you really believe Grandma Vi now?"

"Do you not?"

I shook my head. "I'm not sure *how* I could know, but somehow, I know she's right. I feel it. Like Fate herself is telling me it's true. Does that sound insane?"

He wrapped his arms around me. "No more insane than the fact fated mates actually exist. Besides, I feel it, too. As though, on one hand, I don't know you enough to know if I even like you but…"

"Also like you've known me forever?"

He nodded. "Exactly like that."

I leant my face to his chest. "I feel like two people. Or I'm seeing two timelines at the same time. One where I love you and one where I still kind of hate you. Like you said, I don't know you well enough to…not."

He chuckled. "Then I guess we should start at the beginning, then."

"I thought you didn't date?" I sassed and he hugged me tighter.

"Until now, my heart didn't beat. Until now, I didn't realise I could ever need someone so strongly that I'd consider killing myself if I lost them.”

I batted him. “Dramatic much?”

“I’ve told you, Angel. I prefer not to lie to you. I’m not proud of my reaction, but it was the one I had. No vampire would willingly announce to our kind that they felt that way about a mortal, but I have still never heard of it before. If that didn’t convince me of the bond between us, the return of my heartbeat would have been enough.”

I tensed as I thought of something, not sure if I should bring it up or not.

“What, Angel?” he asked gently.

“Strix said that…” At the sound of his name, Rune went stiff, but I continued. “He said that girl you made jump of the tower… That she said your heart didn’t beat because it–”

“Lived outside me,” he finished, and I nodded. “She did say that.” He looked me over. “I have to wonder if she was talking about you.”

“Do you think she was?”

He shrugged. “I don’t know. But there is a poetry to it.”

We sat together for a long time, not feeling the need for words, just relishing the chance to hold each other again after what had happened. I dozed against him a little and didn’t properly wake until the wee hours of the next morning.

Rune was asleep beside me, his colouring looking a little better.

“He has fed and is resting. He will recover far quicker than you.”

I looked over and saw Grandma Vi in the shadows.

“Creepy much?” I teased and I saw the whites of her teeth

flash.

"Protective of what is mine."

"Where do we go from here?" I asked.

"You find out what it means to love each other. You work out how. No one can tell you what your love should look like. Only the two of you can work that out. My only caution would be keeping silent on Fate's part in the piece."

I nodded. "I guess that makes sense."

"It comes to no good, Lena. Never," she said, her voice full of broken passion. "Let them believe you are caught in a whirlwind of young love, but never let them know you are fated."

"I'm still getting my own head around that one."

She nodded. "It will all make sense in time."

"Will it?"

A mournful caw sounded from the window, and I turned to see Atlas on the sill.

"He refused to leave your side," Grandma Vi said.

"You mean, refused to leave Rune's side?"

She shook her head. "I do not."

I looked back to Atlas and could have sworn I felt something very like relief sweeping through me. Except it wasn't mine. I might have been wrong, but it felt like it belonged to the raven.

The whole family took the rest of the week to recover and regroup. We needed a plan of attack. Not only was Grandma Vi adamant that no one know about the whole fated mates thing, but Etienne wasn't risking Rune's 'recklessness' – as he put it – causing issues for the family.

Not that Rune much cared what his father thought.

At school, I was declared more than off-limits. There wasn't just the unspoken knowledge that no one touches a le Rege, but there was the very real threat that Rune would end anyone who touched me. After all, it hadn't taken long for the rumours to spread that Rune killed Strix over me. So far, they were still just rumours. There was a competing rumour that Strix had been so heartbroken over me that he'd left Knightsbridge. I wasn't buying it but, without proof one way or another, no one could do anything about either rumour.

Rune wasn't the only le Rege impatient for me to turn because that was the only way I was guaranteed to be able to defend myself against any future attack – including but not limited to old age, disease, hunters and rogue vampires.

But the family agreed to give us the time to look for the witch who was supposed to be able to answer our question. It was almost the summer holidays and Rune and I had plans to look for her. Mia joined us in the library every night, looking for information about her and where she could be found.

"I'm so pissed off I'm not going with you," she huffed.

Rune gave her a look. "I'm not going away with my…" He looked at me. "Girlfriend? Mate? Whatever. And having my little sister tag along."

"You're not going on some fuck fest odyssey," Mia said with a pout. "You're going on a grand adventure to find a witch!"

"And why can't it be both?" was Rune's answer before he went back to the bookshelves in search of another book.

I shared a smile with Mia. "Etienne is not going to cope if we all go."

Mia sighed, "Yeah, I know. He's going to hate it when we're all out living our lives far away from this forsaken place."

I nodded. "He will. But who knows. Maybe he'll have his dhampir by then. What did he do when the rest of your siblings moved out?"

Mia looked at me weirdly. "No one else has ever lived with him."

Well, so much more made sense now, then. He might have had a shit load of kids, but he'd only been playing daddy for less than twenty years. I wondered what that did to his quest for his dhampir. Did it make him more or less zealous about it?

"You know, I guess that makes sense why," Mia said cryptically, and I looked at her in confusion. She shrugged. "You seemed surprised that you just went along with everything, but it was fate. Fate guided you to us, to Rune, to accepting our world and who we were. If you hadn't, fate would have lost and she's not about to let that happen."

"Is that like a thing, or just something you came up with?" I asked.

She shrugged again. "Just something I came up with."

I sighed as I sat back. "It's as good an explanation as any."

My eyes wandered over to Rune as I thought about her words. It was a conversation he and I had regularly. What was fate and what was love? It was one reason we were taking this slowly. I didn't know if we'd ever know the answer for sure, but at least we'd know that we didn't just bow to fate's design. We tried to make it our own.

"Daydreaming, Angel?" Rune asked, with a cheeky tilt to his

lips.

"Shut up," I retorted, trying to hide a smile.

He didn't bother trying to hide his. "We leave in little over a month, and we still don't know where we're starting."

"Like I don't know that," I sassed as I passed him on the way to find a book of my own.

He wrapped an arm around me and pulled me close to him, dipping his nose to my neck. "You want me to bend you over and punish you for your cheek?" he teased.

"Not with little sister's present, thank you," Mia called, her nose still buried in her book.

Rune let me go, slapping my arse as he stepped back. I couldn't help but smile as I got back to work.

CHAPTER TWENTY-TWO

RUNE – JANUARY

I could smell human blood coming through the wood as Atlas swooped towards me.

And what have you brought me today? I asked him.

He was weirdly silent. Not that I minded as she came into view. Long auburn hair pulled back in a ponytail. Bright green eyes as she took in her surroundings like she wasn't quite sure where she was. She was… Attractive, but I wouldn't have called her the most stunning creature I'd ever seen. And yet… There was something about her that…

I inhaled deeply, trying to place her.

Whoever she was, she hadn't been here long enough for the smell of her owners to seep into her. It could take months, depending on how often they fed from her, how recently they'd fed, and how often they used her for other pleasures.

"This probably counts as not close to the house," I heard her say quietly as she clearly tried to get her bearings.

"And who might be missing you?" I asked her, still in mist-form.

She turned around in circles as she tried to work out where I was. *Stupid mortals.* I walked out of the fog and, when her eyes landed on me, I heard her heart stutter in her chest. Desire wafted from her in a thick haze and wrapped around me. I could feel my fangs aching for a taste. But they weren't the only part of me that desperately wanted a taste. Wanted to sink in her.

I felt Atlas ruffle his feathers agitatedly and I wanted to ask him what was wrong, but I was too captivated by the creature in front of me. Who was she and what was she doing here? No vampire I knew let their food just wander around. And yet she was just… Her pulse quickening dangerously as she looked me over. I felt things stirring I wasn't known for bothering to control, let alone being able to. But I hadn't lost control yet.

"You're new to Knightsbridge," I said as I walked towards her.

She nodded as her heart thudded. "I am," she replied.

I gave her a nod, feeling my feet take me a step closer to her. Her heart beat rapidly and I breathed deeply to maintain my control. I could feel it wavering. Not as much as I would have expected based on her reaction to me. But it was still something I fought in the back of my head.

"Are you attending the Academy next term?" I asked, looking her over carefully, as though that would give me any more information about her.

"I am."

I felt the corner of my lips tug. "Are you capable of saying anything else?"

She caught her lip in her teeth and I felt numerous things in me straining to be free. "I am."

That tug broke into a half-smile. "Well played." And it was.

For a glamoured human in Knightsbridge, she was still quite witty. I liked that.

"I'm Lena," she said.

"Call me Rune," popped out of me like I had lost control after all, just over my voice of all things.

Rune, you're positively flirting with her, Atlas teased with a shrill cry. I smirked.

Lena looked up at him and no doubt wondered what he was doing there, and what his interest in us was.

He's not interested in you.

Aren't I?

Are you?

You are.

"I should let you get back," I told her, not sure what my behaviour would turn into if Atlas kept pushing. "No doubt someone is missing you by now."

The shake of her head surprised me. "I doubt it. I'm sure they don't even know I'm lost. I guess that's what I get for wandering too far from home."

"Well, I'm glad you did."

"Really? Why?"

Why, indeed. Because then I could begin my seduction. "Because I found you." I paused to let that sink in, and saw it landed well. "I'll see you at school," he said.

She stepped forward. "Maybe I'll get lost again sometime before then."

By the blood, I hoped so. "Maybe you will."

I slipped into mist, not too quickly as to startle to human, and Atlas took a moment in following. We whisked away to the apartment I kept in a town down the mountain for those times my father really annoyed me. I told myself I'd hide out there until school went back. Miss the wedding. Miss the new 'family'.

But it took all of a few days before I couldn't resist looking for her again. This tantalising creature who had come out of nowhere. I found her in the woods again.

Will you not tell me what you know of her? I asked Atlas. Because the bird had been awfully stubborn the last couple of days regardless of how often I asked him what he knew. And he clearly knew something.

He shook his wings out. *I will not.*

That amused me. The raven and I shared a bond no other vamp I'd ever heard of knew. The closest similarity was a witch's familiar, but I was definitely no witch. Not that anyone batted an eyelid about it; singular vamps were known to have powers held by to no other.

Why not?

I can only caution your intentions, the raven answered.

I have to talk to her.

Except, you do not.

I felt myself smile despite no corporeal body. *I am…compelled.*

By a human? I heard the amusement in his mind-voice.

Obsession is nothing new for my kind.

You do not know who she is.

Because you will not tell me, I reminded him.

I cannot.

Then surely, playing with her cannot be that dire.

Rune… Atlas' voice was a warning and I looked at him, as best

I was able in mist-form.

If you will not tell me who she is, then I will play with her, Atlas.

Be careful, Rune.

I don't need to be. You'll tell me when I've crossed a line.

He shook himself out again. *I am not here to be your conscience.*

Then why are you here?

We stared at each other as I solidified and walked towards her. I dared him to try to stop me. He didn't, but I felt the displeasure flowing from him to me. Funny how I could compel one mortal to kill themselves and he doesn't flap a wing, but I want to play with this one and that ruffles his feathers. Still, if he wouldn't tell me who this mortal was, I would take what I wanted.

And I wanted her like I had never wanted another mortal before.

She was like a freshly bleeding wound, begging to be licked and worshipped and drained. It was all I could do to control myself. If she was in Knightsbridge, then she would be compelled to accept the existence of vampires, but all mortals still had a base wariness that made playing with her as one of her own, to start with, a much more fun experience.

Lena saw me and I heard as much as felt her pulse quicken. Her breathing grew more rapid. She liked what she saw.

"Lena," I said, and Atlas gave me one more mournful warning. "Lost again?"

"I am," she said, and I had to appreciate her quick mind, even for a mortal.

"On purpose?" I hoped so.

She nodded vaguely. "Perhaps."

"Good." I stepped towards her, and she stepped towards me like there was an invisible string pulling us closer together. "You never said where you were staying."

If I could work out who she belonged to, then maybe I could work out why Atlas was so cagey about her.

She surprised me with her easy, "I didn't."

Compelled mortals never denied a vampire anything that was asked. And yet…

"I sense you're not going to."

She smiled. "You sense right. The force is strong with this one."

I had never once cared that Knightsbridge vampires kept themselves cut off from the mortal world as much as possible. But her using what was clearly mortal popular culture without me understanding was the first time I began to wonder what I was missing out on.

"The force?"

She frowned. "You know." She put her hand over her mouth and wheezed, "Luke, I am your father."

Obviously, it was something I was supposed to know as a teenager. So, I could only pretend I did.

"Right. Of course." Time to move on. We each took another step closer. "Will you tell me anything about you?"

One more synchronised step closer. She shrugged. "Will you tell me anything about you?"

This wasn't the behaviour of a compelled human. But no mortal passed through the wards of Knightsbridge without succumbing to the lowest level of compulsion before one of us got our eyes on them. Why then was she pushing back? How was she pushing back?

I couldn't complain. Just the sight of her – the scent of her – had me hard. But she was the first mortal to defy me who was still alive. And, weirdly, I had no immediate wish to cut her lifespan even shorter.

The fabric of our clothes was very nearly close enough to give a whisper of contact, and I could feel she was nearly vibrating with my closeness. It was a feeling I was starting to notice hummed in me as well. My cock was already straining to claim her, but my fangs throbbed in my gums to make her theirs as well. It wasn't just about feeding – which was always more exciting during a rough fuck. I wanted to take her long and slow, penetrate her deep and feel her come undone around me.

I looked down at her and felt something stirring deep inside me that I couldn't really comprehend. I was enjoying my effect on her. I was confused and aroused by her effect on me. And I desperately needed to know everything about her. But as I looked down at her, I felt myself locked there. She held me as surely as I held her.

But her eyes were clear. As clear as they could be with lust gripping her. There was no glassiness, no clouding, no sign of one either compelled or falling for compulsion. She was affected by me, but my compulsion wasn't what was doing it.

"What would you want to know?" I asked, pushing all my power of compulsion into my words. Her eyes lost some focus, but nothing like they should have.

Her heart thudded. Her pulse ran deep and steady. Her breathing was even. I could smell the need on her. The arousal. I felt the monster rise up in me. It bucked and demanded to be free, to make her submit to us.

I quelled it with the promise she would, but not until we had answers.

"Everything," was a simple breath upon her lips and my stomach bottomed out.

Who was this mortal? Who was this mortal who held my attention like no other? To make me want her with a deep, consuming hunger but make me restrained enough to not – as disgusting as the thought was – scare her away.

She stumbled into me, and my hands went to steady her, if not keep her there. As soon as we touched, mere skin to clothing, it was like I'd been electrocuted. My heart was in serious danger of restarting. It seemed to stir in my chest, like a bear questioning if it was time to awaken from their hibernation yet. I cut off every feeling I could.

Rune... came Atlas' warning.

When I didn't heed him, he shrieked loudly, and I involuntarily took a step away from her.

Either tell me why I can't have her or fuck off, I snarled at him.

I could tell the raven was torn. There was something larger at play here and he knew all of it. Of course, he did. Ravens were a thread to the Otherworld. They saw things with little effort even the most skilled psychics couldn't. They spoke to the dead. Or the very nearly dead, such as me.

I supposed I should listen to him. This time.

I didn't want to walk away, but I knew what would happen if I didn't. "I'm sure I will see you again, Lena."

She nodded. "At school, at least."

If I had no answers before that, I should be able to find them then. "At least."

I walked away, dissolving into mist but unable to stop myself curling around her before we left again.

Despite whatever his obvious misgivings were, Atlas brought her to me only a few days later.

Humans seemed to like it when we were enigmatic, and I did enigmatic so very well. So, I waited for her by a bridge under a lamppost and looked wistfully into the water. Atlas alighted on the bar of the lamp above me and I knew when she walked out of the trees as much from my body's reaction as hers.

"It seems you found me today," I said, my eyes still on the water.

"Did I?" she replied, moving to lean on the wall beside me.

She was far too close, but I couldn't bring myself to step away from her. She wasn't close enough, but I knew it would be dangerous to touch her.

"Or perhaps you were led," I suggested.

Rune... was Atlas' one-word warning.

"Is there always this much fog?" she asked and I wondered exactly what she'd been told by her owners when they brought her here. I still couldn't smell them on her.

"In Knightsbridge, yes. Something about the..." Telling her the truth might have been a problem. "Environment."

"Oh."

"Have you been this far from home before?" I asked,

wondering why I gave a fuck.

"Considering I don't know how far away I am from where I started, or how many circles I went in to get here, I can't answer that. If," she paused. "you're referring to my accent. No. This is my first time out of Australia."

Australia. Why was that familiar to me? I mean, obviously I was aware it was a country. We did geography at school like anyone else. I just couldn't place why that should mean something to me. Oh, well. I ignored a good majority of what most people said to me. I was sure it wasn't important.

I gave her a smile. "Well, welcome to Knightsbridge, Lena..." Maybe if she gave me her last name, then I could piece who she belonged to.

"Just Lena will be fine. Rune...?"

Two could play at that game. "Just Rune will do."

Something was niggling at me. Had I actually cared about anything in this world, I'd have thought it wasn't something I wanted to know. But I couldn't imagine not wanting to know something. What possible purpose would I want to ignore knowledge in me?

My musings were interrupted when Lena tried to sit up on the wall and started falling backwards. Despite her mortality, my reaction was something I definitely couldn't control.

I stepped between her legs and wrapped my arm around her waist, pulling her into my body hard. As though it was instinct, her legs tightened around me and fuck. But that had been both the best and worst idea I think I'd ever had. My body went haywire. My cock stiffened. My teeth ached. I felt the tingle-like stirring under my eyes that heralded my full vampire face.

Her breath was short and shallow, her heart thundered, but I felt the need dripping off her. Her reaction. It was excitement. It was want. It called to me and stoked the burning embers in me that I was trying desperately to control. I'd always had impeccable control for my age. Somehow, Lena made it both harder and easier to maintain. I felt on the verge of breaking out in full vampire and giving it all over to the monster. And yet, at the same time, I knew I wouldn't hurt her accidentally.

By the blood, I wanted her. And I didn't know why I shouldn't just take her and be done with it. Clearly, whoever had brought her here wasn't making any decent use of her. So why shouldn't I?

She held me, enthralled, and our bodies shifted closer.

Rune.

I breathed heavily, made sure she was standing safely and stepped back as far as I could bring myself to go.

"You want to be careful," I told her.

She wasn't the only one disappointed. "I will. Thanks."

I knew I should leave, but I couldn't. We both turned back to the water for a few moments and I wracked my brain for something to say to her. Something of my usual charm and sophistication. But there was nothing. She'd rattled me. Me. A mere mortal had rattled me.

Finally, she cleared her throat. "I guess I should find my way back."

"I guess you should. If you told me where you lived, I could walk you back."

She smiled. "Maybe on our...fifth meeting," she told me.

"I look forward to it."

She gave me a small nod and started walking back the way she'd come.

Make sure she gets back safely, I said to Atlas.

I will.

I don't suppose you'll tell me where that is?

I won't.

He swooped after her and I told myself I felt nothing for them both leaving me there. When he came back, he berated me for how close the call had been.

Are you worried I'll kill her, fuck her, or both? I asked him.

I'm worried you don't understand what you're playing with.

That was an interesting word choice. *What or who?*

Just be careful, Rune. There is only so much I can do to clean up your messes.

I rolled my eyes. *Then the least you can do is make sure she makes it to next term for me.*

You say that like I haven't already been keeping an eye on her.

Fine. Then keep doing it.

And he did. I was supposed to keep well enough away. But I knew she walked the woods. I wondered if she was hoping to see me again. But I promised Atlas that I wouldn't interfere. Not that I did. On purpose.

I found her walking with Atlas and she was talking to him like it was the most natural thing in the world. I heard her mention fate and Atlas did not enjoy that response at all apparently. Instead of asking him why, I felt myself solidify. Not that I'd meant to.

What are you doing here? Atlas yelled into my mind and my ear.

I was meant to be mist, I explained to him.

But I felt it. Whatever he was worried about. It thrummed between Lena and me. It made the monster growl and rail and demand release until I wasn't sure how much longer I could deny it. As though, the time I hadn't seen her had done the opposite of nothing for this build up of obsession in me; it had only grown it.

I knew I had to leave, or I was going to do something Atlas would probably kill me over. Then suddenly, Lena had crossed the distance between us, and her hand was on my arm.

Her scent enveloped me, and the monster thrashed for freedom. I breathed slowly to keep it in check. Especially once her heart started racing. Her skin flushed. I felt held in place by something stronger and older than any magic I had ever felt.

I blinked and it seemed the spell broke.

"Before you go, Rune–" she said, and I heard how breathless she sounded. It undid me.

I took her in my arms, and I kissed her. Just as I heard her heart stop for a moment, it was like I could almost feel an echo in my own chest. Like an answer or a reminder to hers. But then she wrapped her arms around my shoulder and had pressed her body to mine. What I wouldn't give to make her mine. Right there and then. My hand slipped up her side and hers slid down and gripped the lapels of my jacket like she wanted me closer. Then her hand was in my hair and I was trailing my fingers up her thigh, imagining her gripping my hip like she had at the bridge.

Fuck.

"Lena," I groaned.

Atlas shrieked and I knew he was right. I didn't even bother arguing with him with time. I just left as quickly as I could and knew that going back would be more than a bad idea. I didn't know who she belonged to. I didn't know why she had such an effect on me. Left to my own devices with no answers – because Atlas was being decidedly unhelpful on that one – I knew I could make a mistake even I couldn't get out of.

I could wait a few more weeks until school went back. I could wait until her scent was diluted by everyone else's. I could wait to get answers in a place that I'd have a better handle on my control.

◆◆◆◆

Except, I couldn't. Because after Mia's unrelenting insistence, I acquiesced to appear at my father's wedding.

Mia had told me that I would want to meet our new stepsister. That she was great, and she defied even the great Rune le Rege to feel nothing for her. My interest was piqued. Father had forbidden me from playing with my new stepsister, but it could be just the thing to take my mind off Lena until school went back.

So, to say I was less than impressed when I instantly recognised the girl Father was talking to when I arrived would be an understatement.

I was pissed.

Australia. Of course it had been familiar. My Father had told me his new wife and her daughter were Australian.

She didn't smell like anyone. Because she wasn't a feeder. She wasn't a toy. She was a daughter. Family. A first in Knightsbridge, but it still should have flicked a switch in my head.

No, I'd been so obsessed with her that I hadn't wanted to know she was the very thing I wasn't to play with.

Atlas cautioned me, as usual.

You knew, I accused him. *You knew who she was.*

I did.

Why didn't you tell me?

That is not the only reason I have counselled caution.

And I suppose you won't tell me that either?

He didn't answer. Which left me even more pissed off. Fine. I couldn't play with her the way I wanted? That didn't mean I couldn't play with her at all.

Vampires of Knightsbridge

If you liked *Monster of Fate*, share the love and let me know!
There are three more instalments to come.

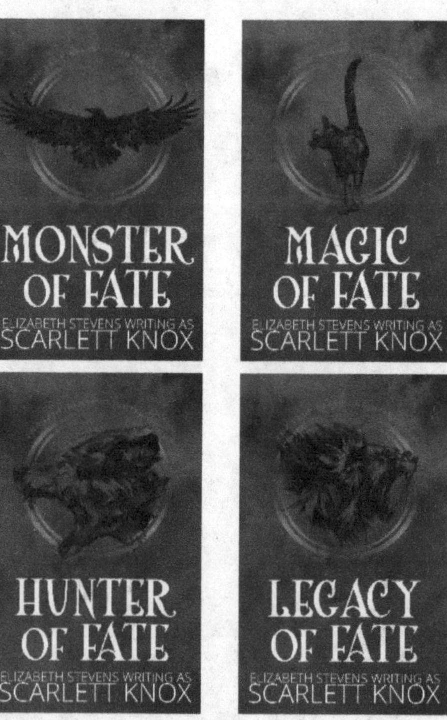

WANGED

Did you know Eternal Academy is actually a series I'm writing? If you liked *Monster of Fate*, you might also enjoy *Wanged*. An upper Young Adult darker, paranormal romance. https://books2read.com/EA1-Wanged.

From Elizabeth Stevens, writing as Scarlett Knox, comes…
An awkward heroine totally out of her depth, the long-lost twin sister who hates her, and the two guys who make this one hell of a complicated romance.

One day, I'm your average teen. Last year of school. Suffocating under homework. Fiercely loyal friends. Totally oblivious crushes. Weird parents who've forgotten what it's like to be a teen.

The next… Well, the next, I died. Got wanged in a car crash and died. But I didn't stay dead.

Thrust into a world so unlike the one I've known all my life, it's all I can do to keep my head above the constantly revealing secrets that threaten to drown me.

I used to know exactly where I fit. Now I straddle two worlds. Two equally new and foreign worlds. Neither of which want me… Not alive anyway.

It's a new school and whole new rules. Rule #1 being there aren't any. Rule #2 being that nobodies like me do not look twice at vampire princes. Although, to be fair, I'm pretty sure he looked twice at me first.

And chief among my tormentors is the blood ruby child, Stasie Couvreur. The Academy's top student. Heir to a seat on the council. And the girl who shares my face.

My name's Minka Morgunova. The first Vampire/Hunter hybrid in known existence. A genetic experiment gone horribly wrong – or horribly right. And as far as I'm concerned, my long-lost twin could have stayed lost.

THE DAMNED TRILOGY

If you liked *Monster of Fate*, you might also enjoy *the Damned Trilogy*. An upper Young Adult darker, paranormal romantic comedy. Book 1 is *Damned if I do*. Get it here: https://books2read.com/damned-1

From Elizabeth Stevens, writing as Scarlett Knox, comes…

The devil always collects. And so does his son.

Drake

Most guys like their dads.

Most guys aren't the son of the literal devil.

When Daddy Dearest tells me its unseemly for the last living son of the Lord of Hell to be unmarried, I hate to think who he has in mind. Until, I remember I'm technically already married. Yeah, she's human and I was all of eight at the time. But, still counts.

Now I just need to get my wife to Hell for a meet and greet with Pops and send her back home. Except, our marriage won't technically be legit until it's consummated. And I don't know that I want to send her home…

Wren

Most girls live normal lives.

Most girls aren't married to the devil's son.

There is something weirdly familiar about the new guy next door, but I can't place it. Then a weird little demon thing turns up in my room to tell me a prince of Hell wishes for an audience with me. Oh, yeah. And, apparently – while I'm not even eighteen yet – he's my husband?

So, I find myself stuck in Hell with a husband. And, I guess I don't hate it as much as I thought I would. There's always something going on and things to discover. And soon, I don't know that I want to go home.

GODS & ANGELS

If you liked *Monster of Fate*, you might also enjoy *Gods & Angels*. A New Adult darker, high school, bully romance. Book 3 is out soon! Get it here: https://books2read.com/u/38yaGw

From Elizabeth Stevens, writing as E.J. Knox, comes…

A ruthless god. A sinful angel. And the princess between them.

My life is perfect. My life is planned. My life isn't mine.
Promised to a man I love. A man I hate. Not even a man. A god.
Apollo Callahan is that and much more.

My life is broken. My life is fractured. My life isn't free.
Craving a man I hate. A man I need. Not even a man. An angel.
Valen Kincaid is nothing I could ever want.

Though the Saints rule the hallowed halls of Saint Benedict's College, they're anything but saintly. Behind closed doors, they call themselves the Sinners. Sex. Fast Cars. Drugs. Money. The odd assassination or two. Nothing is beneath them, except the next in a long line of women. Can one little princess, searching to break free from her prison tower, bring these mighty lords crashing to their knees?

The stunning first book in the Sinners of Saint Benedicts series.

MONSTER OF FATE

Thank you so much for reading this story! Word of mouth is super valuable to authors. So, if you have a few moments to rate/review Lena and Rune's story – or, even just pass it on to a friend – I would be really appreciative.

Have you looked for my books in store, or at your local or school library and can't find them? Just let your friendly staff member or librarian know that they can order copies directly from LightningSource/Ingram.

If you want to keep up to date with my new releases, rambles and writing progress, sign up to my newsletter at https://landing.mailerlite.com/webforms/landing/y1n6q2.

Follow me:

THANKS

It has been so long since I really let myself get back to vampires and I'm really glad that this is not only the book officially launching my Scarlett Knox penname, but also that it's probably most people's introduction to my real paranormal side. The one I've been harbouring and feeding off to the side since I was about seven. It's really awesome it's not only back in the light, but also that I've got quite a few of them planned in the next few years.

Thanks primarily goes out to my beta team this time around. We haven't done one like this is…perhaps forever and I had such a great time talking to you about this one and can't wait to see what book two turns into! Because we all know it won't be what any of us expect.

I'd like to, weirdly, issue a bit of an apology for those of you who are waiting on the next books in other series I've started this year – I just have so many ideas in my head and I'm excited about them all. Plus, I just know that if I push myself to just do one series at a time that they will suffer for it.

Thanks to all my new uni peeps; for all your insights and bringing up things about writing this year that I hadn't thought about yet. I'm so glad I met you all.

Of course, thanks to my family. Mum for helping me with the Sprog while I work, and Hubby for yet again dealing with my terrible (self-inflicted) work hours. At least this one was a little better than usual.

MY BOOKS

I'm working on Scarlett's list, but you can find out about what I have planned at my website, as well as have a look at my older YA and NA books; www.elizabethstevens.com.au.